I0562814

Patriot's Blade

by

Susan Leigh Furlong

Copyright Notice
This is a work of fiction. Names, characters, places, and incidents are either the product of the author's imagination or are used fictitiously, and any resemblance to actual persons living or dead, business establishments, events, or locales, is entirely coincidental.

Patriot's Blade

COPYRIGHT © 2025 by Susan Leigh Furlong

All rights reserved. No part of this book may be used or reproduced in any manner whatsoever including the purpose of training artificial intelligence technologies in accordance with Article 4(3) of the Digital Single Market Directive 2019/790, The Wild Rose Press expressly reserves this work from the text and data mining exception. Only brief quotations embodied in critical articles or reviews may be allowed.
Contact Information: info@thewildrosepress.com

Cover Art by *Lisa Dawn MacDonald*

The Wild Rose Press, Inc.
PO Box 708
Adams Basin, NY 14410-0708
Visit us at www.thewildrosepress.com

Publishing History
First Edition, 2025
Trade Paperback ISBN 978-1-5092-6158-1
Digital ISBN 978-1-5092-6159-8

Published in the United States of America

Dedication

This story is dedicated to the brave men and women who sacrificed their comfort, time, and often their lives for the promise of freedom. This courage echoes through the ages and into today's world, and while it may be an oft repeated sentence, its importance cannot be lessened. "Thank you for your service!"

Chapter One

Three days after the Battle of Bunker Hill, June 20, 1775

Birch Johansen stumbled along the worn path, pain racing through every muscle and bone of his battered body. Blood seeped out of the musket ball hole in his side and covered his shirt and torn breeches with splashes of grotesque crimson. Other men's blood dripped off his shaggy blond hair and streaked his cheeks. He wiped it out of his eyes, but his vision blurred, and he had to fight to keep moving. Exhaustion was his only friend now.

Even the sounds of the woods, the birds chirping and the leaves rustling, couldn't distract him from the echoes in his mind—the roar of musket fire, along with the anguished cries of his wounded and dying fellow soldiers. He lifted one arm to his head to stop the noises but to no avail. His feet shifted over the uneven ground, and he struggled to stay upright.

"Keep walking," he muttered.

Then he saw it, a small house with the words "Dr. Samuel Dougal" painted over the door. Here was help, his beacon in the darkness. He took two more shaky steps before falling into unknown arms. His long legs gave out, and his knees hit the ground.

"Help me with him!" a woman called to two men who dashed up and took Birch from her. "Get him inside."

For a moment, his weary eyes locked on hers, and time stood still.

Hers was the face of an angel sent to rescue him from the fear, despair, and brutality of the battle. An angel in a stained dress, a vision with dark auburn hair tumbling loosely around her head, held back by a yellow scarf, and round green eyes that spoke of a promise he was safe. He sighed and let his eyes close despite the unrelenting pain.

As they carried him over the threshold, the intense stench of death nearly overwhelmed him, along with the rancid smell of infection, and the sobs and moans of other injured Continental soldiers lying crowded together on the floor of the front room.

"Put him over there," she said as she pointed to a door wedged between two overstuffed chairs in the front parlor. The men laid him carefully on the makeshift table.

"I know him," said one of them who, although a shorter, huskier man, was still able to easily lift the taller, leaner one. "He's Birch Johansen. We fought beside each other. Birch, it's me, Joseph."

Birch gasped, "Joseph. We made it."

"Yeah, luckily we found this place after our army doctor was shot in the head."

"Mark, get me a fresh bucket of water," said the woman. "Find out how many bandages and pads are left and hand me my scalpel."

A young boy took the instrument off the seat of the chair, wiped it on his pant leg, and handed it to her. "Here, Dr. Sophie."

"No! You know better than that. I want a clean

one. Put it in that pot of water on the fire and get me another one. Hurry, I'm going to need it soon."

"Yes, ma'am," said the boy as he scurried to do her bidding.

She tore open Birch's shirt and saw the dirty ripped rag wrapped tightly around his belly and hips. Dried, crusted blood clotted along his left side. "Whoever tied this around you saved your life, but now it's my turn. Hurry!" she called. "I need those bandages now!" She cut off the makeshift dressing on his stomach and carefully pulled it away from the dried blood.

"Get his shoes and breeches off him. This is starting to bleed again," said his angel of mercy as she dipped a torn cloth in a fresh bucket of water and squeezed it over his stomach so she could wipe the blood away with her hands.

Joseph tugged Birch's muddy shoes off his feet while another man ripped his breeches along both sides and yanked them down.

"Now, wait a minute," said Birch in a raspy voice. His body stiffened. "Not…in front…of her."

Sophie put her hands on her hips and glared at him. "Listen, soldier, I say they come off."

The taller man with an Irish accent said, "Stop being a wee one, Johansen." His dark hair fell over dark eyes. "I didn't believe a *cailin* could do it either, but she's a grand doctor, and she's seen all there is to see. She's a fine fixer, and I've been soldiering in these colonies for five years, so I've seen it all. Quit giving it out." He tore again at Birch's stained and filthy breeches and pulled them off his legs.

Birch finally quit protesting when the woman draped a towel over his stomach and thighs.

3

"Tom Hickey," he asked, "is that you?"

"Who else? Where's me bucket of water?" Another teenage boy appeared at Tom's side with cold water fresh from the well. Tom dropped another rag in it and cleaned off Birch's face and chest. Wet, crusty mud mixed with blood soaked the floor under the door.

Birch's words came out in short gasps. "Are you really a lady doctor?"

Tom said, "Shut yer yap and let the *cailin* here work."

Over the next hour, agony splintered through every part of him each time her knife bit into his side. He struggled to get free of the pain, but Joseph and Tom held him tight. "Stop digging that knife into me!"

"The musket ball went clear through your side, but the hole is already festering. I cleaned it out as best I could, and now I'll stitch it only part way so it can drain."

"Stop it!" he shouted. "I can't stand it!"

She put her hands on her hips and frowned at him. "I can stop, and you can die, so make up your mind quickly. Others are waiting, and I'm too tired to argue with you."

He opened his eyes to look at her, and in his muddled mind he could almost see the angel wings behind her. Even when she scolded him, her voice somehow comforted him.

He gritted his teeth. "Go ahead. I'll try to keep quiet."

"No need. There's nothing between here and heaven I haven't already heard." She kept working on the wound on his side. "What took you so long to find your way here? Most everyone got here a few days

4

ago."

"I helped clear some of the wounded off the field. I was one of the last to leave."

"Good thing somebody tied that rag around you, or you would've bled to death long before now."

Birch groaned as she started to work on his side again.

Joseph squeezed his hand. "Hang in there, Birch. You can make it."

"Ye two better make it," growled Tom Hickey. "Colonel Prescott put me in charge of ye newbies, and he'll take my head if ye kick off."

"We did our best," said Joseph. "I'm just a storekeeper, and I never shot anything before."

"And Johansen never shot nothing but rabbits, but I'll whip ye into shape, if ye live the night."

Sophie looked up. "You there, Irish, we don't need talk like that. Check outside and see if anyone's bleeding through their bandages or isn't breathing. Let me know what you find."

Tom stared at her for a moment before scowling. "All right, doc, I guess ye can handle him from here."

Birch wanted to take in a deep breath, but the air reeked with the stench of injured men crammed together on the floor, in chairs, and leaning against the walls. Even the stiff breeze blowing through the open windows didn't seem to make a difference, but worse than the smells were the screams and sobs of men enduring surgery or amputations in a nearby room beside the stairs.

"Lie still," she said.

Someone lying on the floor cried out, "Help me!" Birch turned his head to see a man with a thick dirty bandage covering half his face.

She pulled her skirt out of the man's clutches. "You're next."

"I want a doctor."

"I am a doctor."

Sophie poured a cup of water over Birch's stomach again and cleaned off the lingering dirt and blood. "Mabel, I need fresh water again," she called to a young girl as she came from the kitchen carrying a folded pile of white rags in her arms. The girl said, "Justine will have more rags dried soon." She put the cloths on the only empty chair in the room and grabbed the bucket.

"That's my Justine in the kitchen," said Joseph, still holding Birch's hand to steady him. "I wondered where you got to after the fighting. I was worried."

Birch nodded toward a bandage wrapped around Joseph's head above his eyes. "What happened to you?"

"I got a scratch." He lifted his curly brown hair off his forehead and raised the edge of the bandage, revealing a gash much deeper and wider than a scratch. "I just got nicked, but Justine pitched a fit until Dr. Sophie got it washed and wrapped. I have six stitches under there."

"Justine is here with you?"

"My wife would follow me into the gates of Hell. You know how wives are."

"No, I don't."

"When the smoke cleared on the hill, she came looking for me, brought me here in the wagon, along with a few others, and got roped into helping. This lady doctor can talk a good game, though it didn't take much to get my Justine to stay. She wanted to help. Right now, she's boiling the blood out of rags to be reused, along with cooking up mush to feed anyone who can eat."

Birch sucked in his breath against the pain and closed his eyes. "So, you're the doctor," he said to the woman leaning over him.

"Lie still," said Sophie. "I wish we had more wine to clean this out, but we ran out yesterday. And, yes, I'm a doctor. My father has the official title because he's been to medical school in Scotland, but he taught me everything he knows."

"Why didn't you go to medical school?"

She cocked her head, her dark auburn hair falling across her forehead into her eyes. She pushed it back with her wrist and gave him a mocking look. "Even as dirty and bloody as I am, you must have noticed I'm a woman and obviously not allowed the privilege of going to school, but I've been apprenticed to my father since I was a child. Believe me, he's as demanding as any professor at school. Now let me bind this. Then you'll wait here for a couple of weeks or more to see how you fight the infection."

"What does your mother think of you doing this kind of man's work?"

"I wouldn't know. She died when I was three."

She pulled him up to sit so she could tie strips of torn cloth around his belly, but Joseph had to hold him up to keep him from falling over. When she finished, she said, "Now don't move around too much. Sit wherever you can find space against the wall or sit outside in what's left of the grass. We'll feed you, and if you need to use the outhouse, go ahead, but don't let any part of you touch anything that should stay in the outhouse." She pointed to Joseph. "You there. What's your name?"

"Joseph Gallagher, ma'am."

"All right, Joseph Gallagher ma'am, see if there are any clean clothes left from the dead soldiers. Justine can find you some, but make sure she's washed them before you put them on this one. Then help him find a place to sit."

She eased Birch off the makeshift table to his feet. He leaned against her, and she held him steady. With one hand, he clutched the towel around his waist until Joseph helped him into a clean but wrinkled shirt and a pair of breeches. Putting them on proved to be daunting, and he bit his lip with each movement, however small. When, at last, he was dressed, he took a couple of cautious steps toward the nearest open space against the wall with Joseph carrying most of his weight. He turned his head back toward the doctor. "What's your name again?"

"Sophie Dougal. Mark, help me get this one on the table." She pointed to the man curled up near her feet with the bandage on his eye. Together they heaved the man, little more than dead weight, onto the door.

"I'm Birch Johansen."

"I won't remember. Go sit down."

An older man burst through the archway leading to the room beside the stairs, shouting, "Sophie, I need you in here! Now!"

Sophie lightly patted the man lying on the door. "My father needs me in surgery. We won't ever be able to use it as a dining room again! Mark, keep him calm until I get back. Don't let him move around or touch that cloth on his eye." The boy pressed his hands against the soldier's shoulders as she disappeared through the swinging door.

"You're going to be all right," said Joseph to Birch as he carefully set his friend on the floor in the corner. "I've seen her save men I thought nobody could. A lot of them won't be any good as soldiers anymore, but they'll be alive."

Birch slumped against the wall and closed his eyes, letting his body succumb to all he'd been through in the last three days. In his troubled sleep, Birch's dreams raced between the terror of the battlefield and the remarkable face of the lady doctor.

****

Three days earlier—June 17, 1775—at Breed's Hill (the battle commonly called Bunker Hill)

Birch kept his eyes on the redcoats marching in perfect formation up the hill from the river, stomping their feet to a drum cadence that vibrated the ground. Birch shivered as he knelt on the wet grass, but he held his musket in position. This was his first time in battle, and although he'd been told what to expect, the reality of it hit him hard. Sweat dripped down his neck.

"Save your powder!" shouted Continental Colonel Prescott. "Don't shoot until you see the whites of their eyes!"

The pulsing marching stopped, and the first row of King George's men knelt while a second row stood behind them. Birch held his breath, wondering how a musket ball entering his body would feel. Then on command, both redcoat lines fired. The piercing sounds from their muskets echoed in Birch's ears, and the smell of gunfire burned his nose. The incoming shots went over the heads of the ragtag and mostly untrained

Continental soldiers or into tree trunks, but the patriots' return fire was accurate, and the redcoats fell where they stood.

The patriots scattered and searched for cover again behind the stone walls, fence rails, and hedges. The few houses and stables left standing on the hill also provided hiding places.

The British retreated briefly, but advanced again, stepping over their fallen comrades who now lay as tumbled piles of red wool. The colonists fired, increasing the bloodbath of the lines of enemy soldiers. Those who could walk staggered away. Many more were dragged off by their comrades. Officers shouted orders but weren't heard above the chaos of the horses snorting and stomping, and the men crying out in pain and shock.

Birch's stomach turned, but he held his position.

Minutes of uneasy calm passed until they saw the British plunge ahead for the third time. Now, finally, learning from their mistakes, they spread out, but the colonists were low on powder and could not return fire. Many started to desert from the hill.

"Get your knives ready!" hollered Tom Hickey. "Go in low, under their bayonets. We ain't got none for our muskets, so look out! We're not done for yet!" He chased two retreating men back to the battle line after giving them both a sharp thump to the gut with his musket barrel. "Ye're not going anywhere! Stand and fight!"

Birch hurriedly reloaded his musket with the last of his powder and shot while Joseph, kneeling next to him, fired. "That's the end of my ammunition," he said. "They keep coming!"

British soldiers descended on them in a rush, and the intense hand-to-hand combat gave every man a good look at the faces of their enemy. The clashing of swords and knives coupled by the grunts and shouts of so many men drowned out any thoughts of strategy. It became all survival instinct. Kill or be killed.

Once the enemies were face-to-face, they became real breathing men, bleeding men, and it didn't matter what continent they were from. The enemies became men just like themselves, with families, hopes, and dreams, and watching them die right in front of them at such close range made war more than slogans and rhetoric, but a reality, a deadly reality.

****

Three hours later, Sophie shouted from the doorway of the surgery room, "Hey, you there! You, the one sitting next to Birch Johansen, we need you to carry a man out of here and bury him."

Birch jolted awake at the sound of her saying his name, and, thankfully, the memory of the battle vanished into the darkness of the room.

Birch nudged Joseph in the arm. "Wake up. The doctor needs you."

Joseph opened his eyes and eased himself to his feet. He yawned and gave a groggy reply, "Yes, ma'am."

She pointed inside the surgery room. "Put him with the other bodies behind the barn. Get a couple of the more able-bodied to help you bury them. Can you read and write?"

"Yes, ma'am," said Joseph.

"Write their names in this book." She wiped a smear of blood off the corner of the book with her finger. "We keep records so we can notify their families. If you don't recognize them, ask around until you find someone who does. If no one does, take a button or anything that might be in their pockets, and put it in that box over there, and write it all in here." She handed him the small black ledger. "Don't lose this. It could be months before the army gets around to needing it."

"Yes, ma'am."

Joseph took the book from her and started toward the former dining room. Just before he reached the doorway, a woman with deep brown braids, a generous curvy figure, and a splatter of freckles across her nose came out of the kitchen at the back of the house.

"Joseph!" she called.

His eyes happily flashed as he ran over to her and planted a kiss on her cheek. "Justine, my love, what is it?"

"I heard your voice, and I had to see you. It's been two days."

"Dr. Sophie wants me to carry a man out to be buried."

Justine brushed his hair off his forehead and ran her fingers over his bandage. "Does it hurt?"

"No." Even if it did, he wasn't going to tell her. He couldn't have her worrying too much. "I've been helping with Birch. He's going to be fine, just needs rest." He kissed her again, this time on the lips. "Birch can take care of himself tonight, so I'm going to spend it with you." He shot her a knowing wink and wiggled his eyebrows. "I'll find you."

She smiled as her cheeks reddened. "I'll be waiting. Hurry."

"My heart is with you always," he said as he walked through the surgery door.

Across the room, Birch straightened up as much as he could and felt a jolt of pain on his side. He grimaced.

Sophie, stepping over several injured soldiers on the floor, stood beside the man still lying on the door. Bending over, she lifted the cloth on his eye. A minute later, she dropped the edge of the cloth before pressing her hand, and then her ear, against his chest. Her face fell as she dried her hands on the only clean spot on her apron and spoke softly, "The bayonet sliced right through his eye. He bled out waiting for me. Forgive me, and God rest your soul."

Birch watched her press her wrist into her eyes to keep the tears at bay. He understood her sense of loss, but wondered how she could still have tears after all she'd been through.

He said, "I thought you said you wouldn't remember my name."

She smiled and shrugged.

Later that morning, Birch finished a bowl of Justine's mush. It was bland with no honey left to sweeten it, but it filled the hole in his belly. "I need some fresh air," he said to Joseph who had eaten the last of his own mush. "Help me outside. The air in the house is choking me."

"I don't know how Sophie stands it," said Joseph while he draped one of the few remaining clean blankets around his friend, a blanket with frayed edges and black stains that would never come out. He walked Birch out to a tree beside a sleeping Tom Hickey.

"He falls asleep at the drop of a hat. Ever wonder what he dreams about?"

Without opening his eyes, Tom slapped Birch's leg. "Hey, any news from the Tree family?" Even in the short time he'd known him, Birch was used to Tom's derogatory remarks about him having been raised on a farm in southern New Jersey surrounded by his close-knit Swedish family. Tom especially ridiculed any stories about Birch's two brothers and two sisters—calling them the Tree family—since all of them were named after trees or flowers, Linden, Ash, Birch, Daisy, and Tansy.

Strangely, Tom's criticisms brought back good memories of growing up where people tousled his hair, kissed him good night on the forehead, and taught him the value of respect. None of these kindly feelings existed here during a war.

Birch spoke. "Milk production's been good, and we're getting more orders for lumber every day. I'll bet—"

Tom's eyes sprang open. "Yeah, yeah. Listen to me. I got nobody to keep me down, no family, no knots. No one to tie me to a cow or a tree, like ye." Tom rolled over to his stomach and buried his face in his arms. Seconds later, he gave a snore.

"That's too bad," said Joseph. "Nobody should be alone in the world."

Birch leaned back against the tree and looked up at the sunlight glittering through the leaves. "He told me once that this was the same sun that shone over County Cork where he was born and lived on the streets. The same sun that shone over him on the boat sailing to the Americas after he was arrested for pickpocketing, and the same sun in Philadelphia when he landed in the colonies as an indentured servant. All he wants is to be far away from those places."

"You can never escape the sun."

"Did many die during the night?" asked Birch.

"Three more. Tom supervised their burial in the back field. It took me a while to find him to tell him I needed help, I guess off gambling again. I've only known him a few weeks, but he's found a game, cards or dice, every night."

The crisp wind and the sunlight continued to brighten Birch's mood until a man over by the fence along the road called out, "Redcoats!"

Chapter Two

Two soldiers in bright red uniforms limped up the path, one held his belly and the other dragged one leg behind him.

Tom Hickey bolted awake and stormed across the yard, followed by several other ambulatory soldiers who formed a tight circle around their enemies.

"What do ye want?" barked Tom.

"We need help," said the smaller of the two men with a heavy British accent. "We've been separated from our unit, left behind because we couldn't keep up. He's bleeding badly." Then he pointed behind him. "The man on the road back there said there was a doctor here. Please, we need a doctor."

The bleeding man lifted his head and said in gasping breaths, "We don't have any weapons. We...need...help."

"No help for lobsterbacks around here," said Tom sharply. "Go back where ye came from." He gave the man with the broken leg a shove, knocking him to the ground. "Go before we finish ye off!"

A cheer went up until Birch limped into the crowd, leaning on Joseph, but the men's voices became silent when Birch said, "If we turn them away, that will make us just as bad as they are, maybe worse. They're no threat to us, hurt like this."

"Yer a bosthoon!" said Tom. "A soft-hearted, weak

16

bosthoon. Can't show the enemy any mercy!"

"Tom, I was in the same battle as you, and men were hurt on both sides. Maybe showing a little compassion—"

"I got none for any Brits!"

Dr. Samuel Dougal stepped out of the house into the yard. "It doesn't matter who inflicted the wounds. I took an oath to help the sick and wounded, an oath to do no harm. It doesn't matter who they are or where they're from. Now step aside and get them in the house."

Tom scowled and clenched his fists, but seconds later he moved to let the doctor pass.

Samuel, a small thin man, looked even frailer now that he was exhausted, yet he grasped the shoulders of the Brit with the fractured leg and helped him hobble across the yard. Sophie pushed through the crowd of soldiers toward the man with the bleeding belly. "Joseph, can you carry him?" Joseph lifted the man into his arms.

"Tom, help my father bring that one in," she said, pointing to her father and the redcoat with the twisted leg stumbling toward the house.

"We don't put up with no loyalists," said Tom Hickey. "I won't touch him. Ye'll regret this, lady doctor. Down with the king!"

Several men joined in the chanting. "Down with the king! Down with the king!"

The crowd followed behind the wounded men, still chanting, but none came close enough to stop them.

"Enough, men!" Tom finally said. "We'll see that no more of them redcoats come here."

Most of the recovering wounded settled back in

their places in the yard while Tom led the stronger ones down the road to look for more of the enemy. A few grabbed their weapons off the ground, ignoring how useless they were. They had no powder or shot.

Birch followed the British wounded men inside the house but lingered in the doorway. "Dr. Samuel and Sophie, helping these men could come with consequences. We might have made a mistake. A lot of people who were run out of Charlestown won't take kindly to us doing this for their enemy."

"Some folks'll think you're a traitor," said Joseph after laying the soldier on the door between the chairs. "We've heard of Loyalists being tarred and feathered and run out on a rail."

"We're doctors, not soldiers," said Sophie. "We've always treated whoever came to our door, and we'll keep doing it. Besides, who's going to come after us with all these soldiers around? Wounded or not, they could still put up a fight. Make yourself useful. Get me water and bandages." She pointed to the shelves with a dwindling supply of dressings.

To the British soldier, she said, "You just rest easy. We'll get you cleaned up as good as new."

She looked in Birch's direction. "I appreciate what you said out there. Not too many men would have stood up against their fellow soldiers like you did."

"My brothers and I fought a lot, picking on the weaker one, usually me as the youngest, and every time our father took us to task, he'd say this quote from the Bible. 'Blessed are those who have regard for the weak; the Lord delivers them in times of trouble.' Psalm 82:3. It's something worth living by."

Sophie ripped open the man's uniform as she

thought about the words of the handsome soldier with a heart for the weak and compassion for the injured, just like she had. A rare man.

She exposed two musket holes in this Brit's chest and one in his stomach. He'd been bandaged, but the wounds were still bleeding and oozing stinking green pus.

Her father reached across the table and touched her hand. Lifting his eyes, he shook his head, and said softly so only she could hear, "It's been too long. There's nothing we can do."

To the soldier on the table, he leaned in and spoke in his ear. "You rest easy, young man."

The Englishman gave a nod of his head and sucked in a gasping breath. "Help…Peter…first."

"We're going to take care of your friend, and then we'll be back for you."

Samuel turned his attention to the other Englishman sitting on the floor near the fireplace with his leg twisted under him. He pointed to Joseph. "Take this one into the surgery. We'll do the best we can to save his life." He pulled Sophie close and whispered, "He'll likely lose the leg. I'll need your help."

Later, Birch, clutching his belly against the pain in his side, followed Joseph and Tom to the back field behind the house to bury the unknown British soldier and the leg of the other. Birch wanted to help dig the graves, but a short prayer was all he had the strength to give.

He felt a twinge in his chest for the loss of men he didn't even know. Still, the cause of freedom would always be strong in him, and death was an unavoidable tragic result. He tried to reconcile the two realities in his mind, but he couldn't. He would fight with those thoughts for a long time to come.

****

Word of a nearby doctor spread. For the next two weeks, stragglers from the battle continued to arrive at the house at all hours of the day and night. Most had walked away from the fighting having received only minimal care or no care at all. Festering wounds covered with old and dirty bandages were as common as broken legs and arms that had not been set properly.

Sophie bandaged wounds, set broken legs, dug musket balls out of every part of the human body, all the while keeping her eye on the tall blond man with the seeping wound on his side. She told herself her concern was about the possibility of infection setting in, but she had to admit that Birch Johansen was an intriguing man, not like any she'd met before.

"What do you know about this Birch?" she asked Justine while taking occasional sips of soup from the cup Justine held out to her as she stitched a bayonet wound.

"He and my Joseph met at camp a couple of days after they both enlisted. They got along just fine from the start. Birch is real smart and my Joseph is real practical so they go together, and they started looking out for each other. Here, take another sip."

Sophie swallowed the last of the broth from the cup. "He seems different from the other soldiers. Birch, I mean."

"I think it's because he came for a reason, not just to fight and count how many redcoats he takes down. Some of them brag about how they fought in the battle, every detail, but not Birch, he just does it. He acts the same whether anybody's watching or not."

Sophie bandaged the bayonet wound and moved to the next patient, a man with a broken jaw, when she spotted Birch in the corner of the parlor reading aloud from one of her father's books, *Gulliver's Travels.* Three men sat nearby listening while five others lay on pallets on the floor, too wounded to sit up. His voice, although not deep, rose and fell with the tension of the story, and the men listened intently, thankful for the distraction from the pain and slow recovery of their injuries.

Chapter Three

Later that week, Sophie sat down on the stairs to rest and, exhausted, fell asleep with her head leaning against a spindle on the carved railing. Birch watched her for a while, admiring how peaceful she looked compared to the frantic pace she usually set with the wounded.

He moved to sit beside her on the stairs, whispering, "Here we go, lean into me. Sleeping on the step is no good."

Gently, he moved her head to his shoulder, and her body shifted closer to his. She snuggled in and draped her arm over his chest. Her breathing slowed as she fell deeper into sleep.

Lifting a loose strand of her hair off her cheek, he tucked it behind her ear. The rich, reddish-brown color was much like that of a burgundy wine he'd sipped once. He didn't much care for the taste, but the color was extraordinary, just as she was. He'd never met a woman like her, educated, determined, and skilled, and yet one who carried softness deep inside. She had a captivating soul, a sensitive heart, and a strong mind.

Often, he saw her sitting on the floor beside a patient, listening to him talk about his home and his family, and when one of them died, she bit her lip and brushed away the tears. She never let the men see her cry. She'd rather it be easier on them, even if it was harder on her.

Sophie was a woman beyond any he'd ever known. He'd grown up with his beloved sisters, Daisy and Tansy, beautiful and strong in their own rights, but he'd watched Sophie calm a fearful or restless man with a gentle touch and then minutes later use a firm hand and voice with a patient who was uncooperative or whiny. She never let a man feel sorry for himself. He was here to heal, and she would do her best to make it happen. From the first day he had seen how beautiful she was in face and form, and now he knew exactly how beautiful she was in her heart. He felt drawn to her in more ways than he should have, and if this had not been an uncertain time of war, he could easily have fallen in love.

Maybe he already had.

Sitting next to her, he wished he were bold enough to kiss her forehead, but instead he leaned back against the riser to let her rest more fully into him. He wanted her to know she was safe with him, and to know so much more, but that would come later.

People walked past the stairs, and as each one passed, Birch put his finger to his lips and whispered, "Shh." Each passerby nodded. A few minutes later, her father came out of the surgery room, wiping his hands on a bloodied cloth. He stopped at the foot of the steps. "Let her sleep," he mouthed. "She hasn't slept in nearly three days."

Birch nodded.

About an hour later, when Birch stretched his back to work out the kinks, she roused, looked up at his face, and then nestled back into him. "You're the softest pillow I've had in days," she murmured, closing her eyes again. "The warmest, too. Any more wounded arrive?"

"No," answered Birch." Go back to sleep."

"I really shouldn't."

"I say you should." He brushed his hand over her hair, and she relaxed into his chest again.

Despite how tired she looked, with dark circles under her eyes and a smear of blood on her forehead that ran into her hair, he longed to kiss her pale lips. He pulled her closer and imagined taking her for long walks in the moonlight when they would talk and they would kiss, and he would be happy.

Sophie jolted awake. "How long have I been asleep?"

"A little over an hour. No one needs you right now. Go back to sleep. I don't mind being your pillow." He put his hand on her head and tenderly pushed it down, but she jerked it back up.

"I have work to do," she said as she stretched her arms over her head and yawned. "Thank you very much for being here. Let me see if Father needs me, and then I want to look under your bandages. You might be going back to your outfit soon. Talk is that General George Washington is organizing troops here near Cambridge."

"What if I don't go back? What if I just stayed here?"

Her smile filled her tired face as she shook her head. "You know you can't do that. The army would arrest you." She looked at him for a few more seconds. "But I wouldn't mind if you stayed."

Some of the men who'd been sleeping quietly when she first sat down on the stairs now groaned in pain, and one started to bleed through his bandage, so she went back to treating the seemingly never-ending crush of patients.

Three hours later, she finally found a moment to sit in the kitchen and do nothing more than watch Justine and Mabel soak bandages while cleaning her scissors, scalpels, and lancets. She laid her head down on the table and closed her eyes as her mind floated back to Birch, the man who had held her so tenderly on the stairs.

He was a man of quiet strength. He never bullied or flaunted his influence, but the men listened to him. Never once did he grumble like some of the others, saying that because she was a woman, her doctoring skills were questionable. If others sneered or refused to cooperate with her, he took them aside. She never knew what he said to them, but they never questioned her doctoring again.

****

Boredom haunted Birch as he healed. Unlike many of the recovering soldiers who were content to sit in the garden, either sleeping or playing cards, Birch needed something to do. He pestered Sophie until she let him help take care of the remaining soldiers.

Sophie taught him how to apply pressure to stop bleeding from deep wounds, how to steady a patient while she dug out musket balls or rebroke and reset limbs, and she even let him treat the smaller cuts and scrapes by himself. He fed mush to anyone unable to eat alone, cleaned up soiled sheets, and supervised the burial of the dead. The work was tiring, and he only escaped the never-ending stench of disease and death by brief walks outside.

After another especially busy day, he sat on the staircase, rubbing his tired back until Sophie carried over two bowls of soup and sat down beside him.

"It's amazing what Justine can do with a few vegetables and some broth," said Birch as he scooped up a mouthful of the soup.

"This is the last of the broth," said Sophie. "All the cows and chickens in the area are gone, eaten, or confiscated by renegades. I'm not sure what we'll feed the men next."

She sighed and set her bowl on the riser.

He handed her bowl back to her. "Not eating will not solve the problem. If you get sick, these men left here will die. Eat."

She picked up her spoon. "You like taking care of people, don't you?"

"My parents came here from Sweden right after my oldest sister, Daisy, was born. Then came three brothers and another sister, so we had to take care of each other. We're all named after trees or flowers, Ash, Linden, Birch, Daisy, and Tansy."

Sophie giggled. "I love those names. So why did you decide to join the army?"

"It's hard to explain, but I've been raised with pride about how my family created an independent life in their new country. We own a large dairy and cattle farm, and we're just starting to get into the lumber business. We've all put in so much work, and we won't let anyone take away what we've built."

She blew over the soup in her spoon before taking another swallow. "Do you think we'll ever get our independence?"

"George Washington told me that at first he was in

favor of trying to work out a peaceful agreement with England, but not now."

"You've met General Washington?" she said, astonished.

"Yes, two years ago. My brother Ash and I went to George Washington's Mount Vernon home to deliver a bull for his herd. Our herds are well known for their high quality, and we spend a lot of time breeding them. One big part of our business is helping other farms increase their herds by bringing them new cows and bulls."

"George Washington raises cattle?"

"He had intended to build a business making milk and cheese, but the biggest thing on his mind even then was the trouble in the colonies. He talked about it with us. At first, he hoped for a peaceful solution, but when King George and his taxes and restrictions to free trade became more egregious, he started to consider we might have to go to war."

"What military experience does a country gentleman have that the Congress would make him head of the army?"

"He's done a lot more than just be a country gentleman. He served in the army for many years, but mainly as a messenger or a general's aide. He admitted to us that his career had its ups and downs, some victories, and some defeats, but he learned from them all. He's got a good mind and a dedication to our new country."

"Sounds like you admire him."

"I do, and I hope to be the kind of clear-thinking, logical, and resolute soldier he is."

She nodded. "Now that the war is real, what do you

think of our chances of getting our freedom from England?"

Birch waved his hand toward the injured men. "I hate the fighting and all that goes with it, but right is right, and freedom is just and proper. What do you think about it, knowing the destruction it brings?"

"Besides my father, you're the only man who's ever asked me that."

"I learned early that my sisters have opinions on everything. All you have to do is ask, and sometimes you don't even have to ask. So, what do you think?"

"I think, like you, the destruction and loss of human life is horrific, and a just cause must be strong enough and right enough for a man to give up his life. I pray freedom is that just cause. Otherwise, it's all for nothing."

A long thought-filled pause settled between them before she asked, "Did your brother Ash join the army with you?"

"No. Only two Johansen sons are still at home now. Daisy is married and lives in New York City. Tansy and her husband, Alden, live on his farm in Pennsylvania. Ash believes he can best serve by supplying the army with milk and beef, so he's back home in New Jersey working with my father and my brother Linden."

"Tell me more about your family."

"Well," he began, "as I said, we've built our herds of cattle and dairy cows and are starting a lumber business. We're proud of our reputation for transporting cattle by boat or on specially made wagons to other farms as needed."

"No, I mean about your family, how you grew up."

He chuckled. "I remember how my older brothers picked on me until I gave Linden a black eye and Ash a bloody nose. After that they treated me as an equal, and much to our father's dismay, it made us a trio to be reckoned with. It was a good way to grow up. What about you?"

"My story is different. My mother died when I was very young, and I don't remember her at all, but my father filled the gap by training me to be a doctor. I couldn't have been more than four or five years old when I started helping with the simple things."

"So, did you always want to be a doctor?"

"My father kept me busy helping him, so I never felt lonely, and I guess that's how it became my calling." She paused, remembering with a faraway look in her eyes and a slight smile on her lips. "If I cried, Father tickled my chin until I laughed. It made things all better."

Birch reached over and wiggled his fingers under her chin. She giggled, and he smiled for the first time since he joined the fighting.

"My father took me to Scotland for three years when I was eleven," she said. "He went to study medicine in Edinburgh, and I sat on the floor by his chair during the lectures. Every once in a while, he'd reach down and tickle my chin just to see if I was still awake. I usually was. The practice of medicine fascinates me."

All at once a commotion of men shouting sounded from the front yard.

"Someone's here. A soldier on horseback."

Birch jumped to his feet and ran toward the front window with Sophie right behind him. The men recovering in the yard were already gathered at the gate as the rider entered.

A soldier in a clean blue and white uniform sat astride a sorrel mare. "I've come with orders from General George Washington. Who's in charge here?" he asked in a commanding voice.

A low murmur sped through the men until the soldier on horseback repeated even louder than before, "I asked who is in charge here?"

"I am," called out Sophie from the doorway. "These men are all my patients."

The rider dismounted. "You're the doctor, ma'am?" he asked with a hint of doubt in his voice. "Where is the real doctor?"

She put her hands on her hips. "Standing in front of you."

"She's the doctor all right," said Birch. "All of us are alive because of her. A lot of the injured have been sent home, and the dead are buried in the field out back. We're all that's left. About twenty of us."

The man cleared his throat and said, "The Continental Congress has ordered General Washington to assemble all the remaining men for the new Continental Army. He is setting up his headquarters at Harvard College in Cambridge, and he orders that all able-bodied men report at once for assignments and training. I am Captain Husen. Ma'am, may I have a list of all the men who are well enough to serve?"

"Of course, sir. Won't you come inside?"

Birch's heart sank. He'd gotten comfortable here. He'd spent most of his days following Sophie from patient to patient, cleaning wounds, changing bandages, and helping men walk around to get their strength back, but most of all, he'd gotten to know Sophie as more than a doctor. He'd started to feel things he hadn't felt before, deeper feelings, more intense, and now he would be leaving. His heart wanted to stay, but the fight for freedom called him, and he wouldn't refuse.

Captain Husen talked briefly to Sophie before stepping outside to announce, "The British have removed their wounded and dead from the hill and are now in full retreat to the peninsula of the city of Boston. Other militia groups will be joining us as we harass the enemy, forcing them into the sea or into the heavens above, whichever comes first. By orders of General George Washington, Commander of the Continental Army, gather your weapons and follow me."

Some of the men clamored to be first in line while others held back, but before Sophie would release anyone, she inspected each man's bandages and decided on their fitness for duty. She released Joseph Gallagher and Tom Hickey first as their injuries were slight. "You two have been just what we needed around here, and my father and I will miss all you've been doing."

"May I say goodbye to Justine before I go?" asked Joseph.

"Of course, she's in the kitchen wrapping slices of bread for each man to carry."

Joseph ran toward the house while Tom groused, "I don't like leavings, so I'll say..." He ducked his head. "Ye, Miss Sophie, treated me better than anyone ever had, so...goodbye."

She patted him on the arm.

She sent three men grumbling back into the house because their wounds hadn't healed properly. "Give it a few more days, and you'll be ready."

She also had complaints from some when she said they were fit for duty. "Doc, let me stay for a while. I don't feel so good," two of them pleaded.

She shook her head. "I did my duty too well, and now you have to go back and do yours."

Birch was last in line. She opened his shirt and gently padded her fingers along his injury to his side. "You're ready to go, but I'll miss everything you've done for me."

"I'll miss working with you," he said as he tucked his shirt back into his breeches.

He put his hands on her arms and stepped closer. She rested hers on his waist. The air seemed to crackle around them even though they were the only ones who could hear it.

"I don't know when I'll be back here," he said quietly, "but there's one thing I want to take with me."

"What is that?"

He leaned in. His eyes met hers, his blue to her green. He would have the kiss he'd wanted for so long, but he knew the moment his lips touched hers, he'd be lost in her forever. He had his duty as a soldier in this war, but she would have his soul. Could he risk this kiss, knowing he might never see her again if the worst happened? He felt her rise on her toes, and in that instant all hesitation vanished; his lips touched hers. They were warm and soft and melded into his. He moved his mouth slowly against hers, deepening the kiss. Her breath tickled his cheek.

She moaned low in her throat, and he pressed closer, shifting his lips across hers, pulling her into him. She broke off briefly to whisper his name before returning to the kiss, this time stronger and deeper. His hands splayed across her back and slid down to her hips. He felt her hands copy his movement on his own back. He had expected to give her a kiss, but had not expected to get one in return, and he was overjoyed when he did.

"Johansen, we're moving out!" shouted Tom Hickey standing near the fence.

They both shuddered at the sound of Tom's voice, but Birch's lips lingered on hers. How could he leave what he had just found?

Her scent was strong and certain, and he breathed it in. When he finally lifted his head, he looked down at her face. It was flushed. Slowly, he released his embrace and took her hands in his, softly rubbing his thumbs against her warm palms. "I have to go," he said in a voice thick with regret.

Her tongue swept slowly over her lower lip as if to taste him again. "Keep yourself safe. Doctor's orders." After brushing a lingering smudge of dirt off his cheek, she held her hand against his head until Hickey shouted again. "Johansen!"

Suddenly they were apart. She took a step back and gave him one last look before she turned and walked back toward the house.

The fifteen men healthy enough to march to the camp lined up with their muskets at their sides. "What about powder and shot?" asked one man. "We don't have either."

Captain Husen said, "When we reach the encampment, you will receive proper ammunition. Until then, shoulder your weapons and march as if you are prepared to fight. The enemy doesn't need to know otherwise."

As Birch walked out the gate, he looked over his shoulder for one last glimpse of the woman he knew he loved, but Sophie was out of sight. A heaviness settled in his chest.

****

She couldn't watch him leave, not the way she watched the other men who had left her care over the last month, some of them healthy and strong once more, and others limping home to live out their lives away from the fighting. Their leaving didn't bring her sorrow, not the way Birch Johansen's did. Maybe it was because she knew him better than the others, and maybe it was more than that. She'd never been in love, never met a man she wanted to care about in that way, and she realized she'd fallen in love for the first time in her life. And the man she loved had kissed her, and now she knew he felt the same.

Chapter Four

September 1775
Birch's first glimpse of the encampment at the newly formed Continental Army shocked him. Harvard Yard had been grassy acreage edged by college buildings on three sides with tall straight trees of elm, oaks, maples, and evergreens, but once turned over to the army, and the students moved to Concord for their studies, its serene beauty disappeared. Now there were more stumps than trees, and what was left of the grass was nearly covered by the remains of a torn off metal roof that had been melted into bullets. Birch covered his nose and mouth as they walked past a large hole dug in the center of the yard. Judging from the sight, and the odor, it was the latrine for the camp.

Soldiers called out when they spotted the new men, "Got any bread? Or a biscuit? Any whiskey? Just a swallow?" When the newcomers shook their heads, one of the men growled, "The general eats plenty in that big house over there." He pointed just beyond the former student buildings to Washington's headquarters. "But what about us?"

Another man shouted, "Hope your last meal was fine 'cause you won't get nothing much here but orders and more orders."

"Yeah, every morning he reads us a new list of things he wants us to do," said another. "He's trying to make us la-dee-dah fancy like he is. Today he complained that when we wash in the river by the bridge, we run around naked when ladies are walking up top. So how else are we supposed to get clean?"

Yet another man called out, "The ladies like it! That's why they come by!" Laughter spread through the troops along with snorting noises and kissing sounds.

The fifteen men from the Dougal house stayed together and walked to the back of the yard close to one of the buildings where a little grass remained. "At least we're out of the mud," said Joseph, "and about as far away from that pit as we can get." He tossed down his pack and stretched out with his hands behind his head. "I guess we're having Justine's bread for supper."

There was little activity in the camp until late in the afternoon when the boredom was abruptly broken. The Marbleheads from Massachusetts, who occupied most of the Harvard Yard, began hooting and hollering at new arrivals from Virginia.

"Will you look at that?" said one. "Wearing fancy ruffles and fringes! Now the ladies are fighting with us!"

A roar of laughter went up from the Massachusetts men. "Well, if they ain't all hat and no cattle. Dressed fancy but got no fight in them!"

"I ain't seen such pretty clothes in a long time. Pretty linen frocks with ruffles and fringe! Do you want to dance, m'lady?"

The fighting men of Virginia returned the insults. "Want to see what us fancy-dressed can do? Or are ya chicken?" The regiment started clucking.

A Virginian in the front called out, "Sound like a bunch of chuckleheads to me? What do ya think, boys?

All talk or just puppies with no bite?"

Four of the men who came with Birch stood up and moved forward but stopped when Birch jumped to his feet and stretched out his arms to hold them back. "Stay out of it. It's not our fight. Stand steady! Right now, it's just words, and none of them aimed at us."

Men from both Massachusetts and Virginia bolted forward, and soon they all were throwing punches. Over one hundred men fought to defend their unit's honor with their fists until the sound of hoofbeats came bearing down toward the Yard.

"It's General Washington himself," called out Joseph.

The general stopped at the edge of the crowd, jumped off his horse, and pushed his way into the middle of the melee. Men fell or leaped out of his path. He seized two of the biggest men from each unit by the back of the neck, his grip choking them and shaking them nearly off their feet. His booming voice silenced them all. "We are here to fight the enemy, not each other! Soldiers are trained fighting men, not barroom brawlers!"

The men from both sides took off running for cover, rather than face the wrath of the general. Soon the only men left standing on the field were Washington, the two fighters, and the men from the Dougal house.

Washington finally released the two combatants who sheepishly walked away. The general brushed the dirt off his jacket and breeches before getting back on his horse to ride slowly through the camp, giving scalding looks to anyone who might think of challenging him. None did.

As he passed by the men from the Dougal house, he nodded, saying, "Welcome." Each one saluted before watching their commander ride back to his headquarters.

Once he was out of sight, Joseph said, "I guess that settles who's in charge around here."

All agreed.

****

October 1775

After most of her patients were back on duty at the army camp, Sophie recognized a familiar face standing in the doorway.

"Willow!" she called out as soon as she saw the thin, sharp-nosed woman with a receding chin on the front step. "Your bonnet is lovely." She always tried to say something complimentary about Willow's outfit. Lord knows, she couldn't say the young woman was pretty, but one didn't need good looks to be a prostitute, and Willow was good at her work. "Won't you come in? I haven't seen you in a long time."

Willow walked directly over to Sophie and, taking the bowl of water from her that Sophie was using to rinse a wound, headed toward the kitchen. "I've been visiting in Rhode Island with…a friend, ma'am."

"How nice. Did you have a good time?" Sophie washed her hands and wiped them on a clean dish towel, saying, "Just dump the water out on the garden."

Once Willow was back inside, Sophie asked, "Would you like a bit of tea? It won't be very strong. We haven't much left, and who knows when we'll be able to get more."

Willow nodded. "Thank you, ma'am." She pulled out a chair by the table, and fluffing out her skirt until it draped neatly over her legs, she sat down to wait while Sophie prepared their cups.

Sophie asked, "Have you come for the cure again?" Both Drs. Dougal were known in the community for providing treatment for syphilis and other transmitted conditions. It did not give them a favorable reputation among the ordinary citizens, but for the "ladies of the night" and their clients, discreet treatment was a blessing. The usual cure involving mercury was tedious, lengthy, and rarely successful, but at a patient's request it could be done. Sophie, on the other hand, preferred to treat the sores and pustules on sensitive areas by relieving the pain and hoping her patients would practice discretion from now on.

"No, ma'am," said the girl. "I've been real careful. I have a letter I'm supposed to deliver."

"To whom?"

"I don't rightly know, just to someone British, but I got to thinking about it, and maybe that's not such a good idea. Maybe General Washington needs to see it."

"Who's it from?"

Willow wrung her hands together nervously. "Uh, it's from a personal friend of mine. I swore I'd never tell. I wanted Godfrey Wenwood to send it, you know, the baker who makes Wenwood Butter Biscuits. Sells a lot of them in Rhode Island, that's where he lives near the British navy. That's where I was."

"Why do you need to deliver it? Why doesn't Godfrey do it himself?"

"Well…" She paused and took a sip of tea. "It's not really his letter. I asked Godfrey to deliver it to British military, but he paid me a gold coin to do it instead of him, but I'm afraid, so I'm asking you."

Willow forced a smile. "Will you, please?"

Sophie gave her an uneasy look. "What's in the letter?"

"I don't know. That's why I'm scared to give it to the general." She hung her head. "I'm sorry to bring this to you, but I don't know many people who'll even talk to me, let alone do me a favor. I could pay you," she said.

"No need to pay me. I just want to know what I'm doing. Let me see the letter."

Willow handed it over, and Sophie opened the seal. She gave it a look before saying, "What in the world is this?"

Illegible and unreadable markings covered the folded paper. "Can you read this?" Sophie asked.

"No, ma'am, I can't even read regular writing, and this is some sort of funny writing. I never opened it, anyway, just gave it to Godfrey."

"If I'm not mistaken, it's written in code, which makes me suspicious about why someone would want you to carry it, especially carry it to the British."

Willow chewed on her lips. "I can't give it to the general myself, not an important man like him, I just can't! I'm going to throw it in the fire and forget I ever saw it. Give it to me." She held out her hand.

"No, it could be nothing, or it could be important, so we'll go together to the army camp, and I'll get one of the soldiers I know to give it to the general."

Willow gulped to get the lump out of her throat. "You'll hold my hand the whole way? You won't ever let it go or leave me alone?"

"No, Willow, I'll never let you go. You can count on me. The soldier I can give it to is a good friend of mine. His name is Birch, you know, like the tree. You can always depend on a strong tree, so don't worry."

She tucked the letter inside her bodice and patted it. "All safe and sound." Then she took Willow's hand.

Sophie never let go of Willow's hand on the three-mile walk to the army encampment. Twice Willow tried to pull away and escape, but Sophie clung to her and spoke comforting words. Willow's nervousness escalated once they got close enough to camp to hear the low undercurrent of conversation from the soldiers gathered in small groups.

As they walked closer, Sophie, who put cleanliness next to everything, gagged at the smell of unwashed bodies and a makeshift latrine. Willow didn't seem to mind. She was used to these things. She tried to pull her hand away again, but Sophie held tight. After a minute someone noticed them.

"Look, the Good Lord has sent us ladies!"

One man called out, "Come to me first! I'll give you a wild ride. Give me the redhead!"

Willow spoke up in a firm voice that Sophie had never heard before. "Quit acting like you don't have all your buttons! You can't talk rot like that to her! She's a doctor and a lady, and you ain't nothing but rot! Even I wouldn't have you!"

Stunned by her outburst, a couple of the men asked in gentler tones, "Who you looking for?"

"Birch Johansen," said Sophie. "Birch Johansen and Joseph Gallagher." She shouted out both their names and was relieved when she spotted them running toward her.

"What are you doing here?" asked Birch when he put his arms around Sophie, who despite the urge to hug him back, didn't let go of Willow's hand.

"We've got something for you to deliver to General Washington."

"What?"

"We have to talk privately first. The four of us."

After repeating the entire story for the men, Sophie handed the letter to Birch. "We can't figure it out. It's in some kind of code, so it might be something important. We don't know, but we wanted to do what was right."

"Are you sure this is all right?" whispered Willow in Sophie's ear. "To give it to them?"

Sophie nodded. "These are both good men and loyal to the general. Don't worry."

"There is one thing I need to know," said Birch. "Who is this letter from? Who wrote it?"

Willow started to cry, tears smudging the kohl around her eyes. "I can't tell. I promised. Please don't make me."

Joseph spoke up. "We understand that you gave your word, but sometimes a promise is the wrong thing, especially if someone is hurt by that secret, especially if it's a military message. War is often terrible, but necessary for men to be free."

"Please tell us," said Birch. "I swear on my life that the only other person on this earth who will hear the name from my lips is General Washington."

"You can believe him," said Sophie. "He's honorable and trustworthy. I promise you he is."

Wiping the tears and black streaks from her cheeks, she whispered, "Dr. Benjamin Church."

Joseph's face blanched. "Do you mean the former member of the Sons of Liberty who tried to liberate

Boston?"

Willow nodded.

"I can't believe he'd do anything suspicious. He's a member of the Massachusetts provincial congress."

Willow shrugged. "I got the letter right from his own hand, I swear."

"We believe you." Birch took the letter from Sophie. "We have to get this to the general as soon as possible and see if anyone can translate it. Sophie, take Willow home. We'll let you know what he says."

Both Joseph and Birch headed toward the house that served as General Washington's headquarters.

Commander-in-chief Washington scanned the coded message, and he could hardly believe his ears when they told him the name of the writer: Dr. Benjamin Church.

"Church is one of us," said Washington. "I've never had reason to doubt him. He's a respected physician, and he fought with the Sons of Liberty in Boston. I consider him a friend." But after a long thoughtful pause, the general spoke with brutal detachment. "I must hear this from his own mouth. Johansen, gather five or six men and arrest the doctor. Bring him directly to me. Dismissed!"

The next day, Dr. Benjamin Church stood before his friend, General Washington. "It's a letter to my brother-in-law, John Fleming. We write in code as a game, to see who can decipher it correctly. It's a challenge, a contest between brothers."

"Then decipher it."

Church held up his chin. "It is private correspondence, and I will not. I demand you send my letter to Fleming."

Washington's reply dripped with irritation. "Then you won't mind if I get men to decipher it into plain English."

Dr. Church didn't answer.

Washington found two teams of people near Cambridge who were willing to tackle the task. After only a few hours, both teams came up with virtually the same translation.

Washington read the deciphered letter aloud. Everyone in the tent was shocked, except for Dr. Church who did not change his stalwart expression.

The letter contained information on troop status and numbers, along with critical details about weapons supplies, and even battle strategies of the Continental Army. The worst was that it clearly was intended to be sent to General Gage, Commander of the British forces in America.

Washington shook the translation pages at Dr. Church. "How do you explain this?"

Church looked around the room at the soldiers ready to arrest him but still held his chin high. He fixed his eyes on the general but flicked his thumb against his fingers in a nervous gesture. "It was intended to give General Gage false information," he said firmly. "I am a patriot."

A stunned silence seemed to pull the air out of the room until Washington spoke. His voice was cold. "It is better to offer no excuse than a bad one." He turned his back on Dr. Church. "My heart sinks at this treachery of a formerly trusted friend. You have betrayed your position as a respected patriot, betrayed all who put their trust in you. You are a traitor and a spy, and I believe you have been sharing information with the enemy for longer than I care to know. You are under arrest, and I hope to never set eyes on you again. Dismissed."

Once the soldiers led Church away to a prison cell, Washington called for Captain Caleb Gibbs. "Gibbs, this betrayal survived under our noses for too long. That will not happen again. From now on we will answer every British spy scheme with one of our own.

"I now charge you with putting together an elite guard that will report only to me. These must be dedicated soldiers whose loyalty cannot be questioned. You will conduct extensive investigations, and I will give you my specifications for these men. As soon as that is done, I expect to meet with the chosen men so I can select the best and the bravest. Understood?"

"Yes, sir!"

"Dismissed!"

Chapter Five

Late October 1775

"Another seven showed up today," said Justine. "We don't have any more room in the house."

"The only thing we can do now for these refugees from Boston is to let them sleep in the yard," said Sophie. "See if we have any more clean blankets for them. I'll check them for smallpox."

"How much longer can this siege of the city last? We're out of bread again, and if I make some loaves today, we'll be out of flour, and last night, somebody raided the last of the vegetables in the garden, and they milked the cow before I had a chance this morning."

Samuel Dougal came into the kitchen, holding the bleeding hand of a young boy dressed in a satin jacket and breeches fit for a stroll in the city, but not for trekking through the countryside. "Now don't you worry, boy, I can fix that cut right up. Let me rinse it under the pump. Then I'll wrap it." The boy mumbled agreement.

After Samuel had bandaged the cut and the boy was on his way, he said, "These people escaping from Boston are certainly not prepared to look for food and shelter. What's worse is they're carrying smallpox with them. How many sick do we have in the greenhouse?"

"About sixteen," said Sophie. "Four died last night. Judge Beal sent two of his workers here to help us last week, and they've dug graves almost nonstop. I wish we could give them proper burials, but it's too dangerous. We did tar the sheets to bury them in, but we have to burn their blankets and bedding."

Justine walked over to the window in the front room. "Another bunch from Boston is walking past the house. They can see we're too crowded for them to stop."

"And undoubtedly, they'll carry smallpox with them, and it'll spread," said Sophie.

Samuel sighed. "The only good thing to come out of this long siege is that it gives George Washington time to train his troops."

"Nothing good can come out of this siege, only more death."

A week after the first smallpox victims arrived, Sophie called her helpers, Justine, Mabel, and Mark, into the kitchen. "Don't become alarmed, but I want to know if any of you have ever had smallpox?"

All three shook their heads, and at once tears welled up in Mabel's eyes. "Do we have it now? I didn't touch any of them. You wouldn't let me."

"No, no," said Sophie. "It takes time for symptoms to appear, but smallpox spreads quickly, and we are bound to see many more sick ones passing by here. I want to be sure you don't get it."

"I ain't taking no magic potion!" cried Mabel. The thirteen-year-old girl stomped her foot. "You can't make me!"

"It's no magic potion. It's a medical treatment called inoculation. Both my father and I were inoculated when we lived in Scotland, and now we are immune, meaning we can't get the smallpox."

"Inocu—what? What's that?" asked Justine, not so much frightened as curious.

"It was first introduced in England about fifty years ago, but they'd done it in Turkey before that, and it's very effective."

"But what is it?"

"The process is simple, and nothing to be afraid of. You take some pus from a pustule of a person who already has smallpox, and you scrape a little of that pus onto a thread and then slip that thread under the skin on the hand of a healthy person."

Mark's eyes opened wide. "Won't that give them smallpox?"

"Yes, but a very mild form of the disease. That person will only be sick for a week or two, sometimes less, with much milder symptoms, mainly a slight fever and some weakness, but they'll survive. That's what's important, and there will be fewer pock mark scars. See, I only have two on my face and both are close to my hairline." She pulled back her hair to show them two small round pox scars over her ear. "I have a few more on my back, but that's it. Even Queen Charlotte of England approved of it and had her children inoculated. If the queen wasn't afraid for her children, there is no reason you should be."

"Our preacher says it's a curse from God on the unrighteous," said Mabel.

"That's impossible," said Sophie. "Very small children can get the disease, and they're too young to be unrighteous. I promise you; it can save your life. I want to inoculate you three. Believe me, I would never do anything to harm you."

"What about the soldiers here?" asked Mark.

"Most of them are still too sick to be treated, but as soon as they're healthy enough, I'll inoculate as many as I can. Will you trust me?"

An uneasy silence fell over the kitchen until Justine blurted out, "I trust you." She stepped forward and held out her arm. "Come on, you two," she said to the others. "Be brave."

After a moment's hesitation, Mabel and Mark stuck out their arms, too. "Will it hurt?" asked Mark.

"Only a little, but we need to get things ready first. You three will stay in the upstairs bedroom as long as you have symptoms, so I can take care of you and not spread the sickness to the others. Bring your things, your extra clothes, soap, anything else you might need, books or games, if you have them. I'll take samples from some of the ones who are already sick in the greenhouse and get the inoculations ready."

A little over two weeks later, Mark was the only one still complaining of symptoms. He stayed in bed, delighting in the extra attention from Justine and Mabel, until Sophie pronounced him well enough to bring in some firewood. He reluctantly put on his shoes and declared himself cured to anyone who would listen to him about his victory over smallpox.

Chapter Six

November 1775

Henry Knox, a twenty-five-year-old bookseller from Boston, Massachusetts, had a bold idea to end the siege of the city. "The soldiers are restless, and the country is eager for victory, and I have a plan to do both," he said to General Washington.

"I've listened to many plans and none of them are feasible," said the general. "What's so different about yours? What does a bookseller know about wartime strategy?"

"I've always had an avid interest in military history, and I'm part of a local artillery company, so I do have a lot of military knowledge. My plan to break the stalemate is to bring cannons here from the deserted Fort Ticonderoga to use against the enemy."

Washington gave him a dubious look. "So how do you propose to get them here? It's over two hundred miles."

Knox remained unfazed. "If you will assign me twelve men for the trip north, then once at the fort, I plan to dismantle the cannons. I'll hire more men to build the sleds and load the cannons, and enough oxen to do the job of bringing them here. It should only take about twenty days."

"Give me more details, such as how you plan to take the cannons apart and how you will stow them on these sleds."

Knox had all of that worked out, and Washington didn't need much time to give his approval. On Thursday, November 16, Washington issued orders for Knox to take any supplies he needed from the artillery corps. He then was to go to the New York Provincial Congress and eventually to Albany to ask for more supplies and funds for the trip. Both the bookseller and the general were pleased when the Congress approved everything.

Days later, Henry Knox, cash in hand, left Cambridge for northern New York State with his brother, eighteen-year-old William. Marching with them were twelve men of the Continental Army that included Birch Johansen, Joseph Gallagher, and Tom Hickey.

After a long uneventful trek north, the weather changed for the worse as the thick stone walls of the deserted star-shaped fort came into view. The men, now shivering and covered with wet snow, spent the night in the empty housing in the center of the fort.

"At least we've got a roof over our heads," said Joseph.

"We're going to need more than a roof if this weather keeps up!" said Tom as he moved closer to the wood-burning stove in the center of the room.

"Rest up," said Knox. "At dawn, William and I will go out and find local men to build the sleds and bring them back here as soon as we can. In the meantime, you twelve will start dismantling the cannons so they're set to load when the sleds are ready."

****

"Heave, Hickey, heave it this way!" shouted Birch. "Joseph, get over there and help him!" Even with twelve men working together, loading the sleds with the cannons was a challenge. One slip of the heavy equipment could break a leg or crush an arm.

First, they tied the barrel of the cannon and the undercarriage onto a flat wooden sled with heavy rope. On top of that all the smaller parts, such as chains and bolts, were nestled into the empty spaces. Finally, the wheels were lashed on top, making the sled and the entire load ready to transport.

"I bet we've used a mile of rope," said Joseph, wiping the sweat from his forehead despite the chill in the air.

"I'm betting more than that, but we've only got an hour of daylight left and four more sleds to load. Knox thinks we can leave tomorrow."

"Not if we don't get the oxen," said one of the local men hired by Knox. "I know George Palmer, and he won't sell anything for less than double what it's worth. If he won't sell, your man'll have to get horses, and they won't last as long on a trip like this."

Tom spoke up. "Quit yer griping. You're getting paid to do this while I'm under orders, so I get nothing but a sore back. Let's get this train of cannons moving!"

The next morning Knox announced to the men, "Mr. Palmer will not sell the oxen at the previously agreed price, so we'll have to use horses to pull the loads. We could be delayed by as much as three weeks before we reach Boston."

A groan went up among the already tired men.

"Our mission is vital to the war effort. General

Washington is counting on us. Stay strong, men, and pray the snow lets up."

It did not.

Birch, Tom, and Joseph stood on the bank of Lake George. "It doesn't look completely frozen solid," said Joseph. "I see watery spots with only a thin layer of ice under it."

William Knox, although only eighteen and inexperienced, took charge. "Don't worry men. Our flat-bottomed gundalows are made for just this sort of thing. It sails easily in the water, matching the currents' speed, but it can also glide over any thin ice patches. Our skipper has made this trip many times before. Load up the sleds on the gundalow, making certain to balance the weight."

After the gundalow finally set sail, Henry Knox went ahead in a small skiff, confident that all would be well. He arrived at Fort George.

The cannon-loaded boat did not.

The eerie cracking sound of the floating slabs of frozen ice melting in the sun or bumping into the gundalow sent shivers up the men's spines, but panic set in when the cannon parts on one of the sleds shifted. The entire sled slid toward the edge of the boat, forcing the gundalow into a tilt to the side. Men grabbed onto anything they could reach, the ropes, the sleds, even the cannon parts, to keep themselves and their cargo from falling off into the icy water.

"Haul back on the ropes!" shouted Birch. "Don't let it slide anymore! Pull, men, pull!"

Bracing their feet against the other sleds, the men grasped the ropes of the sliding cannon and heaved with all their strength. After several long minutes of straining, the sled moved back into position, scraping hard against the wooden floor of the deck, and the boat righted itself. With a sigh of collective relief, the men relaxed until one of them shouted, "Man overboard!" He pointed to someone floundering in a hole in the ice. "It's Tom Hickey!"

"Secure the load!" shouted Birch as he flung off his heavy coat. "I'm going in!"

"No!" cried Joseph. "Throw him a rope," but it was too late. Birch had already climbed down the side of the boat until he could lie on his stomach and scoot toward the ice hole. "Hang on, Tom. I'm coming!"

Tom flailed and splashed, breaking off pieces of the edge of the hole that now threatened to swallow him. "Help me!"

"I'm coming!" Birch called, even though he could barely be heard over the wind and the shouts of the men on the boat.

"Careful! It's cracking! Come back!"

The ice chilled his chest through his shirt, and where the material slid up, his bare skin clung to the ice. Birch did his best to ignore the tearing of bits of his skin as he stretched out until his fingertips finally reached one of the broken edges of the ice hole, and Tom grabbed his hand in a vice-like grip. He choked out, "Help me!"

The men on the boat shouted encouragement. Birch's arms throbbed as he dragged the water-laden Tom out of the hole. "Kick your feet!" he ordered Tom as the ice groaned under their weight. Tom kicked his feet in the water and slid out a few more inches, but not nearly enough.

"Hang on, Tom. I got you."

Using his feet for leverage, Birch maneuvered the two of them back toward the gundalow. By this time Tom was little more than dead weight, and his whole body, face, hair, and clothing were covered with ice crystals.

"Here's a rope," shouted Joseph from the boat. Birch felt the end of the rope flap against his back, but he couldn't let go of Tom or twist around enough to reach it. The bitter wind continued to blow nonstop, and both shivered violently. The cold spread through their bellies and moved out to their trembling arms. Tom shook so badly he lost his grip when his water-soaked glove slipped off his hand and out of Birch's grasp. Birch stretched his arms and slowly wrapped his fingers over Tom's bare hand. "Don't give up, Tom!" cried Birch. "Hold on to me. We're almost there."

His muscles ached and his breathing labored as he dragged Tom, now too cold to move or help, across the ice. After what seemed like forever, his feet touched the side of the gundalow. He felt a hand on his boot, followed by a loop of rope sliding over his ankle. He glimpsed back to see Joseph dangling over the edge of the boat with two men holding him by the legs as he reached for Birch and tugged the rope loop tight around Birch's ankle. "I've got him! Pull!" he shouted.

The two men onboard heaved together and lifted Joseph back to safety while four others pulled the rope on Birch's leg and dragged him awkwardly up the side of the boat. The aged wood sliced more pieces of skin off his legs and stomach.

"Don't let go!" shouted Joseph. "You're almost there!"

First Birch and then Tom finally found themselves

on the floor of the boat, shivering violently. "Get them warm," called Joseph. Two men took off their jackets and draped them over Tom and Birch while rubbing their arms to get the circulation moving until they could bring blankets to wrap their shipmates in.

"Get his water-logged clothes off him, and his boots." Soon, Tom was naked and wrapped up in four or five heavy wool blankets and a tarp.

"Get them both on their feet and make them walk. Rub Tom's hands and feet before they fall off."

The gundalow rocked as more ice cracked beneath it, and she floundered slightly, taking on near-frozen water, but, by the grace of God, her gunwales at the top edge of the sides of the boat stayed above the water line and the men were able to bail out any water.

Two days later the gundalow reached the southern end of the lake and met a worried, but now relieved, Henry Knox. The men tied up the boat and gathered on shore around small fires. Birch held onto Tom's arm to steady him as they stepped onto the ground.

"I still can't feel my feet," Tom said, struggling to walk. Three toes on Tom's right foot had turned an ugly black and blisters formed on them. Birch's little finger on his right hand had the same symptoms.

Tom sat down hard on the edge of a large boulder beside one of the fires on shore.

"I'll get you something to eat while you sit and warm up," said Birch.

"Ye don't have to treat me like a baby. I'll get my own food." Tom started to lift himself off the rock, only to fall back down with a grunt.

"Just sit there. I'll bring you something, but don't expect it to be more than hardtack and crackers."

Just then a group of men from the gundalow walked by the pair. "Johansen, you sure did some pretty nice ice fishing out there, but if I were you, I'd throw him back, too small." He gave a hearty laugh.

Another man slapped Hickey on the shoulder. "Did you forget how to walk on the water, my man?"

The third man joined in. "I would have waited until summer to go for a splash! The weather's better then!" All three laughed and walked away when one turned back and said, "Good work, Johansen. Took guts."

Tom watched them go before he said grimly, "Ye tell 'em to say that?"

"No."

"Ye just played the hero again." He spit out the words. "Like always. The big man, Lieutenant Johansen, the leader of men. Fearless and brave. Defender of the weak."

"Stop it, Tom. You don't have any right to take it out on me. I went out on the ice for a friend. You should know that by now."

Birch understood how Tom's early life had shaped him, making him angry and jealous. Tom had fallen from his proud and celebrated reputation as a thief and pickpocket in Ireland to being a lowly soldier here in the Americas. Still, nothing of his former life was reason to act like this. Birch didn't expect him to say, "Thank you," but a little gratitude would be nice.

Tom glared at him before dropping his head to his chest saying, "Yeah, get me something to eat. Save me from starvation."

Tom hardly spoke to Birch as the Noble Train of Artillery made its way south to the Hudson River, and once there Knox realized the water wasn't frozen hard enough to carry the heavy sleds. To add to that, all the men he'd hired near the fort had gone home, claiming to be too exhausted to continue the trip.

"Looks like this is as far as we go," said Tom.

Knox answered him with, "I will not give up. I made a promise to General Washington, and I intend to deliver the cannons. I'm going to New York City to hire teamsters to haul the sleds along the shore of the river. While I'm gone, repair the sleds, retie the cannons in position, and be ready to leave upon my return."

Knox brought back a crew of hardy teamsters who had nothing but scorn for the exhausted men who had carried the weapons this far.

"Step aside," said one New York man to Tom. "I'll push the sled through the drift. How about you ride on top, and I'll move both of you."

"My pleasure," said Tom with disdain in his tone. "Up there I can make sure ye do it right."

"I'll do it right!"

"We'll see." The ensuing fight left Tom and the teamster with black eyes and cut lips.

Four times the train of cannons had to cross the barely frozen Hudson River, and four times a load of cannons slid off into the water.

On the last time across, Birch and one of the New York haulers stood waist-deep in the icy water struggling to lift a cannon out of the river and back onto the sled. "Thank God, you cut the lines on the sled before the horses were dragged under," said Birch.

"Good thing that skinny Knox gave us all axes. How'd that johnny raw greenhorn get in charge of this anyway?"

"It was his idea. Loop that rope around the end of the barrel. Then we can pull it out."

"I don't care whose idea it was, just so we're not squashed by falling cannons, and he pays us when this is over. Heave!"

****

Transporting the Ticonderoga cannons to the outskirts of Boston, first estimated to take sixteen or seventeen days, took forty, and they finally arrived on January 25, 1776. With the help of more soldiers, they reassembled the weapons in near secrecy along the Dorchester ridge across the river from Boston.

The teamsters went home with coins in their pockets, leaving the soldiers of Washington's army to stand guard for nearly two months before the gunpowder arrived. That night, the bombardment of the city began, and the British army deserted Boston for Nova Scotia, Canada, on March 17, 1776.

Now, finally released from duty for three days, Birch and Joseph headed for Cambridge and the little house with the words "Dr. Samuel Dougal" on the sign over the door.

****

Justine Gallagher came down the stairs carrying blankets when she heard a familiar voice call, "Anybody home?"

Her heart skipped a beat as she dropped the blankets on the steps and jumped over them to get to the front door. "Joseph! Joseph! Is it really you?"

He flung his arms around her and twirled her off the small porch into the yard. Before either of them said a word, he kissed her firmly on the mouth, and she responded in kind. Cupping her cheek with his hand, he wiped his thumb over her tears.

"Hold me up," she said. "My legs are like mush. I thought I'd lost you. It's been so long."

"You don't need to worry. Not even the devil himself could keep me away. You own my every breath." Wrapping his free arm tightly around her waist, he lifted her off the ground again and moving his hand from her cheek to the back of her neck, kissed her.

When they finally separated, Justine spoke in yearning gasps. "Let me look at you. Are you hurt? Have you lost weight? I'll get Dr. Sophie." She started to pull away, but he tugged her back.

"I'm not hurt, and I haven't lost weight," he said, patting his round, but firm belly. "Well, maybe a little, but I'm still strong as an ox."

"Where have you been? It's been months since we heard word."

"We've been in the far north. I've never seen so much snow and ice, and I hope to never again."

"Where? Why?"

"Henry Knox had a plan to get the lobsterbacks out of Boston once and for all. He had a crazy idea to go to Ft. Ticonderoga in upstate New York and bring back the cannons from the deserted fort. All he needed was some soldiers and some money. Washington said, 'Yes,' so Birch and I were assigned to go with him."

"How did you bring them back? Cannons are heavy."

"It's a long story of frozen lakes and horses pulling the cannons on sleds, and frozen toes, and teamsters from New York City. When we got back here with the guns, we set them up south of Boston in just one night, and those dunderheaded British never knew a thing until Washington started shooting into the city. They turned tail and sailed to Canada in the middle of the night."

"We heard rumors they had left, but who knows what to believe. We even heard the cannons booming too, but we didn't know what was happening. We thought we were under attack. Every night and every day I prayed for you to survive."

He lifted one of her braids and brushed the loose end of it over her cheek. "I wasn't in any real danger, just exhausted mostly. The man next to me lost three toes when a cannon part slid off the sled, and, oh, Tom Hickey fell through the ice."

Justine gasped.

"But Birch saved him. It was pretty exciting."

"Exciting? It sounds dangerous."

"Enough of that. I've got other things on my mind right now. I've only got three days before I have to be back. The army is moving out, heading toward New York City."

"Leaving again? Kiss me, man of my heart!"

Sophie watched them from the doorway for as long as she could stand it before blurting out, "Did Birch come with you? What did you say about him saving Tom?"

Joseph lifted his head. "He'll be here tomorrow, and he'll tell you all about it. He's been promoted to lieutenant, so he has to get his squad ready for travel."

"How is he?"

"He lost the tip of his little finger to frostbite," Joseph shouted over his shoulder as he and Justine ran, hand in hand, toward the woods surrounding the property. "I'll bring her back." A few seconds later, he added with a grin, "Maybe."

"Joseph, wait!" called Sophie. "Tell me what happened to Birch!"

Her father, coming up behind her, put his hand on her shoulder. "Leave them be. They need to be alone."

"But I want to know about Birch."

Samuel dragged out the words as he patted her softly on the back, "Sophie, he'll tell you himself soon enough."

"They better be back here before dark or I'm going after them!"

Joseph and Justine returned to the house just before sunset to an anxious Sophie. "Tell me about Birch!" she said before they were even through the door.

"He's fine," said Joseph, "just tired and worn out like the rest of us. We almost lost a couple of cannon parts, but we were able to dredge them up from the water. Took a day to do it. Those things weigh 1000 pounds, you know. Then Birch saved Tom Hickey."

Justine took Joseph's hand in hers. "You didn't tell me how it happened. Is he all right?"

"Tom slid off the boat when one of the sleds tilted, and he fell through the ice. Birch got right out and stretched out on the ice until he could reach him. Then he dragged him back to the boat. Tom shivered for a week, and he wasn't much good for most of a month, but he was fine by the time we got the cannons here."

"I'll bet he was grateful."

"You know Tom, not much to say about it. I'm not sure he knows how to be grateful."

Sophie wasn't listening but had a preoccupied look in her eyes. "Frostbite can be dangerous. Are you sure

Birch'll be here tomorrow? I want to look at his fingers."

Joseph nodded. "Tomorrow. He promised."

Chapter Seven

Late that evening

Lieutenant Birch Johansen gently shook her shoulder. "Sophie, you fell asleep on the stairs again."

Her eyes fluttered open as they adjusted to the darkness and to the man kneeling on the step below her. "Is that you?" she asked. "I'm not dreaming?"

"It's me."

Relief flowed through her like the stream behind the house. Her body went limp, and her voice quivered. "It's you."

Before another word passed between them, he lifted her off the step into his lap and nuzzled her neck. She melted into his arms. The world was right again now that he was here.

In a breathless voice, she said, "Tell me everything. Everything."

"There's nothing important now that I'm home with you."

She rubbed her fingers across his cheeks, chin, and shoulders. "You've changed. Your face seems thinner, but your shoulders are broader, stronger." She squeezed his arm. "My father would call you a strapping young man."

"Hard work will do that. I was promoted to lieutenant, and I have the command of some new recruits."

"A lieutenant, that's wonderful! You'll be a fine officer. Joseph told us about nearly losing the cannons. And nearly losing Tom."

Birch shook his head and smiled. "That Joseph can't keep anything to himself."

"Tom must have been grateful you were there."

"Not so you'd notice, but I understand why. He grew up on his own with no family, so he always holds himself apart from everybody else. He always wants more."

"More what?"

"More money, more authority, more prestige. He thinks I made him look weak."

"But that's not what you did. You saved his life."

"Why are we talking about Tom when all I want to do is kiss you?" So, he did.

The kiss felt like dancing to music that only the two of them could hear. Their lips melded together, and the sensations rose and fell like a symphony. They moved as one, and then apart without leaving each other's arms. The kiss ended softly and quietly.

Sophie was the first to speak. "Things aren't the same when you're not here. I didn't know I could miss someone so much."

"You're giving me too much credit. Kiss me again."

She leaned in, and she never wanted that kiss to end, but when it did, she finally felt whole again. Running her finger from button to button on his jacket, she said, "I look in every soldier's face for pieces of you. Are his eyes like yours? Are his lips? The answer is always no."

With a sudden jerk, she sat up, grabbing his hand.

"Let me see your finger." Birch held out his hand, and Sophie studied it as only a doctor could. "Someone did a good job bandaging it up. I can rewrap it and check for infection."

"Not now. I don't have much time here. Our company is heading out in a couple of days, marching to New York City. Washington's certain the British will try there next."

"How long can you stay?"

"Only two days after this one. Until then, I won't leave your side."

And he didn't.

****

For Birch, the hardest part of being with Sophie for only three days was that it was only three days. He found her after his first battle at Bunker Hill, left her for the army camp a couple of months later, and was gone on the trek to Ticonderoga until now. He'd be leaving again all too soon. Even though he had only spent a little over two months with her as he healed from his musket ball wound, he now had never been so sure of anything in his life. He was certain. He needed her and wanted her above all else. She made him more of the man he wanted to be.

The next morning Dr. Samuel Dougal left the house to tend to the sick in the area who'd been neglected during the treating of the battle wounded. "I'll be back in a couple of days. Send word if you need me."

"The four of us can take care of everything," said Sophie as she kissed his cheek. "Joseph and Justine can take care of the house while Birch and I see to the patients. Don't worry but be careful. Not everybody agrees that the fight for freedom is worth it, and there are people on both sides you have to look out for."

"I can take care of myself, and I'm sure Birch will take care of you."

Birch nodded. "You have my word, sir."

Birch and Sophie worked hand in hand with the wounded, but Sophie handled the smallpox victims in the greenhouse by herself, always scrubbing down and changing her clothes afterwards so no one else could get infected. "I want to inoculate you, but there isn't enough time for you to recover before you have to leave."

"When I come back, I'll take the cure," he said. "Until then I'll be fine."

In the evening, they walked in the moonlight, each of them sharing dreams they never knew they had.

"You've changed my life," he said that evening under the tree in the yard. "I always knew I wanted a family of my own like my sisters and my brother, Linden, but it was so far in the distance, I could barely see it. When I saw you, the first words in my head were a grateful, 'Oh my.' Your wonderful face, your smile, your eyes, got my attention, but after watching you take care of me and the others, I knew my future was closer. It was here, and you had to be in it."

Sophie spoke quietly, but her eyes never left his face. "In the beginning, I was confused about how I felt and even why you stirred something in me." She rubbed her finger softly over the back of his hand. "The men I meet are either wounded or sick or farmers scratching out a living. Throw in a few shopkeepers, and that's all I see. Intelligent men of courage are hard to find. Then I met you."

He tugged her closer and wrapped his arms around her. "Maybe I should thank the redcoat who shot me."

"When you do, tell him I won't let this war keep us apart, not in our hearts."

She raised her hand and gently rubbed the beard he'd grown during the New York winter. He hummed quietly at her touch. "I never imagined you with a beard before, but I love this one. It's a darker blond than your hair. You look very handsome."

He lifted her hand away from his beard, but she put it right back, this time raking her fingers across the hair on his chin. "I don't want to forget how you look or how it feels." She took in a soft breath. "I wish I could turn back the clock, so I could have found you sooner and loved you longer. No matter how long I live, it will never be enough for me."

He kissed her gently. Her soft lips melted like taffy into his. "I wouldn't have met you if it weren't for this war, and now it's taking me away from you again."

"I thought my life was complete here in Cambridge, in this house, that I'd be content fixing and mending people for the rest of my life, but you filled a void I didn't even know I had. When you're near me I feel so sure, and when you're gone, I can't keep you out of my thoughts."

The evening moonlight found them through the still bare branches on the trees. He leaned in slowly until their lips met again. Soft and moist, warm and tender. She purred as his mouth moved against hers, his tongue lightly licking her lips, and she opened her mouth a bit, asking him in.

He felt her heartbeat against his chest as her fingers danced through his beard and into his hair. She clasped her hands at the nape of his neck. His leg stepped between hers, and she shifted her hips, bringing him even closer.

An owl suddenly hooted from an overhead branch, and their kiss broke, but their hands still held each other close. She leaned her cheek against his chest, and they stood motionless as a soft wind blew around them.

In silence they walked back to the house. Tired and content, they checked each patient before carrying blankets to the space under the stairs and piling them against the wall. They only intended to stay and talk awhile before she went upstairs to her bedroom, and he spent the rest of the night on the blankets. But despite good intentions, they couldn't bear to leave each other, and contented together, they fell asleep.

Through the night, Birch dreamed of having her fully and completely, but tonight was not the time. Maybe soon.

The next morning, Sophie and Birch, neither wanting to leave the warmth, stayed wrapped in the blankets. Finally, she said, "I have to change the sergeant's bandage, but I'll be right back." She tossed off the first of the several blankets covering her.

"No, wait a minute. I want to show you something. I carried a notebook in my jacket pocket on the way to and from Fort Ticonderoga, and I wrote in it whenever I could. I wanted you to know what was in my heart, even if I never had the chance to say the words to you." He handed her the small book, and she pressed it against her heart before opening it.

She read the first line to herself, then handed it back to him. "You read them. I want to hear you say the words."

He took the book from her and read each line, slowly and honestly, pausing between them to see her expression. She tapped the book when she wanted him to continue.

"You're the one I've been waiting for."

"I'm lonely without you and complete when you are near."

"I never knew the world could be so colorful until you came into my life."

"I feel a part of me is missing until I see your smile. Then I am full and content."

"I can't wait to show you how much you mean to me."

Snuggling into his chest, she put her arms around him. "Are there anymore?"

"Not on paper yet. Do you want to keep the notebook?"

"No."

He winced. "You really don't want it?"

"No, because I want you to write more lines in it. Write down things that I can read later, but right now, I have to change the sergeant's bandage. Then I'll make us some bread with jam."

She stood, but he tugged on her hand. "I have something to ask before you go."

"All right."

Sucking in a long deep breath, he said in the firmest voice he could muster, "Will you marry me?"

Chapter Eight

She blinked her eyes and tipped her head to the side as if pondering a difficult question. Birch's heart pounded. Would she say no?

Finally, after what seemed like endless breaths, she said, "I never thought I would marry. I never intended to marry. I had enough right here."

Birch's brow tightened. "If we're married and something happened to me, you would get my pension."

Sophie's voice became a guttural rasp. "Awww!" And like a bear caught in a trap, she fought her way out from under the blankets. "You fool! I don't want your stupid pension!" Tears surged into her eyes. "If you died…If you died…" She dropped to her knees in front of him. "I'm going to marry you just so you won't die, because I won't let you. Do you hear me? I won't let you!"

Birch burst out laughing. "So, you will marry me? You're saying yes? You'll marry me today?"

Sophie leaned in until their lips almost touched and said slowly, "You're the only man on this earth I would ever marry." She kissed him, and they fell against the blankets in each other's arms.

"Hurrah!" Birch shouted, raising his arm in victory.

"Hurrah!" Sophie chimed in between their laughter and kisses.

"What's going on under here?" asked Joseph, ducking his head under the stairs. "You're waking up the entire house."

"The sooner they get up, the better!" said Birch. "We have a wedding to plan, and we only have today to do it. Go get the nearest preacher! No, first tell Justine we need a cake or some tarts!" Birch stood up quickly, bumping his head on the slope of the staircase. "Ouch, no, first find Dr. Samuel. I need to ask for his permission!" He shook his finger at Joseph. "No, first get the preacher!"

Joseph grinned. "Yes, sir! I'll do all of it. Preacher first." He headed out the door and down the road to the nearby church. "A wedding! It's going to be a great day!" But once he got to the small chapel one mile away, the preacher was not as enthusiastic.

"Who wants to be married?" he asked. He was a portly man with a long black beard and a bulbous nose that jerked and wiggled every time he spoke.

"Sophie Dougal and Birch Johansen."

"I know Sophie, but I'm afraid I don't know this Birch fellow. Is he from around here?"

"No, his family's from New Jersey. Birch is a soldier in the Continental Army, and they met when she removed a British musket ball from his side."

The preacher's face suddenly turned crimson as he shook his fist just inches from Joseph's chin. "You've come to the wrong place! I am proud to be loyal to our king, and I will never marry a rebel to one of our own!" The man took a deep breath, filling his lungs with air so he could shout even louder. "It's God's will! The king's will is God's will! Get out of here!" Reverend Massey pointed sharply at the door. "Get out!"

Joseph turned in that direction before he stopped and faced the man. "As a man of God, would you rather they live in sin than be lawfully married?" He took a couple of threatening steps closer to the reverend. "They will be together whether you approve or not, so will you make Sophie a fallen woman, shunned by all because you, a self-righteous, pompous devil-dodger, refused them the sacrament?"

The man turned even redder in the face and sputtered, "I have known Sophie since she was a child. She never had a mother to guide her, no proper direction, only a father who put wild improper ideas in her head about avoiding a woman's duty and allowed her to doctor with him. A woman's place is in the home with her children, not doing surgery on...naked men! No fit work for a woman! I cannot and will not acknowledge such a marriage."

"You will!" Joseph put his shoulder into the preacher's belly and hoisted him off the floor, carrying him kicking and yelling out the door and down the road. Once back at the Dougal house, he dumped the man in a chair and held him there with his hand on his chest. "The preacher's here!" he shouted. The few patients still lying on the floor started to cheer while Massey continued to bluster.

"I'm so glad you could come, Pastor Massey," said Dr. Samuel Dougal, still brushing the road dust off his jacket. "I just got back from seeing some of your parishioners, and rest assured, most are well, but the bride and I will not be ready for a while. May I offer you tea while you wait?"

Massey pushed against Joseph's arm, but to no advantage. "This man dragged me here. I demand he release me!"

"I'm sorry to hear that," replied Samuel. "I'm sure that was a bit uncomfortable, so may I offer you tea while you wait?" Samuel stepped closer to the preacher and lowered his face until they were almost nose to nose. "My daughter *is* getting married to a fine young soldier. You will say all the proper words, and sign all the proper papers, or…" He paused. "Or I will have to reset your arm again."

"My arm isn't broken," stuttered Massey.

Samuel spoke through gritted teeth. "It will be…before I reset it."

Massey's eyes opened wide, and he swallowed hard. "I'd…uh…be glad to perform the ceremony." His eyes moved to look up at Joseph. "Yes, I would like some tea."

****

Two hours later, Birch stopped pacing in the front room and watched his bride make her entrance down the stairs.

He wore a dress uniform that had belonged to one of the dead patients. Over the months, Justine had cleaned all the useable uniforms in the hopes that someday another man might wear it, and with only small alterations, this one fit Birch perfectly. It was a regimental dark blue coat, over a light gray waistcoat, shirt, and breeches, a silk scarf, shoes with buckles, and a tricorn hat.

He moved to the bottom of the stairs and waited to take Sophie's hand and guide her down the last few steps. "That dress is beautiful."

"It was my mother's. All Justine had to do was brush it off and take it in a bit."

The linen dress, a subtle cream color, was sprinkled from collar to hem with dusty blue flowers and designs. It fit well, draping easily over her slender figure. A folded white scarf wrapped around the back of her neck and tucked into her bodice, and as the final delicate touch, white lace draped at her wrists.

He smiled and reached for her hand, but Samuel interrupted him as he followed his daughter down the stairs. He now wore a freshly brushed black wool coat with a black waistcoat under it, and matching breeches with white stockings. "She's not yours yet, Birch," he said firmly. "She's still mine until the proper words are said."

Birch nodded with a wink. "All right, I can wait, but not much longer."

The preacher stood in the center of the room with Joseph's hand clutching the back of his jacket to keep him in place. Justine waited beside her husband, smiling broadly, with her hands clasped in front of her.

"Are we ready to begin?" asked Samuel.

"Yes, doctor," said Massey with a slight tremble to his voice. "Will the couple, please, come and stand before me?"

Massey assumed his Sunday morning preaching voice, deep and resonating, as he recited the vows he had said so often for other couples and reluctantly did now. "The purpose of marriage is for the procreation of children, to avoid sinful behavior, and for the mutual help and comfort of society both in prosperity and adversity."

To Birch, he said hesitantly, "Young man."

"My name is Birch Johanscn."

Massey cleared his throat and with a touch of

sarcasm, said, "Birch, named after a tree, interesting." His eyes flickered over to Joseph before he quickly added, "Do you, Birch Johansen, take this woman to be your wife, to love her, comfort her, honor, and keep her in sickness and in health, forsaking all others as long as you both shall live?"

"I do. I will. I promise." Each word louder and stronger than the one before.

Massey cleared his throat again. " 'I do' is sufficient, young man. Dr. Dougal, are you certain you really want your daughter to wed this renegade?"

Joseph squeezed Massey's arm. "Is my hold too tight? I do hope your arm isn't broken, sir." He gripped it tighter, bringing Massey almost to his knees. "Are you able to finish the vows, sir?"

Samuel said, "Joseph, I'm certain Reverend Massey wants to continue. Am I right, Reverend?"

Massey gulped, nodded, and straightened up as best he could. "Now, Sophie Dougal, are you certain you want to marry this man?"

Sophie squeezed Birch's hand. "I have never been more certain of anything in my life."

Massey choked out the words, swallowing after almost every one before he could continue. "All right, Mistress Sophie, will you obey him, serve him, love, honor, and keep him in sickness and in health, and forsaking all others, keep only to him as long as you both shall live?"

"I will with all my heart."

"Do you have a ring?" asked Massey.

"We do not," said Birch. "Our vows will be our pledge."

Quickly Samuel Dougal thrust his arm between

Birch and Sophie. In his fingers he held a thin silver band encrusted with three rectangular blue sapphires and three pearls, all edged with small diamond chips. "Mother's?" asked Sophie.

"Yes," said her father. "It had been in her family for many years, and I, a poor doctor and having no ring of my own to give Eleanor, was honored to receive it from her father to give to her on our wedding day. Birch, I would be honored if you would accept this ring to give to Sophie on your wedding day."

For a moment, Birch couldn't draw a breath. He had no words for this generous offer. He took the ring from Samuel's fingers and in a choked voice said, "Sophie, with this ring, I thee wed," and slipped it on her third finger. It fitted perfectly.

"Samuel, you may be the only person who fully appreciates what the gift of this ring means to me when I have nothing to give her but my love." He brought Sophie's hand to his lips and kissed it. "Thank you for the ring and for giving me your daughter. I promise I will cherish both forever."

Samuel patted both Birch and Sophie on the shoulder and stepped back into place as he became teary eyed with loving fatherly tears. "Continue, preacher."

With Massey's direction, Birch and Sophie completed their vows to each other.

Taking a small Bible from his vest pocket, the preacher read from the well-known "love" chapter of Corinthians 13 and ended the ceremony with a prayer for their safety in these perilous times. "You may kiss the bride." And Birch and Sophie did so to the applause of Justine, Joseph, Samuel, and the patients who gathered at the doors and windows to watch.

Under Joseph and Samuel's close eyes, Pastor Massey wrote out a certificate of marriage and all present boldly signed their names.

Afterward, Joseph took Massey by the arm again and gave him a mocking smile. "Would you like me to escort you back home?"

Massey vigorously shook his head. "I'll walk."

****

The house was eerily quiet. Sophie had protested the moving of Samuel, Joseph, and Justine along with all the patients into the barn for the night, but her father insisted. He argued, "I am more than capable of attending to them, and privacy is important for newlyweds. Besides, the barn has a pot-bellied stove for warmth, and tonight the wood box is full."

"But what about the smallpox patients?" asked Sophie.

"There are only four left in the greenhouse, and I can check on them. You two newlyweds need to spend your first night together, alone."

Birch wrapped his arm around Sophie, saying, "Come see what Justine has done for us." He led her inside to the front room, which was now completely empty except for a haphazard pile of thick blankets and pillows in front of the fireplace. The firelight bathed the room in a warm glow, inviting the newlyweds to curl up together in the makeshift bed. She laid her head on his chest, and he played with a strand of her hair. No words were spoken as their eyes sparkled with the dancing firelight. Occasional pops of wood made them both turn their heads, but within seconds they only had eyes for each other again.

He took his small journal out of his pocket and handed it to her. "I wrote these words, and I want to hear you read them again."

She opened the book and began to read aloud. "You're the one I've been waiting for. I'm alone without you and complete when you are near. I feel a part of me is missing until I see your smile."

He placed his fingers on the next page and repeated from memory the words written there. "I've waited so long to show you how I feel. I'll wait no more."

She came to her knees and reached for his hands and interlocked her fingers with his. They kissed, a kiss as warm and soft as the fire glow, a kiss that spoke of things to come. He brushed his thumb along her cheek, and his touch sent a shiver through her.

She started to unpin her bodice from her stomacher underneath, but he lightly pulled her hands away. "Let me," he said. His fingers undid each pin slowly and gently until he slid her bodice to the floor. She arched her neck and sighed as his hands slid over her shoulders, pushing open the chemise, until she shrugged it off, and it, along with her petticoat, floated down her legs to the floor. Her breath became ragged as she turned to face him again and tugged his shirt out of his breeches. He lifted it over his head and off.

She kissed his bare chest, moving her mouth up to his neck until he tipped down his head, so his lips could meet hers. These kisses spoke of a passion yet to come that they hadn't dared release before.

"When was the last time I told you I loved you?" he said softly.

"When you wiped the jam from the tart off my chin after the ceremony. When was the last time I told you I loved you?"

"Every time you look at me. Your eyes say the words, and I hear them with my heart."

"Lieutenant Johansen?"

"Yes, Mistress Johansen?"

"I insist that you show me how much you love me right here, in this room, on this bed of blankets right now."

"Doctor's orders?"

"Doctor's wishes."

Birch flipped back the top blanket, letting the perfume waft from the lavender petals Justine had sprinkled there. He eased Sophie down into the pile, and she slid under the warmth. He stripped off his breeches and slid in beside her, pulling another soft wool blanket over them. As he lay back on the pillows, she pushed herself up and put her head against his chest, listening to the steady rhythm of his heart beating beneath her ear.

"I often put my ear against a man's chest to see if he's alive, and his heartbeat assures me. But your heartbeat sounds entirely different tonight. You're more than alive, you're mine, and I'm yours. I think I knew from the first moment I saw you I would someday listen to your heart like this."

The time for words was over. He wanted to be a part of her in the most intimate way.

Her kisses tasted like the tarts they'd eaten earlier, sweet and scented. Their hands roamed over each other as if to memorize everything, every curve, every muscle. He found her soft places, and she found his stronger ones, and when all his hesitation and willpower vanished, and he had to have her, he entered her core. She welcomed him.

Her hips moved to match his rhythm, and as it grew faster and stronger, he felt her quiver. He felt her tightening, and he responded until both understood a release like no other. Breathless, their bodies wrapped each other together.

In the aftermath, they whispered promises of devotion. "We might be separated by distance, but we will never be apart in my commitment to you," he said. "War might take me away, but my heart will stay here with you."

They made love again, and as the firelight burned down to ashy coals, they fell asleep in each other's arms.

They awoke to the sunlight peeking between the curtains on the front windows.

"One more time before you go?" whispered Sophie. "One more time until you come back to me."

He couldn't refuse her.

Later, they both lifted their heads off the pillows when they heard a gentle knocking on the wooden trim around the door leading from the kitchen.

"I'm sorry. You don't know how sorry," said Joseph without stepping into the room, "but we have to be back at camp by noon."

"I hear you," said Birch, never taking his eyes off Sophie. She nodded.

They reluctantly unwrapped themselves from the blankets and helped each other dress. Once more Justine had made the wedding day perfect by washing and pressing fresh clothes. They never saw her drape the clothes over a chair in the corner during the night. Birch tucked his shirt into his breeches, and Sophie tied her apron over a light green dress.

In the kitchen, neither of the married pairs took more than a couple of spoonfuls from their breakfast of bread soaked in milk and swimming in honey. They couldn't keep their eyes off each other as if memorizing a vision they wouldn't see for a very long time. Talk was sparse while longing glances and touching of hands and arms was not.

At the front door, both couples said reluctant goodbyes.

Sophie wrapped her arms around Birch's neck. "Shakespeare said 'parting is such sweet sorrow.' But there is nothing sweet about this at all." She reached up on her tiptoes and kissed him deeply and completely. "Be brave, be strong, and stay alive. I can fix a broken body, but I can never mend a broken heart. Let your last words to me be the same as mine. I love you."

Birch stepped back, saluted, and said in a strong voice, "I love you. I promise I'll be back."

He and Joseph walked down the path to the gate and then onto the road. He looked over his shoulder to see her one last time as Sophie lifted her hand in a heartsick farewell.

Chapter Nine

William Tryon, appointed by King George as Royal Governor of New York, tossed his bag down on the bed in the small compartment of a British ship, the *Duchess of Gordon*, now docked in New York Harbor. The smell of brackish water, a mix of sea water and river water, and the sloshing of the waves against the ship nearly drove him to distraction, but here was the only safe place for him now.

He muttered to no one, "Up until last October, I conducted state business as usual, despite the growing rebellion led by this hooligan, George Washington. Then my own spies delivered a devastating bit of news that put me in danger and condemned me to this wretched boat! The indignity of it all! How could they?"

The fledgling Continental Congress had issued a proclamation. He read enough to infuriate him. *It is recommended that…Councils and committees of safety arrest and secure every person in their…colonies…who may in their opinion endanger the safety of the colony or the liberties of America.*

"Now those rebels consider everyone a threat simply by being English! Now I am in danger of being arrested by those same damn agitators! How has my life come to this? After all I've done for king and country over here in this God-forsaken wilderness!"

He ripped the paper in half. "Damn those rebels!"

"I've begged for security and protection from the mayor of New York City, David Mathews and he refused me. The pompous ass! Even the sausage-wrapper newspapers won't support me." His face turned a bright crimson as he gritted his teeth remembering how he had threatened to order British ships to attack the city if he was harmed in any way, and still no one responded with help.

Alone and without support, his escape last October was entirely up to him, so with the help of his aides, he fled in the dark of night, carrying only a trunk of his papers and a few changes of clothes. He first boarded a small British ship, the *Halifax,* docked in the harbor, but after another meager reply to his entreaties for help, he had no choice but to move to a larger ship, the *Duchess of Gordon.*

"Larger, my ass!"

Dipping his quill into the inkpot, he began yet another letter to David Mathews, the loyalist mayor of New York City, and his onetime supporter. If Mathews hadn't provided help to him personally, perhaps he'd help to put an end to this abomination of a rebellion.

Tryon wrote *We have plans to make. To prevail in these colonies, we must get rid of George Washington by whatever means possible. The people are united around him, and without him they will flounder. Come tonight.*

"Benson, get in here," he shouted to his aide as he folded and sealed the letter with a drop of his unique jasmine-scented wax. As he inhaled the sweet smell, he remembered better times, and promised himself that someday, somehow, he'd get off this ship and teach a lesson to everyone who betrayed him.

"Deliver this message to the mayor of New York. Return with his reply. Your secrecy is worth the cost of your life. Understand?"

The lieutenant nodded and tucked the note into a slit in the lining of his jacket.

The next night, sailors on the *Duchess of Gordon* greeted a man at the dock holding a single lantern. "I wish to be escorted to the governor's cabin," he said. "Mayor Mathews sent me."

As the man entered Tryon's cabin, the former governor said harshly, "I requested Mayor Mathews himself."

"These are perilous times, and the mayor cannot take risks, but rest assured, the mayor and I speak as one."

Tryon gave no reply.

"This is the situation," said the man once he was seated in one of the chairs bolted to the floor in the governor's cabin. "A small number of colonists began this rebellion. But the speed at which they had to create a central government for thirteen independent colonies as well as organize a military has left them vulnerable. Their fledgling economy is in flux, and here is where we can be most effective and do the most damage."

"I'm listening," said Tryon, grabbing the edge of the desk to steady himself as a wave caused by a passing ship slapped the *Duchess*.

The man clutched at his stomach. "I don't have my sea legs yet."

The governor nodded. "There's a pail over there if you need it."

After taking a slow deep breath to calm his

stomach, the man went on. "We have a stronger military force, but an armed victory often creates more rebels than before. However, Governor, we don't propose a military victory. We propose to undermine this new government's ability to sustain a workable economy. If the citizens cannot buy supplies, and the army can't pay men to continue a war, everyone will lose faith in this American Congress, and to that end everything falls apart. We've already begun interference with their foreign trade capabilities by blocking foreign ships with goods headed for the colonies, but it's not enough."

"Are you saying our efforts to win this war militarily are futile? I can't believe the British army could be defeated by this ragtag bunch of riffraff, especially with all the information I've passed on to General Howe."

"Not at all, sir, but we don't necessarily have to win on the battlefield. We can sabotage their government's ability to maintain a stable economy using their newly printed paper notes. If they cannot pay their bills, this upstart government falls apart, and so does the rebellion."

Tryon arched his eyebrow. "Interesting idea. If we work from the inside, these rebels will defeat themselves."

"This Congress does not have enough gold or silver to back its money. The bills will continue to be devalued, and merchants will refuse to accept Continental ones as payment. Then, as the value drops, this Congress must print more, making the bills even less valuable, and a vicious downhill cycle is created."

"How do you plan to implement this idea?"

The man took out several pieces of blank paper from his case and laid them on the governor's desk. The ship lurched, and Tryon rested his hand on the pile to hold it in place before taking one piece off the top. He turned it over and over and then held it up to the light.

"This is a sample of the paper the colonists use for their bills. It is very cheaply made, but we can recreate it exactly in large quantities. We've imported some paper like this and enough ink, and our forgers are already at work.

"As for getting our counterfeit bills into circulation, we have several ideas. One is to advertise through the newspapers to find loyalist merchants and travelers to spend our bills. I call it 'wallpapering the countryside.' "

"Are you certain this paper is identical?" Tryon rattled the paper in his hands.

"Yes, sir, identical." After nervously clearing his throat, the man went on. "We also know a few British deserters who joined the Continental Army but still have loyalist leanings. We are certain they will be willing to spread counterfeit bills among the soldiers through gambling games. There's also word that Washington is forming a personal guard, and with a little incentive, some of them might be willing to do much more, possibly by getting rid of Washington altogether."

"Yes, the rebels have rallied around him, but it's dangerous to depend on only one man. If we can remove him from the picture…"

The man nodded.

"Imagine the embarrassment to have his own men turn against him," said Tryon, chuckling to himself.

"Especially from his precious personal guard. I like this plan already." He stood, shed his jacket, and loosened his shirt collar clinging to his damp skin. "Soon Washington's soldiers won't even be able to buy a cup of rum. Thirsty, dissatisfied soldiers will leave the cause, and Washington fails! Perhaps we can also look forward to Washington being eliminated altogether. Now that is something I would enjoy seeing."

"With him gone and the country in economic ruins, we will surely prevail," said the visitor.

"Those detestable patriots think they are rid of their British governor, but I'll show them what I can do. Even from this floating can, I'll show them." Tryon smiled a wicked smile. "Let's expand our efforts immediately."

Chapter Ten

George Washington's temporary headquarters, Cambridge, Massachusetts, April 1776

Troops waited in the yard for over an hour before footsteps sounded on the wooden porch of the inn, and the moment the man stepped outside, every eye turned in his direction. There was no need to announce him. His straight back, piercing blue eyes, and Roman nose, all framed with self-assurance, said it all.

"Gentlemen," called out the newly promoted Captain Caleb Gibbs from the steps. "General George Washington. Attention!"

Every soldier standing in the yard stiffened their backs. The sound of one hundred sets of heels clicking together resounded, quickly followed by one hundred hands snapping in salute.

"This is it," whispered one of them. "Now we'll find out why we've been called out of our units."

"It's himself!" whispered Thomas Hickey, standing in the third row of soldiers in the yard.

Birch Johansen gulped. "Why does he want *us*?"

"At ease, men," said the general after returning the salutes. He walked out of the doorway to the front of the small porch. His voice carried over the wind with authority as the timbre of every word declared him to be a man of courage and intent, a leader above all. Birch already had profound respect for him, and he knew why the country rallied around him in their fight for freedom.

"Men, you are summoned here because your commanding officers from every regiment in the colonies selected four of their best and finest men for this new battalion. I will choose a suitable number of you to be assigned to me personally. Captain Gibbs, apprise the troops of my requirements." Washington turned on his heel and walked back to his offices at the rear of the inn that served as his headquarters.

Caleb Gibbs, a wiry twenty-eight-year-old, spoke in a clear firm voice. "You have been chosen for a special assignment that requires a special man. You are all known for your sobriety, honesty, and good behavior. Each of you is approximately five feet eight inches tall to five feet ten inches tall, and most of all, you have shown yourselves to be clean and neat, a characteristic the general pays special attention to.

"General Washington and myself will examine and interview you with no consideration given to the colony you hail from or your family origins, which is why none of you are in uniform nor do you carry arms. The only thing required is for you to be perfectly willing to be part of this special guard. Anyone wishing to return to their unit is commanded to do so now. The rest of you may relax in the yard until you are called. Dismissed!"

Birch, his fair skin weathered by weeks in the sun, dropped his sack carried from camp. He leaned against one of the shade trees standing on either side of the wide stone path leading to the front door of the inn. Birch had washed his hair this morning, but tucking his scraggly blond locks behind his ears didn't always keep it out of his eyes.

Tom Hickey sat down on a patch of grass next to

him. "Sit down," he said. "We could be here a while."

"I don't want to get dirt on my clothes." The grass was sparse where the troops had trampled it. "We've been called out from our outfits for this, so it must be important. I want to be a part of it."

"A little dirt won't hurt mine." Tom raked his fingers through his dark hair and tugged on his shirt, tucking a torn cuff into his sleeve. "I don't have no one sending me fresh ones like ye do, Mr. High and Mighty."

Birch was glad his mother had sent a white linen shirt and black pants to him with a newly enlisted man who lived near their farm in New Jersey. Her note said, "Your mother worries, so here is something clean." The date was six weeks ago. He'd been in New York moving cannons, so he hadn't sent a letter in a long time. No wonder she was worried.

"I would have lent you my other shirt, you know that."

"Thank ye kindly, but I'll be stickin' to me own." Tom brushed at a small stain on his sleeve.

The friendship between Birch and Tom had been strained ever since the rescue on the ice, so Birch was glad Tom was finally talking to him again.

"If you didn't want to borrow a shirt of mine, someone would have lent you one. A lot of the others think of you as 'friend,' too."

"That's only 'cause I let 'em win at dice sometimes."

"The captain thinks enough of you to send you here."

Tom jumped to his feet, his voice raspy. "That's 'cause I can fight, but if I get named to this special troop, I'll be on my way up. After five years fighting the Indians with the British and going on that trek in the snow to get the cannons, I've shown 'em what I can do. Maybe I'll be an officer. Wouldn't that be something? Thomas Hickey, an officer!"

"Hush," said Birch, looking around to see if anyone heard Tom bragging, but the other soldiers were lost in their own thoughts. "Don't let anyone hear you talk like that. Washington needs to think we're the best soldiers who only want to serve him."

Tom leaned back against the tree and took in a deep breath of cool air. Spring might be on its way, but there was still a chill. "Yeah, yeah, I remember. I'm no eedjit."

"I never said you were. Just sometimes you spout off too much. I wish Joseph had been chosen with us."

"He's the eedjit," muttered Tom. "Too short, and he's got a stomach like a pipkin. Like the general would want a fat, pot-bellied eedjit."

"Joseph Gallagher may be a shopkeeper from Delaware, but he's a good fighter, and he's not fat. Just built differently. We're long and lean, and he's strong and sturdy. I recall he's beaten you in arm wrestling more than once."

Tom grunted. "Besides, he's married. The general don't like married men. They might be thinking about their women instead of their fighting."

"That worries me, too, now that I'm married to Sophie, but whatever this assignment is, I want to be a part of it."

"The general'll choose ye for sure, pretty lad! I'll make sure he knows ye're just what he's looking for, the perfect soldier. If he knows about the ice rescue, I'll make ye out the mighty hero." Hickey rolled his eyes. "Ye better hope he doesn't find out about yer secret wife."

"She's no secret."

"But ye don't want him to find out. Women and war don't mix." Tom watched Birch for a minute before saying, "I got ye rattled, don't I? Got ye thinking ye might be the eedjit." He laughed until Birch turned his back on him.

After a few moments of silence between them, Birch said, "Won't everyone be proud of us. A chance to be in General Washington's special guard. From raw recruits to personal security."

"So far, but maybe not far enough," murmured Tom who sat down, leaned back against the tree, and looked up at the leaves blowing with the wind. Again, he asked himself the questions that continued to haunt him. *How can I be this far away from where I started, and it still be the same sky above my head? I'm in another place, another time, but nothing's changed. Even now yet another man is telling me what to do, making me go places I don't want to go. I want to be my own man, and someday I will be, come hell or high water, or George Washington.*

Suddenly someone shouted, "Johansen and Hickey, front and center!"

Birch and Tom grabbed their packs and bolted from the yard to the inn.

Birch didn't realize he'd been holding his breath the whole way into Washington's office until he took an unexpected and embarrassing noisy gasp right in front of the general.

"Are you all right, soldier?" Washington asked.

"Yes, sir!" Birch saluted and nudged Tom with his elbow who followed suit.

Captain Caleb Gibbs, a thin but muscled man with blue eyes and a straight nose, stood to one side of Washington's surprisingly small and unimpressive desk. "I have reports from your commanding officer, and I will be asking you several questions to determine your fitness for this guard. First, Birch Johansen, your captain reports you obey orders as easily as you give them to your squad. Why is that?"

"Sir, I learned discipline as a young child, not from coercion or fear of punishment, but because my survival and safety, and that of my family, depended on consistent leadership and order. I do not follow orders blindly, but with the intent as to the outcome of those orders. I give them with the same intent."

Tom spoke up. "He's a right good fella and soldier. The other men listen when he talks, and he's never let them down. Me neither." The wooden floor creaked as Tom centered on his boots.

"Thank you, Mr. Hickey. I will be getting to you in a minute. Johansen, why did you join the army so early in the war?"

"My parents are immigrants, but only my oldest sister, Daisy, was born in Sweden. The rest of us children were born here in the colonies. My father and mother came with nothing but a few belongings and built a life for us, first with a dairy farm and now with harvesting trees for new buildings, but British suppression and taxation became crushing and unjust."

"You look familiar, young man. Have we met before?" interrupted the general.

"Yes, sir. I was one of the men who brought you a

coded message from Dr. Church, but you probably remember me better when my brother Ash and I visited you at Mount Vernon two years ago. One aspect of our family's business is to breed strong cattle stock and deliver it as needed to other farms so their herds may grow stronger. Johansen is a name well known in this part of the colonies."

"I recall you came by traveling partly on land by wagon with the bulls and then by boat the rest of the way to Mount Vernon. Quite a trip."

"We made two stops along the way to deliver bulls to other farms. I don't mind the travel because I enjoy seeing other parts of the country."

"I see," said General Washington.

"When we were at Mount Vernon, you spoke about the need for careful consideration of all sides of an event. War is our last choice, but when oppression becomes suffocating, we must choose. That made an impression on me. I don't have a family of my own, but my brothers and sisters do, so I'll fight for them."

"I remember our conversation now. Your bull was a fine addition to our herd. I had hoped to start a milk and cheese business, but that will have to wait." His face remained stern even though his eyes twinkled a little as if he were pleased. "I understand you are an educated man."

"Yes, sir. My parents insisted on teaching us every evening after chores, and they insisted we do it in English. A lot of Swedes live around us, and we'd trade books. We read anything we could get our hands on, and my oldest brother, Ash, even went to college for a while, but he was more interested in farming production than in learning Greek, so he came home."

"Have you read Daniel Defoe's *Robinson Crusoe*? One of my favorites. What is your opinion on why Crusoe refers to leaving home as his original sin?"

"Well, sir…"

Caleb Gibbs cleared his throat. "We have many men to attend to, sir."

"Oh, yes. We might discuss the book later."

The general turned his attention to the papers on his desk. Glancing over them, he asked, "Are either of you married? I am looking for men without responsibilities outside of their duty to the army. We frown on such connections that may compromise our security."

Tom Hickey quickly said, "I'm not married and never hope to be."

"All right, what about you, Johansen?"

Birch's head swarmed with what he would say. He greatly admired the general, and it would be an honor to fight beside him. He wanted to offer his dedication and determination in this fight for freedom, and he could do that in this new guard, and he didn't want the fact that he was married to deny him that chance.

So, he chose his words carefully. "I am well aware of my responsibilities to my service in the Continental Army and will not compromise that duty in any way."

Tom coughed.

Birch's eyes flickered in Tom's direction. "There was a woman here in Cambridge, but that is where she'll stay. My duty is to the army."

"Again, well said." Washington now turned all his attention to Tom. "As for you, Hickey, do you agree with Mr. Johansen about your commitment to the colonies' freedom?"

Tom rocked on his feet again, making an even louder creaking of the floor. A fresh breeze blew in through the open window, and Tom hoped it would blow away the odor of nervous sweat under his arms and down his back.

"Excuse me, sir. I'm not smart like Birch, but I can read and do my numbers. I never had no family, raised in a workhouse. I came to the colonies so I could make my own way, have a better life. I've been on my own since I was a pup, did things I don't like to talk about, but this country has given me freedom from all that."

Gibbs held up a piece of paper. "Your sergeant says here that you are a good fighting man, but in your off hours you drink and gamble."

Birch understood that Tom may have been the leader in battle, but, like other wounded souls, he struggled to fit in outside of that chaos. He thrived on the adventure, just like he had when he lived on his own on the streets in Cork, Ireland. He wondered what the man would say about that now.

"I used to, sir," said Tom. "A pint or two can fill your belly when the potatoes are rotten. I fought with the Brits against the Indians, too, as my only means to get something to eat, but I don't no more." He paused and looked over at Birch who kept his eyes facing front. "I don't act the maggot anymore. I've never been scuttered when we was going to battle. I wouldn't let my company down that way. As for gambling, it's foolish to risk my money on dice. I want to make something of myself."

Birch looked down at the floor. Both he and Tom had spun the truth about their situations, but getting into this brigade would make better men out of both of them.

"We've heard reports to the contrary," said Gibbs.

"A man can change when faced with a bigger duty."

"I'd fight with him any time," interrupted Birch. "He's smart when it comes to fighting. Does it say in there what he did when we fought at Bunker Hill? It was the first time in battle for most of us and when we ran out of ammunition, Hickey backed us up, and we survived. All of us were new and scared, but Tom knew what to do. He's a fine soldier."

"I take it you're friends," said Gibbs.

"We're mates," answered Tom. "Couldn't have a better one than Birch here."

Birch raised his eyebrows. That was the first time Tom had ever given him a compliment. Tom distrusted kind words, never having gotten any himself. He preferred teasing insults, and because of their recent disagreement, Birch suspected the flattery now was a lie to ingratiate himself with the general.

Gibbs continued. "Hickey, I've been told you received an injury while bringing back the cannons from Fort Ticonderoga with Captain Knox. Are you healed now?"

"Yes, sir, good as a new penny. I fell through the ice, but Birch here came out after me." He paused before adding, "I could have gotten out by myself, but Birch wanted to help, so I let him."

"Sounds like you have many talents, Lieutenant Johansen," said the general.

"Thank you, sir," said Birch.

Gibbs continued, "Your responsibilities will be many and varied, and we need men we can trust implicitly. Do you see those trunks stacked in the corner? They are filled with documents vital to our ongoing war efforts and to the formation of our new government to unite the colonies, and some contain Continental currency used to support our troops. If any of these falls into enemy hands, our cause is doomed. Most importantly, General Washington's person must be protected at all costs. This will be the responsibility of the members of His Excellency's Guard, and it will demand the utmost of your abilities and strengths. Our motto is 'Conquer or Die,' so there will be strict rules of obedience, and your unfailing duty will be demanded. It may be a more difficult duty than that of a soldier in the field. Are you willing to accept this assignment?"

Tom said, "I'll serve ye right!"

"Yes, sir!" said Birch.

General Washington stood. "I will be forthright with you, Hickey. I have reservations about a soldier who drinks and gambles, even a little. I also do not approve of the condition of your shirt. It's torn at the sleeve and could stand to be ironed."

"I don't have another shirt, only my uniform," said Tom.

"He really doesn't have another," said Birch. "But he did wash it in a bucket last night."

Washington nodded. "You did your best, Hickey, and since Johansen comes so highly recommended, I will accept his judgement that you will be a good and brave soldier with this new unit. Welcome to both of you." The general turned away and opened a cabinet door on a bookcase behind him, clearly trusting the rest of this matter to Captain Gibbs.

Caleb Gibbs extended his arm toward a hallway leading out to the back yard. "You are to go outside to meet other members chosen for this brigade and get something to eat. You will wait for further orders. You are dismissed."

Chapter Eleven

"You're too late for fried cakes," said one of the other men as Birch and Tom stepped up to the table in the yard. "Those were the first to go."

Birch and Tom weren't disappointed. They hadn't smelled the sweet aroma of fresh food in a long time. Even after only a little over a year of the war, rations for the troops were sporadic and sparse, but today the tables groaned with plates of fried chicken, loaves of bread, and bushels of apples. Birch and Tom were happy to see a few of the men from the expedition to retrieve the cannons standing around the table. After the tense meetings with Washington and Gibbs, all were ready to relax and enjoy the food. Some were curious about what they'd be doing next, but most didn't care as long as meals like this were on the menu.

Tom picked up a thick slice of bread. "Look here, there's no mold. Are ye sure we can eat it?" He took a big bite.

Birch chuckled. "If you don't die in the next hour, we'll know."

Tom tossed an empty chicken bone into one of the baskets and picked up another piece. "I guess I owe ye for getting me into the general's brigade," he said with his mouth full.

"You don't owe me, but if you want to stay in, you better do what you said in there. No drinking, no gambling."

"I can handle myself aright, and ye better do what ye said, too." He mimicked Birch, saying, "A woman left in Cambridge. She'll stay there." Taking two apples, he walked away and stood by a tree beyond the crowd to finish his food.

Birch put down his half-eaten chicken to watch Tom. Suddenly he wasn't hungry anymore. He regretted his lie, regretted his failure to mention the woman he loved and married, and he knew that the sick feeling in his stomach would be with him for days. Guilt would be his constant reminder of his secret, his burden to bear, and something he couldn't share with anyone, especially not Sophie.

Late in the afternoon, Caleb Gibbs stepped out of the back door. The crowd of soldiers quickly turned in the captain's direction and quieted down.

"His Excellency's Guard stands in this yard. Each of you has been chosen by our general for this specific special mission, vital to the success of this revolution. The ending of the siege of Boston, from which we have all just come, was a victory, but it is only the beginning. The general expects attacks on New York City, and we must be ready. No brigade such as this has ever been in existence, so each of you will set the standard, which will be high.

"You will have two days to get all your affairs in order and prepare to separate from your units. Your captains have already been informed of your names and that you will no longer be under their command. Gather up all the equipment you have, including your weapon, and bring it here. In your absence, tents and temporary sleeping quarters will be set up behind the inn. Each of you has been assigned to one of these officers." He swept his hand toward three men standing nearby. "Captains Martin, Devonshire, and Carter. Upon your return, you will report to your assigned captain for your duties. We will spend a short time in training, and then we will be on the move. Dismissed."

Back with their unit, around a low campfire, Birch and Tom accepted congratulations from their fellow soldiers on joining this elite group. Their friend, Joseph, clapped Birch on the back. "Knew you'd be moving up through the ranks. You'll do us all proud!"

"Wish you could be with us," said Birch. "We'll be fighting along with everyone else with a duty to protect the general. He's not afraid to fight. He's not one to watch from the back, and we're to see he stays alive. I'll miss having you by my side."

"I don't mind. The general would probably want me to button my jacket." He laughed and slapped his stomach. "Hard as a rock, but these jackets are made for skinny ones like you. Congratulations to you, too, Hickey."

Tom only grunted until Birch nudged him on the shoulder while jerking his head in Joseph's direction. Tom sighed. "Thanks, Gallagher."

Joseph's eyes lit up as he patted his jacket pocket. "I got a letter from Justine that she's coming here and bringing Sophie, too. They'll set up tents with the other camp followers."

"Sophie?" said Birch in a voice too loud. "She's coming?"

"There aren't very many patients left at the house since the fighting moved south, and her father can handle them."

"What about the ones with smallpox?"

"There's not much she can do for them. She thinks she'll be of more use here with the soldiers after the battles. The army doctors are spread awfully thin. Only one of them for each regiment."

"She shouldn't come." Birch stared off into some unknown space. "She can't come."

"Why not? The army could use a good doctor, and you need her. You've been off your feed, an unhappy newlywed," said Joseph, suddenly dropping his grin. "Why don't you want her to come?"

Just then three other soldiers came toward the campsite. Eli, a tall lanky one called out, "Well, look who it is? The general's lap dogs? Kissed his backside yet?" He puckered his lips and made sloppy kissing noises.

The two soldiers behind him, planted their feet, and imitated Eli, kissing and swaggering their hips. The skinny one mocked, "Yeah, look, two rippers. So, you're taking the easy way out? Abandoning us real soldiers?"

Eli piped up again. "It don't take too many brains to find a way to the rear of the lines. Looks like you did it, Johansen."

Birch held a grim expression. "Lieutenant to you, soldier. We'll be fighting just as much as you. General Washington is the key to winning this war, so we'll be by the general's side, protecting him in every battle."

"Sounds like the coward's way out." He curled his lip. "You'll be way in the back, protecting the man who doesn't want to face the guns like we do. He can hide behind you."

Birch stood up. "That will be enough, private. I

won't tolerate anyone insulting our commander and chief who will raise his pistol and sword as often as you do."

Tom didn't look up from the pack and canteen in his hands when he said, "Lollipoops and rooks, every one of ye."

"Who you callin' names, Hickey?" said another lean private, taking a step forward. "You ain't no more than a gentleman of three outs with no wit, money, or manners!"

Tom looked up now.

The man tilted his head back and laughed until Tom's pack and canteen clattered to the ground as he stood. He drove his fist deep into the man's belly. The man collapsed.

"Let's get out of here, Birch," Tom snarled. "Eedjits like these ain't worth our time."

In a tone leaving no doubt as to his authority, Birch said, "Not yet, Tom. These three were just leaving." When the soldiers didn't move, Birch narrowed his eyes and added, "Right now!" The three men eased away from the fire, pulling their coughing companion with them. The other men who had seen the exchange said their goodbyes and went back to their tents.

"Sorry about that, Tom," said Joseph. "They got no brains and nothing else to do."

Tom shook his head and gritted his teeth. "I don't take that from nobody," he mumbled. "I'm going for a grind. Don't wait up for me." He disappeared down the road.

Everyone watched him leave in silence. When Tom was out of earshot, Joseph asked, "What's gotten into him? Isn't he glad to be with the new unit?"

"He doesn't like change," said Birch. "He'll come around."

Birch sat down on a small stool near the campfire and put his head in his hands.

"So, why don't you want Sophie here?" asked Joseph. "Seems to be more to it than the danger of her being near any fighting."

In his mind, Birch saw Sophie standing across from him and that familiar yearning in his gut returned. His world receded into a hazy circle surrounding her. He'd never seen a more beautiful creature. She tied her thick auburn hair back at her neck, but long strands dangled around her shoulders. In his vision, when she looked at him and blinked, her green eyes lit up in the firelight. Her body was lean and firm, and when she smiled, her cheeks filled her face.

"Birch, what is it?" said Joseph.

His voice became wooden and distant. "I can't have her come."

Joseph squatted on the ground beside him. "Talk to me. Why can't she come here?"

Raking his fingers through his hair, Birch looked up at his friend. "The general doesn't want men in his special brigade to have entanglements outside of the army. He's worried about the British finding out military secrets through our family connections. The possible invasion at New York City could be a turning point in the war, and Washington has to be ready."

"Does he think you'll tell secrets?" asked Joseph. The sturdy man's face went pale with a new thought. "Or that the British will put Sophie in danger by coming after her if they find out she's your wife?"

"No, no. Only a few people even know we're

married." Birch sighed and turned his face away. "It's more than that. It's more than the fighting and the untrained soldiers. It's that Washington doesn't know who to trust, which is why he's setting up this new troop. We're to be his trusted guard in all matters, in the fighting, in seeing to the protection of the government papers, and to his very person, everything with no exceptions. Secrecy is important, and so is the truth." Birch's feeling of guilt flooded over him.

"I understand you're afraid for Sophie. I'm afraid for Justine, but both of them can take care of themselves. And besides, they'll be far back from any fighting. The camp followers stay way behind."

Birch stood and paced between the small tent and a nearby tree. "I know that, but it's something else, something I did. It's something I don't think anyone can forgive." He swallowed the lump in his throat. "I don't know how to tell you. And worse, how can I tell Sophie?"

Joseph waited patiently.

The constant undercurrent of noise and conversation from the camp grew louder in Birch's ear until it suddenly faded away, and he blurted out the truth. "I lied. The general asked me if I had anyone outside the army to take care of, and I said no. I lied to him to get a chance to be in the general's special brigade."

Joseph shook his head in confusion. "That's not like you, so why did you do it?"

"I don't know, except that I have a duty to the army and to this war. It'd be an honor to serve Washington, and on an impulse, I put that ahead of Sophie. How could I do that? Maybe I thought I could protect her by keeping her away. Anywhere near a war is dangerous."

Joseph stepped between Birch and the tree he'd been picking the bark off. "Sophie's taken on danger before, and it never stopped her. So, what were you thinking?"

Birch twisted the button on his jacket. "How can I tell her that I lied so easily as if she didn't exist? I have to tell her not to come. Then she'll never know the truth about the man she married."

"You'll never have a good night's sleep if you don't make this right."

"I can live with that if I have to, but I can't tell Sophie. She loves me, and well, that's it. She loves me, and I can't let her down. She can't come."

Joseph didn't speak for a long time as he watched Birch pace. "You've always been honest in all things. Your conscience will show you the right path."

"I pledged to give everything I had to protect the general. He's the key to victory. Sophie or Washington, one or the other will have my all, but it can't be both. I thought the lie might solve the problem, but I was wrong."

"The truth is you sound ashamed."

Birch reeled on him. "I am! I can't face her, and that's why Sophie has to stay away. I love her as if she lived inside my skin, but she must understand she has to share me with this war. What if during a battle I hesitate for her sake?"

Joseph shook his head. "Is that the real reason you don't want her here? To protect her or to protect yourself?"

"I can't have her find out I chose the brigade over

her, and I can't have Washington find out I lied. She can't come!"

****

Sophie gripped the edges of the paper, nearly crumbling it in her hands until her father gently took it from her and read it aloud.

My Dearest Sophie,

It is with heavy sadness that I write this. I have missed you every day we've been apart and will always cherish our time together, but I must ask something of you. Perhaps demand of you. Please stay home.

You are the light in my life. Your smile comes to me every night before I go to sleep, and your laughter, like the sunshine, is with me every morning, but I must say goodbye for now. I am part of General Washington's special guard, and we cannot have any obligations outside of soldiering. These are perilous times, and my first duty is to the army and our fight for freedom. I can have no other responsibilities. I know you will understand.

Neither of us can say what the future might hold. I have made a choice, and you must do your best without me. Stay home. Do not come to the army camp.

Birch

"I must do my best without him?" she cried. "Do my best? What am I, a little child learning to buckle my shoes on my own?"

Her father wrapped his arms around her. "He wants to do the right thing for you."

She struggled to escape his grasp, but he held her close. She looked up at him, her face a dark mask as she wiped away the tears with the palm of her hand. "How can he say I'll always be his light and then tell me to stay away?"

Forcefully, she pushed herself out of her father's arms and stormed up the stairs. "How can he say he has no other responsibilities? Doesn't he have a responsibility to me? He promised this war wouldn't keep us apart in our hearts, and now he tells me he doesn't want me with him!"

"His duty is to the army," said her father. "He doesn't want you to get hurt."

"He's hurting me now!"

"Where are you going?"

She reached the landing before saying, "To the army camp!"

Chapter Twelve

On the Duchess of Gordon *in the New York Harbor*

His fork clattered to the floor. "Dammit! Can't this boat stop rocking long enough for me to finish a meal?" Governor William Tryon pushed the half-eaten plate of food to the side. Even with the special meals they brought from the shore, everything still had an aftertaste like brackish sea water and fish. Every bite reminded him that he lived on this damn boat, and even if it was for his own protection, it was still a prison.

In his hand, he held a report from the Continental Congress about a recent vote.

He shouted to no one in particular, "How could that George Washington ask his Congress to have me arrested? The fact that the Congress voted not to act against me is hardly the point!"

He moved toward the open door of his cabin and shouted, "Can anyone out there hear me?" Two sailors stepped into view.

"Do you hear me? He doesn't have the Congressional support he thought he had. Ha! I'll show them that even from this boat, I can control this state. I still have power! This amateur doesn't know who he's dealing with!"

Then he bellowed, "Take my tray!" and one of the sailors dashed into the room to gather up the dishes from breakfast. "Tell my aide to get in here. I want to dictate a letter."

The aide entered a few short minutes later, sat down, dipped his quill in the inkpot, and poised to take the dictation.

"To Major General William Howe, Commander-in-Chief of the British Land Forces: This will report my widespread progress in undermining the stability of the Continental government and threatening the influence of General George Washington.

"I have overseen our considerable success in flooding the country with counterfeit money toward bankrupting the rebel government, and the Continental Congress has made counterfeiting a crime punishable by death. We have them on the run thanks to my work. Even from this boat, my influence is effective.

"We have also contacted a number of George Washington's personal guards and are putting into action a plan to undermine the general's authority, by his death if possible. Many colonials have accepted cash and land to fight with our British soldiers against the rebels. Pursuing this policy continues to be high on my priority list.

"This written correspondence may be the last as Washington's troops will soon occupy the island of New York, and in his fear of my success, he will have my correspondence confiscated. That, however, will not stop me. The British invasion cannot come too soon.

"With respect, Governor William Tryon."

The aide sprinkled powder over the letter to seal the ink, blew off the remaining powder, and handed it to the governor. After a quick read through, Tryon signed it. His aide now sprinkled the signature with more powder.

The governor folded the completed letter and then lit the end of a stick of wax. He was still a man of power and authority. After four drops of warm wax splattered into a small globule on the edge of the folded paper, he took his official seal out of the drawer and pressed it into the wax, thus ensuring the letter's privacy.

The young officer now took the letter and slipped it into a small leather-bound pouch, saying, "This will be placed directly into the hands of General Howe before the day's end." He saluted and left the cabin.

****

"Have you seen Tom Hickey?" asked Birch when he returned to the soldier's camp the next day.

"Try back in the woods," said one man sitting in front of a low fire between the small tents. "A bunch of them are there."

Birch found Tom with six other men, all kneeling in a circle around a pile of Continental bills. Three of them were not soldiers, most likely men from the town. A red-haired man shook the dice, tossed them down, and Tom cheered as he raked in all but one of the bills. "Next roller!" he called out.

Birch touched Tom on the shoulder. "What are you doing?"

Tom looked up and shrugged off his hand. "Having a little fun playing hazard. Next roller. Max, it's ye. Sit here, Birch. Ye got any cash to throw in the pot?"

Birch didn't sit, just shook his head and frowned.

"Don't look at me like that. I'm not scuttered. No giggle juice to drink around here."

"Gambling is also against the rules," said Birch. "You could get expelled from the Life Guards."

"Are you in or out, Hickey?" asked one of the town men. "Or is this one your nanny?"

Tom stood, his face grim. "Johansen, by all the saints, ye make my blood boil. Who's going to tattle on me? Ye?" He glanced around at the other men, raising his eyebrows before turning back to Birch. "Where ye been, mucking about with some floozie at the camp, no doubt." He laughed, and the others joined in.

Birch's eyes flared. "You know better than that."

Tom gave Birch a shove, nearly knocking him down. "Jesus, Mary, and Joseph, go back to the tent and leave me be! Get yerself a kip so ye're rested and ready for tomorrow. Now off with ye." He knelt again. "Who's got the roll?"

Two hours later, Tom gathered up his winnings. "Are ye sure nobody can tell these bills from the real stuff?" he whispered to the man closest to him.

"Guaranteed. It's British made. Pass it around and keep your mouth shut. I'll pay you for doing the job in coin next time."

Tom gave a quick nod of his head.

****

Birch fell into a deep sleep in the tent until someone shook his shoulder. "Are ye awake?" asked a voice. Birch forced his eyes open and saw Tom in the dim light.

"What is it? Are we leaving already?"

"I won twelve dollars. Ye can have a couple of bucks. I'm keeping the rest 'cause I did the work. Here." He held out his hand with several bills in it.

"I don't want your money," said Birch, sitting up and rubbing his eye with his fist.

Tom, closing his hand back over the cash, laid

down on his bed roll and pulled the top blanket over him. With his back to Birch, he said, "I hate rules, especially when it comes to having a little fun."

"I know," said Birch, flopping back on his blankets.

A long silence passed in the darkness before Tom said, "I had to make them think ye made my blood boil by showing up."

"I know," said Birch with a yawn.

"Just in case ye think ye got one over on me about the gambling, remember the general might want to know about that wife ye said ye didn't have."

Birch didn't answer. He stretched out, but he didn't sleep much.

The next morning Captain Gibbs announced, "Change in plans. We will be on the move by midday. Be ready."

Five hours later, a soldier on the march asked, "When are we going to get there? I have a hole in my boot." He stumbled forward, hopping on one foot.

"Don't know where we'll be tonight," said another man, "but look at this." He held out a crude drawing on a scrap of paper. "It could be the flag for our company. What do you think?"

On the left side of the flag, a guardsman held the reins of a horse while a woman leaning on a Union Shield handed him a blue flag on a staff. An American eagle sat on the ground to the right of her, and across the top of the scene flew a gold ribbon with the words "Conquer or Die."

"Who's the woman?"

"She's the Genius of Liberty. She stands for the spirit of freedom and liberty."

"Hey," said a man marching about two rows back, "I heard we're getting new uniforms, and they'll be different from what everyone else wears. We'll stand out."

"Making us easier targets!" shouted another.

A soldier in the row in front of Birch and Tom turned back and said, "Hey, did you hear the cook almost killed Washington a couple of nights ago? She tried to poison him."

"No!"

"I heard all about it," said another soldier with a neatly trimmed black mustache. "The cook turned out to be a loyalist woman who took the job with orders to see what she could do to get rid of Washington. They say that the Tory Governor Tryon is coming up with plots to kill him."

"So, what happened with the cook?" asked Tom. "We would've heard if Washington's been killed."

"No one knows what happened to her. She disappeared in the night. I guess this cook sprinkled some poison on the peas she cooked for dinner. Washington likes peas. Anyway, one of the men serving the food noticed a funny smell and just before the general scooped out the first bite, he grabbed the plate and threw it out the window. Saved Washington's life."

"The next day they found chickens dead on the ground after eating the peas," said another.

Murmurs of shock and disapproval spread through the troop.

"Maybe Washington needs a doctor to travel with him in case something like this happens again."

"Yeah," said Tom, looking at Birch. "Anybody

know a doctor?"

****

Sophie and Justine walked into the camp of the wives and children of the soldiers following behind the troops. It was almost dark, and after a long day's march, everyone hurried to set up their tents, if they had one, and cook an evening meal. They ignored the two strangers.

"We're looking for two soldiers," said Justine to a woman coming out of a small teepee shaped tent. "Joseph Gallagher and Birch Johansen."

"We only know the ones who belong to us. Set up over there, and you can look for them tomorrow."

Sophie laid her cloth market wallet on the ground and rummaged through it for apples and bread for their supper. After Justine found her small axe in her own market wallet, she said, "I'll cut enough wood to start a fire."

"Got a tent?" the woman asked. Sophie shook her head.

The woman frowned. "I got a boy strong enough to carry the makings for our tent, but you'll be sleeping out on the ground until you get one. I hope you got a warm blanket to wrap in."

The woman turned away to run a wet cloth over the face of a girl about four years old. The girl squirmed and her mother said, "Stay still. Would you like your father to see you acting like a baby?"

Just then a slightly older boy came running between the tents, crying and screaming, "It hurts! It hurts!" He held out his hand to his mother. Embedded in his palm was a large splinter. Blood dripped onto the ground. "Mama! Look! It hurts!"

"I can help with that," said Sophie as she put down her sack and lifted out her doctor's kit.

"I don't know you," said the mother, pulling the boy close to her skirts. "No stranger's touching my boy."

"But she's a doctor," said Justine.

"A woman? I never heard of a woman doctor."

"But Sophie is, and a good one. If your husband fought in the Battle of Bunker Hill, she probably tended him. I've seen her work, and I trust her with my life. A lot of men from the army did."

Sophie patted the boy on the shoulder and when he faced her, she took his hand in hers. "That's a big one," she said. "How'd you get it in here?"

The boy looked up at his mother.

"All right, tell her," said the woman as she gave up a sigh.

In between sobs, the boy said, "I was climbing a tree, and I slipped, slid down the bark."

"Was it a big tree?" asked Sophie as she felt around his palm and realized the whole splinter was embedded several inches across his hand with only a small tip sticking out. "You really did a good job with this one." She pinched the splinter with her tweezers and gave it a slight tug. The boy cried out and tried to pull his hand back, but Sophie kept a tight grip on his wrist. About ten other children surrounded them now.

"A big tree can give out big splinters, but not too big for a strong boy like you. Why don't you show the other children exactly how brave you are?" She held up his hand for all the children to see. "This is a giant of a splinter, but you can see the courage this young man has." Then gripping the piece of bark again, she said,

"Show them what a strong soldier you will be when you grow up. General Washington would be proud to have you in his army."

The boy wiped tears off his face with his free hand. Sophie tugged again, moving the splinter only a little. The boy cried out but choked it back when he saw the other children watching.

"The general will be very proud of you." She pulled harder, and this time the splinter came out of his hand, leaving a bloody hole in his palm.

The boy tried again to pull his hand free from hers, but she held tight. "No, not yet. I have to clean out the hole. You wouldn't want it to get infected, would you?"

His mother said sternly, "No, you wouldn't. Stay still so she…the doctor…can get it clean."

The boy obeyed as Sophie cleaned it out with water, squeezing blood and small bits of bark out of his palm. She then smeared a bit of honey on it for antiseptic purposes and put an extra dab on her finger for the boy to lick off. She then wrapped his hand with gauze, and as soon as she was done, he ran over to his friends to brag about his "war wound." When one child reached a finger out to touch it, the boy pressed the hand to his chest. "No, you can't see it. It's mine!"

"I'll look at it again tomorrow," said Sophie to his mother, "but the splinter came out cleanly, and he should be all right. If his hand or fingers start to get red or he complains of a lot more pain, let me know right away. I can clean out whatever pus forms."

Justine piped up. "Dr. Sophie can take care of it. She's healed a lot of nasty infections. I've seen it."

The boy's mother motioned for Justine and Sophie to come closer. She spoke in a low voice. "I lost a child two years ago when she cut her toe, and it got infected. I couldn't bear to see another die from something as plain as a splinter. I'm grateful. If you two would like to share my supper, I'd be pleased. We'll see about finding you a tent you can carry in the morning."

"We'd appreciate that," said Justine. "We'll find our men soon enough."

"I heard we're staying here for a day before moving on," said the woman. "We've been keeping a pretty fast pace because Washington wants to get to New York City as soon as possible."

The next morning after an uncomfortable sleep on the ground, Justine and Sophie packed up what they had brought with them to stow beside their new friend's tent for the day.

"All of us," said a woman, "have children who need looking after, and we're glad to have a doctor with us. Would you check out some of them while we're here? We got bites, cuts, and a couple have fevers. We'll pay what we can."

"Here's some carrots and potatoes that I'd usually sell to the soldiers, but they're yours now," said a scrawny woman with a few teeth missing.

Another soldier's wife handed Justine a blanket and a large piece of canvas. "Since we'll be here for a day, I can show you how to set up this as a tent. One of you can carry both your market wallets and the other one the tent."

"We can't thank you enough, and I'll be glad to look after your children this afternoon," said Sophie. "But, first, can you tell me who I should talk to so we can find our men? Is there a company clerk or such who would know?"

"We'll take care of your things, so you can ask for your men at the camp ahead of us."

"Thank you!"

"Slow down," said a panting Justine, trying to keep up with Sophie's brisk strides. Sophie slowed her pace and then stopped and waited for Justine to catch her breath.

"What are you going to say to Birch?" gasped Justine. "He asked you not to come here."

"I don't know." Her fists clenched at her sides. "I'm so angry with him. He tells me I'll have to do my best without him, but how can I?" She grasped Justine's hand. "I never even considered I would fall in love and marry. But…" She stumbled over her words. "I-I'm so in love, sometimes I can't breathe thinking about it, and I thought it was the same way for him. I never thought love like this could happen to me, and now he doesn't want me."

"I'm sure Birch was just looking out for your safety when he told you not to come."

Sophie stiffened and dropped Justine's hand. "Is that all he cares about—my safety? I should stay away because he loves me? I should do my best without him? What kind of love is that?"

She walked on ahead, saying over her shoulder, "Why didn't Joseph tell you to stay home? Doesn't he love you?"

Justine's face hardened as she crossed to the other side of the dirt road. Fury like a wounded bear sounded in her voice. "You take care of your man, and I'll take care of mine!"

Sophie's stomach tightened, and she felt like she'd fallen through a trap door. Of all the things she might lose, it couldn't be her dearest friend. She stopped walking and crossed over to Justine. "I'm sorry. I spoke too soon without thinking. I'm sorry. Please, forgive me."

Justine wrapped her arms around her friend. Her touch and her voice were now drained of anger. "I understand. You're frustrated and worried, but so am I. We will work together to find Birch and Joseph."

They entered the army camp where weary soldiers ate what little remained of their rations, and others unfolded blankets, spread them out, and fell into a restless sleep. All of them looked up when two women walked through their ranks asking after Joseph and Birch. But in an encampment of over 12,000 men, just two were hard to find. Some men knew the names but had no idea where they might be.

"We're looking for two soldiers. Can you help us?" the women asked of the next cluster of men.

Several men stood up and one gave a predatory look as his eyes scanned Sophie up and down. "You can stay with me for the night," he said. "We can keep each other warm. How about it?"

Sophie put a broad smile on her face. "What's your name? I never stay with a man if we haven't been introduced."

"It's Davis Worthington." He reached out his hand to her and motioned with his fingers for her to come this way.

"I appreciate the offer, Davis Worthington. I will be sure to mention your name to my husband, Lt. Johansen."

The man blanched. "I spoke out of turn, ma'am, but I can take you to him."

"What about Sergeant Joseph Gallagher?" said Justine.

"He's just up there." The soldier pointed. "See him by the oak tree?"

Justine searched for the tree. When she found it, she started to run, darting around and between the men, leaping over the ones on the ground. "Joseph! Joseph!" she shouted.

He turned just before she ran into his arms, nearly knocking him over. Their lips met as they stumbled backwards. When their kiss broke, he said, "Justine, my love, you're here! I'm off duty until morning. I can help you set up with the camp followers. I talked to Maizy Hanson who says she'll find a spot for you." He kissed her again before she could answer.

With her arms still around his neck, Justine said, "Have you seen Birch? Sophie's here."

Joseph's brow furrowed as he set her down. "Sophie's here? Birch told her not to come."

"I know, but nothing gets Sophie doing something faster than to be told she can't."

"Where is she now?"

"Right here," answered Sophie from a few feet away.

Joseph forced a smile on his face. "You came."

"I did, and I want to see Birch. Do you know where he is?"

Joseph sucked in a deep breath and said quickly, "You and Justine need to get settled, and we can find Birch in the morning."

"I need to see my husband."

"Please, Sophie, it'll be dark in a few hours, and it'll take that long to get you two set for the night. It might rain, and you can't sleep out in the open. Please, Sophie."

"I said I want to see my husband." She spoke firmly as a woman used to getting her way.

The soldiers nearby waited as quietly as the mist on the lake to see what Sophie would do. Finally, she said, "All right. A couple of women in the camp said they would help us with supplies and canvas to make a tent. Joseph, you can carry our bags and then cut poles for our shelter." She turned to leave when another voice said, "I can help with that."

"Birch," whispered Justine.

"I heard there were two women with the men. I came to see what was going on."

The late afternoon shadows hid Sophie's face, but her anger and frustration were palpable, and all of it was directed at her husband.

Chapter Thirteen

"I need to talk to my wife," said Birch firmly, and all the soldiers nearby scattered. Joseph and Justine picked up their packs and started toward the followers' camp about a half a mile back. "We'll have the shelter ready," said Joseph.

"We should talk over here by the fence," Birch said, reaching out his hand toward her. "Come this way."

She ignored his hand and strode ahead of him saying, "I'll do the best I can."

A rocky path led to a wooden rail fence along a nearby field. Sophie rested her arms on the top rail while Birch stood beside her.

He cleared his throat. "I didn't mean to hurt you," he said, "but it's dangerous for you to come here. We'll be in a battle soon enough."

"I don't think being near a battle is what's bothering you. I can understand you worrying about me, but to say I'll have to do my best without you. That's not right. How could I ever do my best without you?" She faced him, her voice dripping with resentment. "You wrote that you have to say goodbye, that you can have no other obligations but the army. Goodbye? Are you leaving me, but you're too much of a coward to say it? Do our wedding vows mean so little? Did you say the words and not mean them? I

Susan Leigh Furlong

should slap your face!"

"You should slap me. I deserve it, but not for the reasons you think. Our wedding vows mean everything to me. You mean everything to me."

"Not everything! George Washington means more to you than I do! You chose him over your own wife."

"No, Sophie, no." He took her by the arms. "Please forgive me for that letter. I'd give my life for you and wouldn't hesitate. Never doubt I love you with everything I am. Please, never doubt that."

She shook her arms free of his hands. "So why did you say this is goodbye? Did you mean goodbye to me and our vows? Well, you needn't worry. I'll say goodbye for you. I'm going to the followers' camp tonight, and I'll be gone tomorrow."

Birch stepped in her way. "Please, listen to me first."

She punched her hands onto her hips. "You've got two minutes."

"I'm not sure I can explain it, so you'll understand. I hardly understand it myself. It just sort of happened."

"What did you let sort of happen?"

Birch swallowed hard and feelings of guilt racked him. "I've wanted to serve with General Washington ever since I met him at Mount Vernon two years ago. There's not a man I admire more, not another man I want to walk with during this troubled time." His head dropped as he said in a tight voice, "So I lied to him. He said he wanted men without outside obligations, so when he asked if I had a wife, I didn't tell him about you. I didn't tell him I had a wife. I should have, but I lied."

Her eyes shot daggers at him, and he felt every

prick. "You denounced me?"

"No, no! I just didn't mention you."

She slapped him hard across the face. He nearly stumbled from the force of her blow.

"I fell in love with you without knowing why or what it meant," she said. "I gave my everything to you, and I did it willingly. But the first chance you get you deny me." She walked back toward the camp. "Don't follow me."

"Please, Sophie, stay and listen."

He took her elbow, but she shook him off and stormed away as he silently watched her.

****

The next morning just after sunrise, Birch made his way to General Washington's tents overlooking the encampment. Both were large marquee tents, one for dining and meetings, and the other used as the general's personal quarters. They had no distinguishing stripes or other ornament to display his rank, and except for their size looked very much like the tents his officers slept in. The only difference was that four soldiers with muskets and swords stood guard around it.

"I wish to see General Washington," said Lt. Birch Johansen to the general's aide, William Lee, seated on a small chair outside the tent with a large ledger across his lap. Lee, an enslaved man from Washington's home at Mount Vernon, served as the general's personal valet as well as keeping his records, messages, and correspondence in order.

"Do you have an appointment?" asked Lee.

"No, but I must talk to him. It's important."

"Important to whom?"

"To me, sir."

"Who is it?" came a voice from inside the tent.

Lee stood and opened the flap. "It's Lt. Johansen. He wishes to speak to you, but he has no appointment. When should I tell him to come back, sir?"

"I'll see him now."

"But, sir, you have a full schedule today."

"I will see him now."

Lee sighed. "This way, Lieutenant." He held open the flap for Birch to go in.

Birch walked straight over to General Washington's desk in the center of the tent and saluted as Lee closed the tent flap behind him.

When the general looked up, he gave a quick salute in return. "Yes?"

"I have something I must tell you." Facing this man with his wrongdoing was harder than facing any enemy on the battlefield. Birch greatly admired the general for taking on this job of leader for his country, and now he would lose the general's respect. That tore at his conscience.

Birch did his best to keep his voice steady. "When I interviewed to become part of His Excellency's Guard, I was not entirely truthful." He swallowed hard. "In fact, I lied."

The general's blue eyes fixed on him. "You lied to me?"

"I am sorry, but, yes, sir, and I am here to set the record straight."

General Washington stood up. "Go ahead." He stood several inches taller than Birch, and his stern face made Birch cringe.

When Birch didn't answer right away, the general said, "I'm waiting, Lieutenant."

Birch sucked up all his courage. He regretted that this would cost him his place in the guard, and so be it, but he had to confess to the general before he could face Sophie.

"Sir, I told you I didn't have a wife, but that wasn't true. I am married. Her name is Sophie. I was afraid if you knew I had a wife, it might compromise your perception of my ability to serve you."

Birch stiffened his back and spoke quickly. "You said you wanted men without outside responsibilities, so I told you something untrue. I have no excuse. I wrote her a letter and told her she'd have to do her best without me and not to come here, but she came anyway. Now I have to set matters straight with both her and you. This has been weighing heavily on me, and I am willing to accept any consequences. I apologize and will take any decision you make concerning me and my position with the guard."

"I'm sure you will, young man. Have you spoken to your wife yet?"

"I tried, but she wouldn't listen. I'll try again."

"I am concerned you found it necessary to be less than honest with me about your marital status. I was surprised when you said you weren't married, and that the woman from Cambridge was not in your life anymore, but the truth is, I'd already heard about your wife. I understand she's a doctor."

"You knew about Sophie? You knew I was married?"

"Yes, but you came so highly recommended by your captain and by several others of the men, I decided to take a chance on you and wait for you to prove yourself to me."

"I'm sorry I let you down. I have no excuse."

"No, you do not. If you had not corrected the situation by the time we reached New York City, I would have seen you drummed not only out of my guard, but out of the army. I also would have had you arrested on charges of attempted espionage for trying to get into the guard on false pretenses."

Birch felt his world closing in around him. He deserved whatever the general meted out, but he had hoped it wouldn't go this far. "Again, sir, I apologize and will accept whatever punishment you decide."

"I am interested in hearing more about your wife. I've been told she treated quite a number of our wounded soldiers after the Battle of Bunker Hill. All of them speak highly of her skills."

"Yes, sir."

"You were one of her patients, correct?"

"Yes, sir."

"I have also been told she inoculated several people successfully against smallpox. The disease is ravaging our troops, and I am most interested to hear what she has to say about it."

"Yes, sir."

"Is that all you can say, 'yes, sir?' Don't stammer around. Speak freely. Tell me her qualities as a woman and as a doctor. You denied her once. Don't do it again."

"She's a fine woman. As a doctor she's often not accepted because she's a woman, but that doesn't stop her. She knows what she's about. She also doesn't suffer fools, which I have been lately, and I'm afraid I have a lot to make up to her."

"I've been told she is headstrong and unwavering,

dedicated to her patients, serving their needs before her own."

"Yes, sir. Anyone under her care will receive the best she has. She takes it personally when a patient dies, and I've seen her cry when no one else was looking."

Washington paced the width of the tent before speaking again. "I've decided your punishment for your lie…"

Birch held his breath.

"Your punishment is to earn her forgiveness and to convince her to come here and become my physician. I am most interested in treating smallpox. It could kill more men than in the battlefields, and if she has any way to combat the disease, I want to hear about it."

"I will do my best, sir, but she can be a stubborn woman."

"And I am a stubborn man, so unless she forgives you, and you bring her to me, you will endure ten lashes."

Birch's eyes opened wide. He said with a gulp, "Ten lashes, sir?"

"You said you would accept my decision."

Birch looked down at his boots. "Yes, sir." Ten lashes would be severe, but maybe he could still be part of, at least in some small way, the cause for freedom.

Washington walked toward his desk to stand next to his lieutenant. "Talking to your wife will be more difficult than any punishment I could think of. Are you up for it?"

Birch nodded.

"Now as for this lying to your general, it does give me pause and serious hesitation. I need men around me whom I can trust, completely without a doubt."

Birch stood up as straight as he could. "I understand, sir. I will resign from the guard, but if I may, I want to continue to serve you in this army. If you wish to strip me of my rank, I will do my best to earn an officer's rank again. You will not be disappointed in me as a soldier."

"Yes, Lieutenant, you will have to prove yourself to me, but Captain Gibbs insists you are worth the chance. We both believe you can best serve me as a member of His Excellency's Guard."

With a great sigh of relief, Birch said, "Thank you, sir."

Then the general fixed him with a stern stare. "Don't give me cause to doubt you again. I will not be forgiving a second time."

"Yes, sir. I mean, no, sir, I will not give you cause again. Thank you, sir."

"Before you leave," Washington said, "I want to talk to you about another matter. Sit down." He pointed to a folding wooden stool at the foot of his camp bed. When Birch didn't move, he added, "I said 'sit,' soldier."

Birch sat.

"I have another assignment for you. Captain Gibbs will contact you with all the details sometime soon, probably in a few days. I will tell you it is a dangerous one. I thought from the beginning you had the character to do it, but coming to confess your lie without excuses proves an ingrained courage and honesty. Dismissed."

The general sat down. "And I expect to meet your wife within the week." He turned his attention to the papers on his desk.

Birch saluted again, but when Washington didn't

look up to respond, Birch stepped back and left the tent.

Now to do the hardest thing he'd ever done in his life, harder than any battle, harder than facing the general. He had to find Sophie's forgiveness.

Chapter Fourteen

The next morning Birch wove his way through the unorganized collection of tents and shelters of the camp followers before he spotted her carrying a bucket of water. Her skirt swayed with the movement of her hips, and once again, he never wanted anything so much in his life. Just to touch her. To put his arm around her, to hold her hand. She held her head high, and he remembered how every time she said his name, heaven's gate opened to him. And today he had to walk through. He had to prove to her that his love was strong and forever no matter how it looked right now.

This was his fault, and he had to make it right.

"Sophie!" he called.

She stopped walking and looked back at him over her shoulder. She didn't answer.

He trotted over to her and took the bucket of water from her hand. "I want to talk to you. Is there somewhere we can go?"

She gave him a withering look. "Take the water to Justine over there by the fire." Then she pointed toward a small army tent with patches of mismatched colored cloth covering holes and tears. "One of the women gave it to us. Her husband died of an infection in his arm, so she's going home and didn't need it."

"Sounds like he could have used a doctor."

Her eyes darkened, and her voice stiffened even

more. "Are you mocking me?"

This is only getting worse. "I only meant that these people need a doctor as much as the soldiers do. I know you're angry with me, and I just want to say the right thing." He lifted his free hand to smooth back her hair, but she smacked it away.

When they reached the tent, Sophie went inside, nearly tearing the flap off the stake as she furiously closed it while Birch set the bucket on the ground near Justine. Birch blanched at Justine's grim expression.

"She wanted to go home." Justine put her hands on her hips and raised her gentle voice. "But I talked her into staying with me for a while longer. She's been treating some of the women and children in camp, so they've been helping us out with food and other things we need." Her frown deepened. "I don't understand you, Birch Johansen. How could you send her a letter like that? And after your wedding? How could you be so addlebrained? So unkind? So unthinking?"

He swallowed back the lump in his throat. "I've come to try and make things right. General Washington wants…"

Justine interrupted. "You're here under orders? How heartless are you? Go back to your general and leave her alone." She poked the fire with a stick.

Birch felt like he was drowning in quicksand. "Please help me, Justine. I came on my own. I keep making a mess of this. Every time I open my mouth, it gets worse. Please can I talk to her?"

Justine took a long moment to answer. "All right, go inside, but don't expect me to pick you up when she throws you out."

"Thank you, Justine."

Justine grunted.

Birch cautiously opened the tent flap. "May I come in?"

She didn't answer at first, and Birch prayed he wasn't too late to make amends.

She jerked a quilt around as she forcibly folded it and threw it down on the pallet. "What is it you want to say?"

He knew his words had to be the right ones. This was his only chance.

"I want to say how sorry I am. I wrote that letter without thinking it through, and I've regretted it ever since. Yes, I was worried about you coming into danger, but the reality was that I was ashamed. I didn't want you to find out I told General Washington a lie when he asked me if I was married during my interview for the Life Guards, a lie making him think you didn't exist. I knew if you came here, you'd find out, and I couldn't face you knowing the truth, but you have to know the truth now."

"You told me to stay away! You said this was goodbye! And I should do the best I can without you! How could you?" Tears came into her eyes, and she stomped her foot. "I told myself I wouldn't cry, but I have, and it's your fault!"

Birch's resolve crumbled at the sight of her tears. He fell to his knees and clasped her hand. "It's all my fault. I was wrong, and all I want to do is make it up to you. I don't need you to forgive me. I just need you to love me again. Please listen."

She patted his hand with her other one, her tears on the verge of spilling over again. "I'm angry with you, but I'll always love you." After pulling him to his feet, she said, "Tell me what you came to say."

Birch's eyes never left her face. "I did wrong in writing that letter, and I know that it hurt you deeply. I don't know what I was thinking, except to keep you from finding out what I'd told the general. I never wanted you to know, and I never wanted to hurt you. I want more than anything to work this out."

"So, it was more important to you to stay in the guard than to tell the truth to General Washington or to me."

"You have every right to feel that way but understand nothing is more important to me than you, nothing. To say I'm sorry and that I was wrong doesn't seem to be adequate. I wish I knew how to say it better. I've relived those words over and over and wondered how I could have been so insensitive. I went to General Washington this morning and told him the truth."

"What did he say?"

"He said I had to make it up to you because he wanted to talk to you about smallpox. He says a lot of soldiers are getting it, and he wants your advice."

She flung down his hand. "So again, you are here because of the general, not because of me. Get out!"

His shoulders stiffened. His voice was suddenly firm. "I am here because I love you, and I made a mistake, a serious mistake, yes, and I want to set things right, but you're making this too hard. This war is keeping me away from you, but it's worse to be apart from you in our hearts."

He pulled open the tent flap. "I've said what I came to say, but if this is the way you want it, that's the way it will be." He ducked down and started to step out.

"Wait."

He let the flap fall closed again and faced her.

She rocked back and forth on her feet, and he'd never heard her voice quiver like it did now. "I am used to things being true or false, black and white, alive or dead, and I did that with you. But a marriage should never be like that. A love can never be like that. I need to learn about the ebb and flow of things…like an ocean. I know you love me." She sniffed in a sob. "Just as I know I love you…like an ocean. Forgive me for being so hard on you. Please."

He dashed into her arms and held her as she sobbed. When she had soaked his shirt with her tears, he lifted her chin. "You're beautiful when you cry."

A small smile came to her lips. "No, I'm not."

"Yes, you are. To me you will always be the most beautiful woman God ever created. Am I forgiven?"

"Yes, but only if you forgive me."

"Done and done."

They were still kissing when Justine peeked through the tent flap and said to Joseph standing beside her, "I hadn't heard anything in so long, I thought maybe they'd killed each other, but I can see they've made up instead." Joseph tried to peek in, but she flicked her hand against his to push it away. "They've moved to the quilts, so let them be."

"We should do the same," said Joseph, wiggling his eyebrows scandalously.

"I know a private spot by the stream." And they were gone.

****

Birch came up on his elbows to look directly into Sophie's face as she lay beside him. His bare chest brushed against her breasts, so soft and smooth. Not like her fingers, strengthened and hardened from doctoring the wounded when they moved across his back and buttocks, stimulating deep sensations that stirred him to his very core.

"You taste like sugar," he whispered as he swept his fingertip across her lips and then licked it.

"Justine got a little sugar from one of the women and we had it sprinkled on bread with butter for breakfast. You taste like sliced ham."

He chuckled. "That's what we had for breakfast. The cook found a pig along the road a week or so ago. He soaked it in the brine in a pot for a few days to cure it as we traveled."

"Found a pig?"

"Just wandering, so he asked the pig where he was going, and the pig said he had no place to go, so the cook invited him to dinner. He was a delightful guest and very delicious."

Sophie started to laugh, but he pressed his lips against hers silencing her. He didn't want to talk. He wanted to feel. To feel her and everything about her with his hands, his mouth, and his body. He pulled her over on top of him. "There's nothing I like more than how you feel against me, your skin, your warmth, your touch. It's the best thing I know." He kissed her again.

She pulled her mouth just barely away from his. "We need more times like this," she breathed. "More times when it is just us and the world is far away." Her lips fell on his again.

He smoothed his hands across her back and hips, and she pressed into him. "Us alone, yet us together."

He rolled her onto her back and took her for the second time that afternoon. The first time had been rushed and passionate, as if the moment would be lost before they knew it. But this time they moved slowly and deeply, cherishing every touch, every sensation. She lifted her hips to pull him into her more completely, and he willingly obliged. This time was meant to last until they could be together again.

"Yes," moaned Sophie as she rocked against him. "My love, my heart, my man."

He couldn't speak. He could only feel her, and that was all he wanted.

When Justine and Joseph came back to the tent, Birch was gone.

Justine smiled, asking Sophie, "Is all well?"

"All is well."

****

The next morning, Birch and Sophie held hands as they walked to General George Washington's tent. This time the aide recognized Birch and showed him inside at once.

Birch saluted. After Washington saluted back, Birch said, "Good morning, sir. This is Mistress Sophie Dougal, I mean Johansen."

"So pleased to meet you, Dr. Johansen."

"Thank you, sir, but as a doctor I go by Dr. Dougal. That, however, doesn't change my married name as Johansen." She squeezed Birch's hand.

"I see. I will do my best to keep the two in order. Lieutenant, since I can see that you have brought your marital life back to its earlier state, there will be no need for the ten lashes. You are dismissed."

"Ten lashes?" asked Sophie.

Birch looked down at her and spoke quickly. "Yes, if I couldn't make things up with you, General

Washington determined that would be my punishment."

Her face pinched tight, and she dropped his hand. "You came to me to avoid ten lashes?"

"No, I came to you because I needed to make things right. I couldn't go on the way it was. I would have taken the lashes willingly for how I failed you."

Washington interrupted. "I saw his face when he told me about the letter he had written. His remorse was deep and sincere. Believe me, Dr. Dougal, he would regret the tear in your marriage more than any bites of the whip."

Sophie hesitated for a moment before taking back Birch's hand. "I have faith in you."

"You are dismissed, Lieutenant. I wish to speak to Dr. Dougal about smallpox."

"Yes, sir. Permission to kiss my wife?"

"Granted."

After a quick kiss, Birch was gone.

The general sat down at his desk and motioned for Sophie to sit on the stool beside it. "Lt. Johansen will prove to be an excellent officer, despite his indiscretion during our interview. The fact that he came to me to set things right speaks highly of his character. A lesser man would not have come forward to accept punishment the way he did. He deserves your forgiveness."

"I have always believed him to be an honorable man, and we have settled things within our marriage."

"I am glad to hear that. In other matters, your husband and I discussed your accomplishments as a doctor, and I understand you have inoculated several people against smallpox. You yourself have been inoculated, is that right?"

"Yes, that's true."

"And none of these people have contracted smallpox?"

"Inoculation makes a person mildly sick for a short time, leaving very few scars or pock marks. The body builds up resistance to the disease and that person is safe from contracting the deadly form. Other parts of the world have successfully done inoculations for quite a few years."

"Smallpox is a serious and wide-spread concern here in the colonies, and I believe winning this battle with this disease could make the difference in winning the war."

"Inoculation is the answer."

"You do understand that this process must be done in complete secrecy. The British would use any weakness to attack, especially if they realized a reduction in numbers as our troops recover. Are you willing to try?"

"Of course, General. When can we begin?"

"If we inoculate incoming soldiers first, the enemy should not notice any recuperating time. We could also outfit them at the same time. We'll do most of the work with recruits entering Philadelphia and move our efforts to the Morristown, New Jersey, entry point later. For now, I'd like you to start with the new men arriving here in this area."

"It's most important that we keep them isolated until they have recovered, for some of them three or more weeks. Inoculating, and then sending them out into the public only makes the spread of smallpox worse."

"I have already arranged for a church and three private homes to quarantine the men in this area. Are you ready to begin?"

"Yes, General, I am."

"I will ensure your safety by having an armed guard with you at all times."

"I am confident you will. When do I start?"

****

In the harbor of New York City

As Governor William Tryon's boldest plan took shape in his mind, a plot for revenge and for victory, he summoned the mayor of New York City, David Mathews, to his quarters in the *Duchess of Gordon*.

"I demanded your presence specifically last time, and I did not appreciate you sending me an emissary," said Tryon. "When I ask for you, it is you I expect. We will work together on reclaiming the city."

Mathews sniffed haughtily, wanting to impress the governor with his own authority. "I have something more important to show you first." He handed the governor a broadsheet. "These are up all over the city."

To the inhabitants of New York: WARNING THEM OF THOSE WHO TRANSMIT INTELLIGENCE TO GOVERNOR TRYON. His only purpose in staying on the ship is to facilitate the gathering of information and sending it on to our merciless English enemies, of which he has already been too successful.

Exasperation crept into Tryon's voice as he tore the broadsheet into pieces and tossed it to the floor. "Don't these morons understand that this city can count on the full weight of Great Britian's army to suppress these people who have subverted the rule of law?" He paused before adding, "And what are you doing to stop this travesty?"

"Sir," said Mathews, wanting to brag about this

next bit of news. "Things are worse than this. You've been hung in effigy, the figure burned and dragged through the city."

Tryon's mouth narrowed into a tight grimace. As spittle dropped from his lips, he shouted, "How can the British army allow itself, and me, to be so humiliated?"

Mathews straightened his stance. "The situation becomes more dire every day. I have spoken against it, but the brunt of their insurrection falls on you."

A heavy silence persisted until Tryon stood and spoke softly, never once looking in Mathews' direction. "Those deluded people call me yellow-bellied and weak, but they don't know how wrong they are. My spies are spread across the city, and even into the mainland, and I will use every one of them to bring down that arrogant General Washington."

Tryon turned to face the mayor. "Listen carefully. Whether you want to or not, you will be my eyes and ears within the city. I want the names of any suppliers of weapons that Washington might use to equip his army. We will pay them to only sell to the British and that will quickly dry up any source of weapons that the patriots might need.

"Then I want the names of one or two trustworthy loyalists to recruit men right out of Washington's army who would be willing, for a fee, of course, to work toward bringing Washington down." He rummaged through his desk drawers and pulled out a leather bag. It jingled when he shook it. "Here is cash enough to pay any man recruited. Pay a fee to the man who brings you a recruit and a fee to yourself as well."

Mathews tucked the money bag into his jacket. "I will do what I can, but the only way Washington can be

stopped entirely is to kill him."
"Exactly."

Chapter Fifteen

Two days later, April 1776, the Continental Army nears the city of New York

Every day, Washington's guards were assigned a variety of duties, and today Lt. Birch Johansen drove one of the baggage wagons loaded with trunks holding the general's governmental documents. He'd only been on the road for a few minutes when Captain Gibbs rode up beside the wagon, climbed onto the wagon seat, and tied his horse to the side.

"Johansen, I want to talk to you privately," said Gibbs in a muffled voice, making certain the armed soldiers riding ahead of the wagon and the pair riding directly behind were out of earshot.

"Yes, sir," answered a puzzled Birch as he slapped the reins to keep the horses moving along the pothole-filled road, bouncing Birch on the seat each time a wheel dropped into one.

Gibbs climbed into the back of the wagon, untied the heavy canvas covering, and flapped it open. Kneeling beside one of the trunks, he opened it and peered inside and began talking to Birch without lifting his head as he made a show of searching that trunk. "We will arrive in New York City in two days to defend against a British invasion."

Birch turned back to catch Gibbs' words.

"Don't turn your head. Either nod or shake your

head."

Birch nodded.

"There are traitors at every turn," Gibbs went on, "and we have only sketchy knowledge as to who and where they are. This is where you'll come in if you decide to accept this assignment. General Washington handpicked you and one other soldier to work with the utmost secrecy within the city to find out how far Governor Tryon's treachery has invaded our troops."

This time Birch couldn't resist turning back. "We're all loyal soldiers, I'm certain of it."

Gibbs closed that trunk and opened another one, making a show of checking the contents. "I know you want that to be true, but the general is not so sure. We have already seen evidence. Three of the gun manufacturers in the city have refused to sell to our army, and two of the general's cooks have turned in counterfeit bills they received after going for supplies. We need to find out who is responsible and put a stop to it."

"You don't think I…"

"No, Lieutenant, we're certain of your trustworthiness, which is why I am coming to you now. Meet me in my tent tonight, and we will discuss the details of your mission. Tell no one what I have talked about here and make certain no one knows where you go tonight. Decisions will be made, both yours and mine. Are we clear?"

"Yes, sir. May I ask who the other man will be?"

"No, you may not."

Gibbs closed and locked the trunks, tied the canvas cover back over the wagon, and climbed into the seat next to Birch. After pulling the reins of his horse closer to the wagon, Gibbs climbed astride his saddle. He moved away quickly, leaving Birch confused and curious. For General Washington to think so highly of him, especially after confessing to his lie, was an honor and a privilege, but this was a treacherous assignment where he might be asked to betray his comrades in the guard.

If he were caught spying, would he be willing to have everyone he knew abandon him, including his family, if they heard about it, which they most likely would? Could he risk being imprisoned or even executed by the ones he spied on? Would Sophie understand? Could she accept the shame, even if it was unjustified? A sickening wave of dread welled up in his chest. Could he face that?

He gulped and swallowed his misgivings. He'd made a pledge that his duty would always be to General Washington and the country's fight for freedom, and he would never back down from that. The entire war was dangerous, and this was only another aspect of it.

He slapped the reins again, although his thoughts were not on the horses or the road.

He had another problem. How would he get away from the tents to meet with Captain Gibbs without anyone realizing he was gone?

****

Birch decided on the story that he had a sick headache, saying he'd had them off and on since childhood, and the only relief was quiet and solitude until it passed. In truth, he'd seen his brother, Linden, with these headaches and knew how debilitating they could be. Imitating them would be his perfect excuse to get out of camp alone.

He closed his eyes and pressed his fingers to his temples. Then he forced himself to gag before leaning against a tree. "A bad one," he said, loud enough for anyone nearby to hear.

"What's the matter, Johansen?" asked the closest man.

"I've had these headaches since childhood, and I never know when one's coming on. I haven't had one in years."

"Can I get you anything from the troop doctor?"

"No, the only cure is to wait until it passes. I need to be alone where it's quiet. I'll be back. Don't worry about me." He walked a jagged path through the woods, leaning on trees every once in a while, but once completely out of sight, he headed to Captain Gibbs' tent on the edge of the camp area.

After knocking on the tent post, he asked, "May I enter, sir?"

"Come in, Johansen."

Birch lifted the flap and in the dim light saw two men sitting on wooden chairs inside.

"Sir," said Birch. "I see you're busy. I'll come back later."

"No need, Lieutenant. This matter concerns both of you. May I introduce Sergeant Joseph Gallagher?"

"Oh, we've met," said Birch with a grin as he reached out his hand. "How are you since I saw you yesterday?"

Joseph stood, grasped his friend's hand, and pulled him into a bear hug. "I hear we'll be working together."

"Yes, you will," interrupted the captain. "We must move forward quickly, and it will be less obvious if you two are seen together since people already know you're friends. Still, the utmost secrecy is required. Johansen, you will work within His Excellency's Guard and you, Gallagher, will work within the regular troops."

Gibbs went on to explain what little they knew of Governor Tryon's plan to embed counterfeit money into the colonies through the troops, and at the same time turn as many men as they could over to the British side of the fight. "Right now, the army is the biggest local buyer of supplies as well as paying salaries to the soldiers, which I am well aware have been delayed recently. While there will be other efforts to get this fake money into the economy, right now the army is the easiest and most efficient way."

"What are we to do?" asked Joseph.

"You are to listen and learn. See where, and with whom, this money is going. If possible, discreetly acquire this money and bring it to me. Write down nothing you say or do, and nothing anyone else says or does. Memorize dates, times, and names. Bring me any incidents, however trivial. Neither of you talk in your sleep, do you?"

"No, sir," said both men in unison.

"As of right now we're making it up as we go along. Our end game is to capture any traitors passing counterfeit money and get to the source. We need to know where it comes into the colonies, and who are the loyalist operatives distributing it, and it all has to be done without anyone, and I mean anyone, finding out. You, Gallagher will follow this fake money to its source."

"Yes, sir."

"If you have to let money into use, let it, and don't try to stop it or give yourself away. Simply report to me how and when it happens, and I'll take it from there.

"Johansen, keep your ears open for talk of desertion to the British side and listen for a plot to kidnap His Excellency and possibly assassinate him. Such a tragedy would essentially end the war, and we will have been through everything for nothing, but remember that any man who would kill the general would not hesitate to do the same to either of you. The general and I are asking you to undertake a dangerous mission. You may refuse."

Joseph and Birch glanced over at each other and gave a curt nod. "We understand, Captain, and will accept."

"Are there any questions?"

Both men shook their heads. "No, sir."

"You will meet me at the Colt's Neck Tavern in Colt's Neck, New Jersey, in two days. It is about thirty miles south of Fort Lee where our troops will camp before marching into New York City. You will pose as travelers to a family gathering in Colt's Neck. Make up your story together, and Johansen, no mention of any details about your real family in New Jersey. You will also scout out anything Washington might need to know about British troops along the way. Until I see you next, keep everything in your head for your report. Understood? If you should meet as friends at camp, do not discuss anything related to this mission. You will only report to me. Understood?"

Both men nodded. "Yes, sir."

"Dismissed. Johansen first and Gallagher a few minutes later. Make certain your paths do not cross as you head back to your companies."

****

Colt's Neck Tavern was a busy place, and no one noticed three men sipping ale at a table in the back corner of the room. None of these three men wore uniforms, making them nearly invisible in the multitude of drinkers and card players.

"The Continental Army will cross the river into the city of New York tomorrow," said Gibbs. "While we expect no military opposition, tensions will still be high. Loyalist supporters are everywhere, and it's difficult to know who can be trusted."

Both Birch and Joseph nodded in agreement.

"You are also aware that New York City has a busy red-light district of taverns and readily available ladies of the evening."

Birch and Joseph again nodded. "We both know men who've been laid up because of drink and disease they caught from an evening visit."

"You are to avoid and ignore all such situations. Unless these men are engaged in either counterfeiting or turning traitor, you are to ignore them. Is that understood?"

An uproar came up from the far end of the bar as one man punched another in the gut. Within seconds, two more men were in the fracas, knocking over chairs and tables while the other patrons scrambled to get out of the way. Everyone, except the combatants, froze in place at the ear-shattering sound of a whistle from one of the two barkeeps leaping over the bar. Each grabbed one of the fighters by the collar and dragged them out to the street. Calm returned to the tavern very quickly.

"We can expect more of this kind of brawling once all the troops are on the island. Your job will be to stay out of it. Understood?"

"Yes, sir," Birch and Joseph said in unison.

"The two of you, however, will be most useful within our own guard," said Gibbs. "General Tryon has offered land and money to anyone who will defect and fight with the British. There are rumors that several of our own men in the Life Guards have agreed to this bargain."

"Are you sure it's not only rumors, or do we know any names?" asked Birch.

"That's what you'll find out for us. Gallagher will follow the counterfeit money while you investigate defectors. Gallagher, begin your search with the brothers, Issac and Israel Young.

"You, Johansen, need to get to know Gilbert Forbes, a gunsmith, who, shall we call it, holds court in a local tavern. His name keeps coming up, and because we are only weeks from British ships landing in the city, we must work quickly. General Washington is counting on you."

****

June 1776, 19,000 Continental soldiers march into New York City and occupy the city

Three men arrived separately in a wooded area on the west side of the island known as Richmond Hill, now George Washington's headquarters.

"The city is now Washington's, but still a large number have loyalist leanings," said Captain Gibbs. "That means the two of you need to be even more alert and cautious.

"Whenever we meet it will be here, at this spot, but we will arrive separately, so no one will track us here together. Gallagher and Johansen, you will arrange a weekly time and day to meet. I will arrive as needed to bring information from you back to the general. As always nothing between the two of you will ever be in writing."

"We understand, sir," said Joseph.

Captain Gibbs rode back to headquarters while Birch and Joseph made plans. "This boulder near this overgrown tree will keep us hidden," said Birch. "We'll plan to meet every week at this spot and as close to this time as possible whether we have new information or not."

Joseph added, "Just to be on the safe side, if two meetings are missed, each of us is to consider the mission exposed and now abandoned, and a rescue team of soldiers will be sent to our last known location."

The two friends spent an hour sitting under the tree in each other's company, knowing it might be the last time for quite a while.

****

Joseph spent the next few weeks gathering information about counterfeiting schemes by befriending less than respectable sources, posing as a man able to supply paper for forged bills at a price that included his silence. After a time, one of his sources, a smarmy little man who made his living keeping secrets for a price, named Marcus Jones, introduced him to the Young brothers, Issac and Israel.

"I'm Dobbin Douglas," said Joseph. "Jones said you'd be worth contacting about my paper."

"Jones told us you might be around," said Issac acting bored with the whole conversation. "What makes you think we'd be interested in paper?"

"I know there's money to be made…with paper,

and I was told you two were the men to see about it. If I'm wrong, I can go elsewhere."

Israel forced a smile, but Issac answered hesitantly, drawing out his words, "We might be interested. What have you got?"

Dobbin took two small pieces of paper out of his vest pocket. "Here's an authentic Connecticut bill, and here is identical paper," he said, handing both to Issac. "Print a bill with your own printer. I hear Henry Dawson does the work, and if he's as good as I hear, you won't be able to tell the difference."

Issac fingered each piece of paper. "Where'd you get this?"

Dobbin flashed a superior grin with all the sincerity of a snake. "Now if I told you that, you'd get it yourself and you wouldn't need to cut me in. I can't have that. Are you in or out?"

"We already have a supplier," said Issac.

"Really? Did Israel Ketchum deliver?" He paused for an answer. When none came, he went on. "I take it that's a no, but if you still want to keep printing, I might be able to supply you, if we can strike a deal. A better deal than Ketchum could have offered."

Issac's brother, Israel, blanched as if he'd been caught with his hand in the proverbial cookie jar. "Ketchum tried to get the paper, but at the last minute couldn't go through with it. Besides, we just rent a room in our attic to Henry Dawson. We don't know what he does up there."

Dobbin snatched the paper from Issac's hand. "You want me to believe you don't know Dawson's the engraver? That you don't know there's a heavy, noisy printing press in your attic? That's like expecting a mouse to follow the cat's advice. I'll take my paper to someone else."

Dobbin was out the door and halfway down the street before Issac Young ran up behind him. "We can pay good money for your paper from our profits after we move the money."

Dobbin flashed a superior grin. "I want to see the press, and I want to meet Henry Dawson before we make a deal."

Issac didn't answer until Dobbin started to walk away again, and as Joseph expected, Issac called to him, "Follow me," and they both headed back toward the house.

****

Meanwhile, Birch Johansen lingered at the bar in a saloon often frequented by Continental soldiers and one Gilbert Forbes, a gunsmith. He'd gotten a general description, so looking around the crowded room, he searched for a short, thick man wearing a white coat. A man like that sat at a table with five other men, all talking and drinking ale, all except Forbes who had a ham and bacon biscuit sandwich.

Birch wore his soldier's jacket because it made him stand out in the crowd, and he needed Forbes to identify him as one of Washington's guards. He had to convince Forbes he was just another footloose soldier looking for easy money, so he decided the best way to do that was to be drunk. But Birch, who had a low tolerance for liquor, knew he needed to remember everything he saw and heard, so he pretended to be scuttered.

He walked up to the already crowded bar and asked for a mug of ale. Only sipping at his drink, he elbowed and joked with the other men standing nearby until he spotted a lady standing on the stairs, dressed in a revealing satin gown and most likely looking for a man to entertain for the evening. When he smiled at her, she came over to him and put her hand on his arm.

Sophie would understandably disapprove, but it is only play-acting.

"Are you looking for something, soldier?" she purred.

The lace stitched on the bosom of her dress was tattered, and she had far too much rouge on her cheeks, obviously a hopeless woman in a hopeless job. He suddenly felt guilty about using her in his plans, but he plunged ahead anyway. He glanced over to see if Forbes had noticed him yet. He had not.

"Yes, I am." Still playing a part, he tried to slur his words as if he were already drunk, but she didn't seem to be fooled.

"You probably need another drink if you want to find what you're looking for. Let me order another for you."

He paid for two mugs and sipped at his until she said, "I could take that one off your hands. I wouldn't mind." She ended up drinking both.

He talked quietly in her ear, saying things he thought a lady of the evening would like to hear. "I'm alone in the city for the first time. I wanted some company, just to talk to someone."

"Are you sure that's all you want?" Her eyes roamed up and down his body. "I think there's a lot we could enjoy together."

He blushed.

"But I see that's not what you're interested in, so I'll just keep you company for a while."

"Thank you, ma'am. I'll pay you for your time."

"Of course you will."

For almost an hour, Birch let her do most of the talking while he took glances at the table with Gilbert Forbes and the other men. When Forbes looked in his direction, Birch said, "I have to be going." He slipped a guinea out of his pocket, and she took it from his hand. Then she gave him a kiss on the cheek.

Understanding he wanted to be at the table of men sitting with Forbes, she said, "Let me help you get where you're going." She took him by the arm, and they staggered together over to the table. He stumbled and fell into her. With a scowl, she righted him and dragged him along the rest of the way.

"Take him," she said. "He's too scuttered to be any use to me."

Birch swayed on his legs again and sloshed ale from his mug onto the floor. He patted her on the rump, and she went back to the stairs.

"Sit down, Johansen," said a drummer named William Green, a man with a dull look about him that made Birch wonder how he could be a member of the Life Guards.

Green dragged an empty chair over to the table. "He's one of us. A fine sport. Interested in a lot of things."

Birch flopped into the seat.

At the same time, Tom Hickey put his hand on Green's arm, saying in a low voice, "Are ye sure ye want this knowing codger to be in on our business?"

Green smiled a lopsided grin. "Oh, Johansen's all right," said Green. "Mr. Forbes, this here is Birch Johansen, one of the guards like us."

Forbes leaned across the table and reached out his hand to Birch, and Birch returned the handshake with loose fingers. "Glad to meet you," said Forbes. "We're making guesses as to how this war will come out. Any opinion?"

With lively conversation, the men at the table exchanged views and thoughts about the war between swallows of ale. Birch interjected the occasional "Hear, Hear!" at comments about both the colonists and the monarchy.

Finally, Birch announced, "I think it could go either way. Depends on who you listen to." He hiccupped and slapped his hand on the table to steady himself.

"If you're in the Guard, Washington must think you're a man of integrity and dedication," said Forbes, "even if you've let the drink take over tonight."

Birch gave a long obnoxious burp. "You're right, I have."

Forbes ignored the boorish behavior. "I wonder, Mr. Johansen, if a man of your quality has truly considered all the practical options. There are many opportunities available for a man who makes the right choices."

Birch straightened up yet continued to slur his words. "What kind of opportunities are we talking about?"

Tom Hickey spoke up in a taunting voice. "Money, prestige, and status, all the things a soldier can't get from your favorite general, old George. Ye know, the one whose boots ye like to kiss."

"Shut up, Hickey," said Birch before slurping at his drink. "I don't care who runs the show, but I'm sick of low rations and being paid in that worthless Continental script. This war is playing out differently than I thought it would when I enlisted. Something needs to change."

"Singing a different tune, are ye?" retorted Tom who picked up his mug and left the table.

"Let him go," said Forbes. "I think you and I have better things to talk about."

Green sat up straight in his chair and grinned. "Johansen, I bet you didn't know the governor is giving up land and money to people who make the right choices."

All at once every man had an opinion to share. Birch ignored their pointless chatter to study the faces of everyone at the table, especially the ones who talked the loudest and interrupted the others, men who thought they were always right, even when they weren't.

Forbes leaned across the table again. "Now, boys, no sense arguing. Let me talk to Johansen privately. Maybe he'll see the light. You all wait here. This won't take long."

Birch gave a drunken grin to Green, left his ale on the table, and staggered after Forbes. Once outside on the street, Forbes, even though he was more than a few inches shorter, slammed Birch up against the wall. "I know a drunk when I see one, and you ain't it! You might fool them, but not me! I can see it in your eyes. You're as sober as a can of beans."

Birch blinked furiously. "What are you talking about?"

"I'm talking about a man who thinks I'm a dunderhead, one who wants information and thinks by play-acting he can get it. Come back when you want to talk real business. Now get out of here!" He grabbed

Birch by the jacket and flung him into the gutter. "And if you try a stunt like this again, I'll slice that pretty face of yours!" He stomped back inside the tavern.

Birch, sitting in a stream of trash and waste, pouted. "I didn't think I was that bad an actor. Guess I was wrong." He stood up and brushed off his wet pants as best he could, but the smell would linger for a long time.

He muttered, "The general said this could get dangerous, and it just did. I don't think Sophie would want me to get my face sliced. Me neither for that matter. I have to find another way into the inner circle, but how?"

Chapter Sixteen

I have to find some way back into Forbes' good graces. Who might help me?

Not Tom. Tom is already suspicious. Besides, Tom's been gambling more than usual and bragging about his winnings to anyone who'll listen.

I'll start with someone lower on the influence scale, maybe William Green, the young drummer in the guard. Green loves to gab and tells everything he knows to anybody he knows, and what he doesn't know he makes up. Forbes has already accepted the little man into his tavern group. Yes, that's where I'll start.

Birch's first contact with Green began with complaints. "This Washington's Guard isn't what I thought it would be. We just follow the general around and do nothing of any importance. What was I thinking wanting to be part of this?"

Green nodded his head vigorously. "You and me think the same way. I should be an officer by now. I deserve to be an officer, but Washington's holdin' me back 'cause I'm from South Carolina." He raised his hand in a fist. "George ain't got no regard for proud Southerners."

"Yeah! No matter where we were born, we're all fighting this war together," said Birch. "Washington said he didn't care where we came from, but he can't hide the truth of how he really feels. We, you and me, should stick together. We need stronger leaders!"

"Yes, sirree!"

It wasn't long before Green agreed with just about everything he said, so his next step was to ask for money. "You've always got lots of money, and I need some." Birch paused before adding, "And I don't care where or how you got it or who you got it from."

Green's eyes narrowed. "Why is a knowing blade like y'all trying to run with us cupboard-headed blokes?"

"I'm not running with you, at least not yet. But I need money now, and the army's not giving it out. Things have changed since my wife got to camp, and I need to keep her happy, and we haven't been paid but a pittance in months. And what will I do when this war is over? I'm a third son, so no family land for me, my brothers will get it all. Makes me wonder if I'm fighting for the right side, you know what I mean? I hear rumors, and I wonder if they're true."

Green's eyes lit up. "They're true all right, but you can only talk about it in certain places, you know, safe places with men who think the same way."

"Places like the tavern?"

Green nodded solemnly.

Birch leaned in and spoke quietly, like telling a secret. "If you can take me to the right people, you know, people like Forbes who have influence, I'd be grateful, and in return, I could make things better for you, get you easier duty, or even get you a promotion maybe. I have the general's ear about some things. You could be one of them. Sort of one hand washes the other, you know what I mean?"

Birch almost choked on those words. Here he was

offering to make things easier for a man whose only skill was hitting sticks on a drum, but he needed a way back into Forbes' good graces, and this little man just might do it for him. "I can make it worth your while if you can help me out? Use your influence, and I'll use mine."

Green puffed out his chest proudly. "Always willing to help a fellow Life Guard. I'll let ya know."

Birch, thinking he'd rather trust a rabid squirrel, still stuck out his hand for Green to shake. "Thank you for this, and you won't regret it."

A couple of days later, Green said, "You already met the gunsmith, Gilbert Forbes, a while back."

"Yes, at the tavern. He didn't like me."

"I know. Threw you out in the street. He doesn't usually let men back in, so I'm making no promises, but maybe Mr. Forbes will reconsider if he thinks you might do him some good. He's always looking for men who are officers already, you know, ones who'd have more pull, ones who can do things us enlisted guys can't. Sort of like what you're gonna do for me."

Birch nodded.

"Remember, I'm just bringing you to him. I told him you were sorry, real sorry, but nothing else. I'm not messing up my own deal."

"I understand."

I already failed once to convince Forbes to take me in, and this will be my last chance. I don't want to think about what it will mean for General Washington if I fail again. But this time it involves more than simply gathering information. If I do some good for Forbes, I'll be getting in bed with traitors and thieves. I'll become one of them. So, this time no ale, I'll play it straight ahead with no pretending. I'll really have to become one of them.

The next night, Birch showed up at the tavern. He hesitated at the door, but William Green waved him over to the table where others, including Tom, sat with Forbes. Tom spotted Birch and scowled before whispering something to Forbes who didn't respond.

Birch stood back from the table and tried not to seem too eager. He couldn't be pushy. Forbes had to take him in on his own.

Forbes glanced at Birch, but his eyes regarded him warily before he turned back to speak to William Green. "Private Green, who's the scoundrel you brought with you?"

Birch stepped up closer to Forbes' chair. "Birch Johansen, sir," he said, holding out his hand. Forbes didn't shake it.

An hour later, Forbes shifted his gaze back to Green again and jerked his thumb toward Birch. "I met this man a few days ago. He pretended to be scuttered." Then lifting his thumb in the direction of the woman on the stairs, he said, "He even got Lolly over there to help him fake it. I threw him out, and I don't think I want him back, so why did you bring him?"

Before Green could answer, Birch said quickly, "I'm sorry. I thought I could be more friendly if I were drunk, but I don't hold my drink very well, so I-I faked it."

"And didn't do a good job of it," said Forbes as he scooted his chair around to look in Birch's direction. His expression told Birch he wanted to step on him like a cockroach.

Birch winced. "I know, sir, and I'm sorry I tried to

fool you. Meeting you was important to me, and I made a mistake. It won't happen again."

"It better not." Forbes ran his finger across his throat while making a gurgling sound.

Birch swallowed hard. "Yes, sir."

Turning to Green again, Forbes said, "Is he always this polite?"

"For as long as I've known him," answered Green. "A bad habit of his."

"Don't let his good manners fool ye," said Tom to Forbes. "He's not one for us. I know him, and he's not for us."

Forbes ignored him and nodded in Birch's direction. "Take a seat at the table."

Tom bolted from his chair, and Forbes pulled over that same chair to offer it to Birch. Tom Hickey stormed out the door.

"What's got into him?" asked Green.

Birch shrugged, but he knew what it was. Birch was crowding in on Tom's personal territory and might cut into whatever scheme he had with Forbes. Tom had more money to spend recklessly than he'd ever had before, so obviously Forbes paid well, and ever since the rescue on the ice, Tom complained that Birch was lording it over him, saying, "I saved that man's life more than once, but he thinks he's a better soldier than me." Apparently now Tom thought Birch was stealing his seat at the table.

Several more evenings passed without incident, but Tom didn't show up. Other men came, ordered their mugs, and lingered to talk with Forbes.

A tall, dark-haired man, unknown to Birch, sat down one night and began suggesting a list of things the

British might offer to entice a man to change sides. "I heard the right man could get land and cash and other benefits for turning his musket the other way. If you know what I mean."

Forbes remained tight-lipped, and as often as he could, changed the topic to casual barroom conversations.

The next night, a man who looked more hungry than sensible stood up and shouted, "I will fight valiantly for the British if given the chance. Just give me the chance!" He raised his glass with a shaky hand and promptly spilled half the contents over the head of the man next to him.

Almost at once, Forbes flicked his hand toward a burly man sitting against the wall. Birch had seen him there before, but he never entered the conversations. The man stood up, hoisted the bragging man by the collar, and roughly escorted him out. Without leaving the doorway, Forbes' man threw him far out into the street. The braggart cried out in pain when he hit the road and was never seen around that table again.

The next night, Tom unexpectedly returned to the tavern, but he avoided looking in Birch's direction. Instead, he drank more and then more, and he wandered around the tavern talking to men who he invited to the table to get to know Forbes and his plans.

Forbes leaned over to Birch. "I like a man who keeps his counsel to himself, not one who makes the rounds of this place, talking too loudly and too freely. Hickey talks too much."

"He does love to talk," said Birch.

"But too much, and to too many."

"Tom will always be Tom."

"That's what I'm afraid of. I want the right men around me. Not all of them are going to be ready for the ultimate mission. Not all of them will have the proper character. Do you understand?"

Birch looked down at the table. "I might."

"Tom has been filling my ear with doubts about you. He comes here early in the afternoon when he can get off duty and leaves before the regulars get here."

Birch nodded. "I understand."

"I have to be able to trust those around me, trust them completely. I can't have doubts about anyone."

Birch's mind slipped back to a similar conversation he'd had with General Washington who also couldn't have doubts. He gave a sheepish smile. "I understand, Mr. Forbes. I'll leave."

Just as Birch slid back his chair to stand, Forbes put his hand on his arm. "Just a minute. I believe you're smart and capable, just the kind of man I want, but you have to prove it. I can do things for you if you're willing to do things for me. Understand?"

Birch felt a knot in his stomach, but his job was to expose Forbes. "What is this thing you want me to do?"

"Meet me outside behind the privy where we can talk privately. I'll go first. You follow."

The wooden outhouse behind the tavern sat at an angle in the back corner of the small yard, surrounded by tall bushes. By standing in the right place behind the bushes, one could see anyone coming out the tavern door but not be seen himself. Forbes led Birch to just that spot.

"What I want you to do is very simple," said Forbes. "And if you do this for me, I can do fine things for you."

Birch didn't answer. He just waited.

After a moment, Forbes took a folded and sealed paper out of his breast pocket and held it up. "This must be delivered to Governor Tryon on his ship in the harbor. It's sealed and vitally important that it not be intercepted by any Continental forces. Right now, most of our couriers are known to the enemy by sight, so we need someone who won't be suspected or stopped and searched."

Birch stayed silent and waited.

"If you deliver this to Rupert Gaston who owns the Gaston Inn about six miles south of here, just follow the main road, and he'll deliver it to Tryon personally. When I've received word that you've done this and the letter with an unbroken seal is handed to the governor, you will have proven yourself."

"I understand, sir." Birch reached for the letter, but Forbes held it out of his grasp.

"Failure will result in very unpleasant consequences, not only for me for trusting someone like you, but from others who are not as forgiving as I might be. Are you willing to take a risk to let me know exactly where you stand?"

Birch took in a slow breath and let it out. "I am, sir."

Forbes handed him the letter, and Birch put it in his jacket pocket.

As soon as he was out of sight of the tavern, Birch turned north instead of south, and ran as fast as his legs could carry him. About two miles outside the city, at a designated spot behind a rock hidden by a large overgrown tree, he sat down, caught his breath, and waited. When he heard a horse coming his way, he curled up and pretended to be asleep until a hand shook his shoulder and a voice said, "What have you got for me?"

Birch sat up and smiled at Joseph. "You're late," said Birch with a grin as Joseph moved out of the moonlight and into the shadow.

"What?" said Joseph with a smirk. "You think I got nothing better to do than visit you? There's a war on, you know."

Birch shook his friend's hand and answered with a laugh, "Really, I hadn't heard."

"If you weren't here tonight, I was going to tell Gibbs to call the whole thing off. You haven't been here in two weeks, and I was getting worried they were on to you."

"Tom Hickey's been causing trouble for me with Forbes." He pulled the letter out of his vest pocket. "This is my test. If I make this delivery for him, he'll take me into his confidence. Here, be careful how you handle this. I flicked my finger under the wax to loosen it. Get it to Gibbs to read and then he can reseal it and get it back to me. I have to deliver it to Gaston Inn tonight, so make it quick."

"Do you know what it says?"

"No, that's your job. I'll be here when you get back."

One hour later, Joseph was there with the letter reclosed with the tiniest drop of wax underneath the seal. "The general says, 'Good work.' The letter is about a British invasion on Long Island set for August 27 and now we can be prepared. Forbes trusted you with valuable information, so you must be getting in good with him."

Birch waved over his shoulder as he was already running on his way to the Gaston Inn.

The next day Governor Tryon received the intact letter from Rupert Gaston. Tryon thanked Gaston and paid him two gold coins.

The next evening word came back to Forbes of the letter's safe delivery, so he sat down with Birch privately to share information and tell him which men Forbes believed would be good candidates to join their group. Birch was told to get to know them and report back what he thought.

Birch, although pleased when Forbes confided in him, now realized the need for secrecy was stronger than ever. If anyone found out, on either side, the British or the Americans, that he had delivered a letter to the enemy or that he was now helping Forbes recruit other men, they'd call him a traitor. Between that rock and a hard place suddenly became very uncomfortable.

****

Two nights later Forbes took Birch aside into one of the corners of the crowded tavern. "I believe you are ready to hear more about what's available for any man whose heart and mind are in the right place for victory."

"What would that be?"

"Meet me at a boarding house several blocks north of here tomorrow evening by six o'clock. You'll find out more then." He tugged Birch's head down and spoke the address very quietly into his ear. "Some men are meeting me there, including William Green. It will be rewarding, I promise you."

Birch gave a curt nod.

A scuttered Tom caught up with Birch as he left the tavern. He grabbed Birch by the arm, and slurring his words, said, "What'd he say to ye?"

Birch shook off his grip. "Nothing."

"He did! I saw him. I won't let ye take my seat at the table! I earned it." With both hands, he shoved Birch against the wall. "What'd he say to ye?"

Birch straightened up and easily pushed the drunken Tom to the floor. Tom landed on his backside with a thud.

"Out of my way."

Just then Forbes came up behind Tom and pressed his hand against Tom's shoulder, holding him down. In a commanding voice, he said, "Hickey, you're getting in the way. I don't want a touchy maggot with a big mouth. Get up and go home."

Forbes released Tom's shoulder, and Tom used a nearby chair to help himself struggle to his feet. "Don't believe him!" he said, pointing shakily at Birch.

"It's you I don't believe any more. Get out."

"He's taking what's mine!"

Forbes' enforcer put his hands on Tom's arms, saying, "You heard him, Hickey. You ain't welcome with us good fellows."

Tom glared at all of them as a strong push from the enforcer launched him out the tavern door as he shouted, "Ye'll see! Ye'll see!"

Forbes put his hand on Birch's back. "You can't trust him. Watch out."

"I will."

Birch had no idea how fateful that warning would be.

Chapter Seventeen

On the day Birch first walked into the tavern to meet Forbes, Sophie and Justine walked through the front door of the Congregational church located two miles west of the Continental soldiers' last campsite. They were greeted by twenty soldiers sitting on church benches wearing uniforms so clean they obviously hadn't seen real duty yet. Most had young fresh faces eager to see action and were disheartened at being held back here. The older men were not so ready to join the fight, knowing the horror it could bring. They'd gladly rest here for a while longer.

Hearing the door open and spying the visitors, their sergeant shouted, "Attention!" and the men jumped to their feet.

"Please, be seated, gentlemen," said Sophie as she walked down the aisle with Justine behind her, carrying two bags of medical supplies. "We have a lot to discuss before I begin. Are you their sergeant?" she asked the middle-aged man in the front.

"Yes, ma'am. Murphy's the name." His pock-marked face told Sophie he'd survived smallpox and could not be infected again, the perfect man to lead this platoon.

Sophie continued, "Is the pastor of this church here?"

"I am," said a thirty-something man with a

receding hairline and ears that seemed to stick straight out from the sides of his head. He leaned heavily on a cane with each step. "I am Josiah Jones, and I am glad to open my church for your use. As you can see, I am no good for soldiering, but I can do this for the cause."

"General George Washington thanks you. Have you been inoculated?" The pastor shook his head.

"Then you will be one of the first." She faced the new recruits, again saying, "You may be seated." The benches scraped against the wooden floor as the men sat down. "Sergeant Murphy, do these men understand the procedure and why they are here?"

"They've been told very little. I am also unsure of it myself. Our orders were to report to this church, so here we are."

"Very well. This group of men has been chosen because they are new recruits, and they are to be the first soldiers inoculated against smallpox as per General Washington's orders." An undercurrent of grumbling rose up among the men.

Sophie ignored it. "Smallpox could kill our soldiers faster than muskets, so I am providing a first line of defense. After all of you have recovered from your quarantine, I will travel to Philadelphia and do the same procedure with other new recruits."

Three men shouted out. One said, "Why choose us?"

Another cried, "We could get smallpox and die!" while the third said, "It's against God's will!"

Sergeant Murphy shouted over them, "Sit down! That's an order!" All the men reluctantly sat back down on the benches. "Sorry, ma'am, I've only had them under my command for little over a week. They're not in shape yet."

"I understand, but General Washington insists these inoculations be kept completely secret, and men who have not been in battle yet are the best way to do that. Pastor Jones, how do you plan to keep our presence here undisclosed?"

"Most of our congregation live on farms scattered at some distance and far enough away not to notice any comings and goings. The church is set far back from the road and very few people pass by here anyway. We're not on the way to anywhere. Only three elders know what is happening, and they are sworn to absolute secrecy. We will be holding outdoor services while you are here. The weather is getting nice, and outdoor services are a welcome change. We can continue to do so for as long as you need us. When only two or three men are left here to recover, we have homes to shelter them."

"Your support is greatly appreciated," said Sophie. She stepped up three stairs to the altar level and faced the soldiers. "How many of you know someone who has been horribly scarred by smallpox?" Several hands went up. "And how many know someone who has died in agony from the disease?" More hands went up.

"Most of you come from small towns or farms with little exposure to smallpox, but it is a terrible way to die, and smallpox is raging through our troops right now. Unless we do something, more men will die of disease and our army will be destroyed. Justine, hold up your hand."

Justine held up her left hand presenting a small scar where a thread soaked in pus from an infected patient had been scratched into the back of her hand. "She just scrapes your hand," she said. "It's nothing to be afraid of. Now I can care for anyone without getting sick."

Sophie spoke again. "Some of you may be wondering what I know about this procedure. I am a doctor, fully trained, apprenticed, and qualified."

"She's a fine doctor!" said Justine. "I've been working with her for a long time, and she is the best. After Bunker Hill she fixed a lot of soldiers." She paused. "And just so you know, there'll be no need for you to be naked in front of her."

Murmuring raced through the crowd again. "What if we want to be naked?" shouted one soldier, standing up and grabbing his crotch.

"I'll be glad to oblige," said Sophie. "Believe me, I've seen better men than you, and not one of them has died from my gaze. In fact, most of them lived because I was able to dig out musket balls and stitch up wounds in areas that men keep covered. Besides, you will not be so ill that you cannot take care of your latrine needs on your own.

"Sergeant Murphy, please have the men take off their shirts, shirts only, and line up in single file in the aisle. I must examine them to see if they are fit enough for the inoculations." Despite the continuing complaining in the ranks, the men did as they were ordered.

Later that afternoon, Sophie declared all of them healthy enough to take the inoculation. After ordering blankets and pallets for each man, she had the men lay them on the benches and across the floor to be their beds for the next few weeks. She called the first soldier forward.

"What is your name, young man?" she asked as she

prepared the injection.

"Thomas Carter, ma'am."

"How old are you, Thomas?"

"Eighteen, ma'am."

"Really?" She looked at him out of the corner of her eye.

The boy hung his head. "I'm only fourteen, but you won't tell, will you? I'm strong, and real good with a musket. I want to fight. My pa said it was all right."

Sophie sighed. "Young man, I'm going to inoculate you because it's the right thing to do, but we'll see how you fare before I decide if you need to go home for a while to grow up. Boys your age have enlisted and fought before, but it's men who started this war and men who should finish it. Those who are boys now will need to be the ones leading this country in our new freedom."

She printed his name at the top of a piece of slate with chalk and handed it to him. "Put this beside your blankets, and we'll keep track of your progress on it. When you recover, we can erase your name, and the enemy will never know you were here."

"Thank you, ma'am. I'll prove myself. I will."

She nodded. "And I hope you have a long life to do it."

The four armed soldiers promised by General Washington to protect her stood in each corner of the room. To avoid calling attention to themselves as they came and went every other day on the roads, they didn't wear uniforms. The only thing identifying them was a blue scarf dangling from their belts. All four men had pox scars on their faces to confirm they wouldn't be infected. While on duty at the church, they spelled each other to catch quick naps and to eat before returning to their corners with their weapons. Late every other afternoon, the guards were rotated out and replaced by four new men. One of the new ones was familiar to Sophie and Justine. Thomas Hickey.

"Hello, Tom," said Sophie when she finished checking the men for that day. "Women of the church have prepared food for supper tonight. Be sure to get something to eat."

"I will. Probably eat better than we would at camp."

"Everyone needs a home-cooked meal once in a while."

After eating, Tom sat down on a bench next to a recruit with a bandage covering the scratch on his hand. "The lady doc gives ye orders, too?" Tom asked.

"Sure, sometimes I think she's the sergeant instead of Murphy. Have you ever had that thread stuck in your hand?"

"Nay, I had smallpox as a wee one." He pointed to four large pock marks hidden by his hair around his ears and two on his cheeks. "See?"

"Was it bad?"

"I don't remember. I was too little."

The young recruit went back to scraping his plate for the last bite of potatoes before Tom said gruffly, "Women don't belong in a war with real soldiers."

"I know what you mean. I got a girl back home, and I wouldn't let her come to war."

"I don't got a woman, praise the Lord for that, but I know this one and she gives orders all the time."

The young soldier shrugged and went to lie on his makeshift bed.

The next morning, Sophie and Justine examined each man and wrote on his slate if he had any symptoms.

"Can I train with the men?" asked Sergeant Murphy. "Or will they be too sick?"

"I don't expect any real symptoms for a week or so," said Sophie. "So, yes, you can train with them, but not to the point of exhaustion. They will need their strength when they start to feel poorly, but training will keep them busy. Remember, you cannot leave this sanctuary."

For the next five days, Sergeant Murphy drilled his recruits on weapon care and repair. When all of them could disassemble and reassemble their weapons quickly, he moved on to fighting techniques, and simple hand-to-hand combat. At first the men were clumsy, but soon they were jumping over benches and pallets to "attack" the enemy.

Twelve days later, the first symptoms of fever and malaise appeared in some of the men. Sophie marked this on their slates and ordered them to bed rest. She also ordered buckets of water hauled in from the well out back to keep the men well hydrated. By the end of the second week, the soldiers standing guard were the only ones healthy enough to do the task.

Tom Hickey, having been replaced and returned to this church duty several times, protested to anyone who would listen. "I am a member of General George Washington's Guard, and I won't haul water. Get somebody else to do it."

"There is no one else healthy enough," snapped Sophie. "You never complained about the work before."

He snorted and glared at her before picking up the bucket, muttering under his breath, "I'm complaining about it now. Johansen's woman can't tell me what to do."

"What was that?"

"Nothing, ma'am. I'll bring in the water."

At night, the guards stood outside the building in the corners where they wouldn't be easily seen, one man on each side of the church, but when Tom Hickey was relieved of daytime duty he didn't leave as ordered. Instead, he lingered in the shadows, hiding in the bushes and waiting until the patients inside were sleeping soundly and one of the guards went to relieve himself. He then eased his way inside through the back door, putting his hand against it to lessen its usual squeak as it came open. Once inside, Tom crept toward the altar level. Eventually, he sat down next to Sophie where she leaned against the pulpit trying to get a few precious minutes of sleep.

He watched her and thought that Johansen had everything he didn't, a family to welcome him home, enough money to stay well fed, and the authority of rank in the army. Johansen didn't deserve to also have such a woman as Sophie.

He softly touched her arm. Her skin was soft and warm. She didn't stir, but when he lightly moved his fingers from her wrist up to her elbow, her eyes flew open. She rubbed them, trying to adjust to the dim light.

"Sleeping Beauty," he said quietly, "I thought we could spend some time together. Birch Johansen shouldn't have ye all to himself."

"What?" She sat up straight. "You were dismissed hours ago. Go back to your unit."

He continued to move his hand up and down her arm. "I'd rather stay here."

"Stop it, Tom." She pushed his hand off and started to stand, but he pulled her back down and wrapped his other arm about her shoulders, tugging her close to him.

"Your Mister High and Mighty is everybody's favorite, and Forbes traded him for me. I'm the one with fighting experience. I taught him everything he knows. It should be me."

He sniffed her neck and hair. Then he licked her.

"Leave me be," protested Sophie, struggling to get out of his grasp.

"He'd fancied ye from the beginning, and claimed ye as his, but he can't have everything. I won't lose my share."

"Go away!" she said loudly.

He leaned in to kiss her, but by shaking her head back and forth she avoided his lips on hers. His breath smelled nasty, and his hands were rough. She fought to free her arms.

Finally, she managed to slip one arm out from under his, and she swung her fist into the side of his head. He fell back, smacking his head on the pulpit wall. It stunned him long enough for her to get on her feet, but he reached out, grabbed her ankle, and tugged. She fell on her face with a thud.

In an instant he was on top of her, pushing her hair aside and licking her neck. She tried to call out, but he pressed her face onto the floor. She could barely breathe. She squirmed against his weight until her elbow caught his side. He flinched but continued his assault.

The scuffle awakened Sergeant Murphy, sleeping

against the wall by the windows. He dashed up the altar stairs and put his hands on Hickey's shoulders, but before he could pull him off, Hickey shook Murphy away, causing him to fall back down the steps. Tom lifted Sophie to her feet by her arms and slapped her. She went limp, but he held her up.

"That's enough!" shouted Murphy, grabbing Tom again. Even with Murphy's arm locked around his neck, Tom fisted Sophie in the face. She staggered away and landed on her back on the floor beside her medical bag.

Murphy and Tom continued to wrestle while she opened her bag and pulled out her scalpel. Finally, staggering to her feet, she held it out in front of her.

"Get out of here, Tom! Now!" she shrieked.

Once again Tom pushed the sergeant down the altar steps and started toward Sophie. She held out her arm and swung her scalpel, up and down, across and back. He reached for it. The blade sliced the top of his wrist.

He cried out and, grabbing his cut wrist, shouted, "Ye'll see! Ye'll see!" as he ran out the side door of the church, leaving a trail of bloody splatters on the floor.

By now the recovering recruits had awakened and reached the steps. Two started after him, but Murphy called out, "He's gone. No need to get him now. We know who he is, and we have to see to Dr. Sophie first."

"Are you all right?" asked another young man.

Sophie collapsed to the floor again, breathing hard. "I'm fine. My jaw hurts some." She touched her rapidly swelling cheek. "Just shaken up. I've known Tom Hickey for a long time, and while he was never Mr. Jolly, he was never like this."

"Back to bed," Sergeant Murphy ordered the men. "Smith, bring a rag soaked in cool water for her face. I'll sit with her for a while to make sure she's all right."

Justine didn't wait for instructions before dashing out the front door, grabbing the guard standing there by the arm, and running with him toward the army encampment to find Birch Johansen.

****

Birch held Sophie in his arms, rubbing her back and caressing her hair. He'd ridden as fast as he could, but for him, it wasn't fast enough. He was hot and dripping with sweat, leaving wet stains on her clothes and against her skin, but he wouldn't let her go. He should have been here. It was his responsibility to be here. Instead, she'd faced Hickey alone.

"Let me see your face," he said softly, lifting her chin with his finger. She slowly turned her face up to his and raised the cold cloth off her eye, which was encircled by a purple splotch reaching down her cheek. She winced when he gently touched her under the bruise. "This is my fault," he said.

"No, it's not, and it looks worse than it is. It only hurts when I smile." Then turning her lips down in an exaggerated frown, she said, "Ouch! Frowning hurts, too. Just wait until it turns a pretty shade of green, then you'll know it's almost healed."

She tightened her arms around his waist. "I'm glad you came." She leaned her other cheek against his chest.

"I wish I'd been here when you needed me. I should have been." His lips tightened against his teeth in a grimace as he looked around the sanctuary before calling out, "Where were the guards Washington sent

183

for your protection?"

Justine spoke up. "They were outside like they always are at night. No sense watching everyone sleep. We all thought Tom had gone back to camp with the others."

Birch released Sophie and paced in front of the pulpit. His voice grew louder and louder. "The guards are supposed to be looking out for everything and anything, especially what they don't expect. They failed in their duty!" He turned abruptly toward Sergeant Murphy. "Murphy, where were you?"

The sergeant jumped to attention. "I was sleeping, sir. I came as soon as I heard the commotion."

Birch's expression hardened. "Obviously not soon enough. Dr. Sophie was injured, and I hold you responsible."

Murphy lifted his chest with a deep breath. "It won't happen again, sir."

"It will be on your head if it does!"

"Yes, sir!" Murphy saluted.

Birch walked over to the other four guards standing at attention along the first row of benches. He gave each one a menacing scowl as he moved past. "And what were you doing when Hickey just walked in the door without any of you noticing? Asleep? Playing cards?"

"No, sir!" said the four together.

"One of you will stand guard next to the doctor, always within an arm's reach, day and night, from now on. Is that understood?"

"Yes, sir!"

"This incident will be reported to your superiors and appropriate action will be taken."

Each man forced his shoulders back and looked straight ahead. "Yes, sir."

Sophie touched her husband's arm. "I don't think that'll be necessary. These men have been faithful in their duty, and they couldn't have known Tom would try this. He won't come back."

"I'm going to see that he doesn't," answered Birch as he strode down the aisle.

"Wait, Birch, he's not worth it."

"But you are!" He stormed out the door, and it slammed shut behind him. The vibrations rolled through the chapel.

****

The forest was quiet except for the leaves and twigs crunching under Tom Hickey's feet as he headed to another gambling game. All at once he felt a tingling sensation run up his neck, and he sensed someone was nearby. Tom spotted his former friend moving quickly behind him, and he didn't want any part of the confrontation that was sure to come. He started to run, leaping over logs, and pushing aside branches. The birds scattered with frantic chirping.

Birch kept pace and soon overtook him. "I won't let you get away with it!" Reaching out, he latched onto Tom's arm and heaved him against a thick tree. "This ends now!"

Tom grunted from the force of his spine slamming into the bark but quickly recovered and landed a blow to Birch's jaw. When Birch staggered back, Tom grounded his feet, yanked his knife from his belt, and menaced it in Birch's direction. "Get away from me!"

"Not until I'm through with you." Birch widened his stance and crouched, giving Tom a monstrous stare.

"Whatever is going on between you and me, it's just between you and me, not her!"

"Now listen, Birch," said Tom. "I just meant to put a scare into her." With a deep guttural grunt, he swung his blade out, just missing Birch's eye.

"Only a sniveling coward takes it out on a woman! This time you've got someone your own size!"

Birch ducked under Tom's outstretched arm and jumped forward, forcing Tom back into the tree again. Tom grimaced in pain, but using the tree as leverage, brought his knee up into Birch's stomach. Both fell to the ground in a heap.

Birch bounded to his feet as Tom rolled away from the tree. He grabbed a fallen branch and swung it viciously. Birch put up his arm to deflect the blow and flinched when the stick cut into his forearm. He wrenched the stick out of Tom's hand and threw it into the woods.

"You're outmatched this time." He charged at Tom and hooked his foot around Tom's leg, tossing him to the ground.

Birch dropped to his knees on either side of Tom's chest and pressed his forearm into Tom's throat. Tom choked and went limp as Birch swung his fists again and again, connecting with Tom's face each time.

Tom's nose bled. His cheeks and eyes swelled. A tooth fell out of his mouth. He spit out blood and hissed in a raspy voice, "I just put a scare into her."

Birch snarled. "That's because she cut you with her scalpel, and you ran like a beaten dog."

Spitting out blood and taking a noisy breath, Tom said, "I didn't run. I let her go."

"Good thing you did!" said Birch. "Because the

next time you even touch anything that's mine, I'll kill you. The consequences be damned!"

Birch's fist flew once more into Tom's jaw. Tom lay unmoving on the ground, moaning.

Birch walked away and didn't look back.

****

Six months later, fifteen-year-old Thomas Carter's name appeared on the list of the dead after the battle of Trenton in New Jersey. Sophie cried at the futility of saving young Carter from the plague of smallpox only to have a musket ball take his life.

Chapter Eighteen

June 1776

Looking for a more effective way to stop Governor Tryon's nefarious activities, George Washington enlisted the help of John Jay, a member of the New York State Congress. Jay was soon appointed to head New York's Committee on Detecting and Defeating Conspiracies with the purpose of using teams of intelligence officers and patriot spies to identify and uncover hostile plots.

George Washington's request included, among other things, that there be no leaks of the names and identities of any of those acting undercover. If any operative was exposed, there would be no acknowledgement of them, nor could they be publicly defended from any consequences at the risk of endangering others and jeopardizing the revolution.

This lack of acknowledgement included Washington's own men, Birch Johansen and Joseph Gallagher.

Rumors of a large-scale operation to kidnap or assassinate George Washington, a scheme initiated by Governor Tryon, reached the committee. A name that also surfaced was Gilbert Forbes, whose techniques and plans had been made known to the committee through an unnamed soldier who infiltrated the group. Forbes, known for his ability to encourage confidence and build friendships easily, sat around his table at the tavern nearly every night and made promises in the name of Governor Tryon.

Captain Caleb Gibbs spoke before the committee. "Our infiltrator, a highly respected man, reports if the man takes eagerly to Forbes' friendship, he is escorted to a private location for a personal conversation. Forbes encourages him to decide as to his loyalties. Our infiltrator reported to the best of his memory that Forbes declared, 'all we need to succeed are a few men like yourself. General Washington trusts the loyalty of his soldiers, especially those in his aptly named Life Guards, and will never suspect any of them, which will be his undoing. Could you be one of them? The rewards will be great.' "

Gibbs stated if the man still seemed interested, Forbes assured him that he would be rewarded with more money and future land holdings, compliments of Governor Tryon. All the recruits had to do was take an oath of British loyalty, and they could be taken onto a British ship and protected if their participation was exposed. For each name Forbes delivered to the New York City mayor, David Mathews, he was paid as much as one hundred pounds.

****

June 20, 1776

William Leary of Goshen, New York, stepped into yet another tavern in New York City, noting that this one looked just like all the others except for the name, Hull's Tavern. It didn't take long before he spotted the man he was looking for, William Perkins, one of the four runaway employees of Ringwood Ironworks in Goshen.

Grabbing Perkins by the collar, Leary said, "Gotcha! I'm taking you back to the factory and letting our boss, Mr. Erskine, deal with you." He scolded Perkins all the way out to the street. "Mr. Erskine don't put up with runaways or loyalists! He'd sooner see you dead than turning traitor. You're coming with me! Where are the other three?"

Perkins started to cry real tears. "Please don't take me to jail! I won't stand it!"

"No jail if you tell where the others are right now!"

The little man pointed to another tavern down the street. "He's in there."

Dragging Perkins with him, Leary poked his head into the tavern the man had indicated. Giving Perkins a shake, he said, "You stay here. If you run off again, I'll beat the stuffing out of you and take the bloody remains to the jail."

Perkins' eyes opened wide, and he nodded.

Walking into the saloon, Leary assessed the situation. This second man looked too big and muscled to drag out without a fight, so he changed plans and decided he'd listen and learn what was so important the men had to run away.

Over the next two nights, Leary listened to traitorous talk about a plot to spread counterfeit money and report any information to two British loyalists. If the men around the table agreed to the oath of British loyalty, they'd be protected. The man to give the oath was a short, thick man by the name of Gilbert Forbes who always wore a white coat. Leary convinced Forbes of his loyalty to the British cause and agreed to all Forbes' terms, and eventually Forbes gave him the address of where the oath-taking would take place at a nearby boarding house.

Leary listened to all he could stand before deciding that reporting this news to the Continental authorities was more important than bringing shiftless iron workers home. After extracting promises from the two workers that they vanish so he'd never see them again, he began looking for Continental army headquarters to report what he'd heard and seen as was his duty. Officers took him immediately to John Jay at the Committee on Detecting and Defeating Conspiracies where he testified freely.

The Committee ordered immediate arrests.

****

Issac Young stormed up the stairs to the attic, shouting, "Shut everything down! Shut it down!" Still the printing press continued its clackety-clack.

"Stop!" shouted Issac when he reached the top of the stairs. "Ketchum's been arrested!"

Henry Dawson leaned against the printer to stop it. "What?"

"Ketchum's been arrested for trying to buy counterfeit paper. He didn't have the nerve to go through with it, but they arrested him anyway. He's in the jail and he's talking!"

"Calm down. I'm sure Ketchum won't name us," said Dawson. "We're not caught yet. We'll finish this run. Then we'll set up somewhere else. You get a wagon to carry the press after I get it taken apart." He started up the press again, but when Issac didn't move, Dawson gave him a punch in the arm. "Go now! You fool! While we still have time."

Dawson's mistake was that Issac Ketchum would name anyone or say anything to get out of jail and back home to his six motherless children. He overheard plenty while in his cell, and he willingly told it all to anyone who would listen, starting with the guards, then the head of the jail, and finally to Continental Army officers.

Armed soldiers were already on their way to the attic and the printing press.

****

Two nights later another troop of soldiers headed toward the boarding house at the address given to them by Leary.

Word traveled quickly to Joseph who realized that Birch could be arrested with the rest of the turncoats. He ran to meet Captain Caleb Gibbs at their predetermined place.

Joseph gasped to catch his breath between his words. "Birch is heading to a…boarding house where he's to…meet Gilbert Forbes to take the British oath. He's on the way… there now. We have to stop him."

"Slow down," said Gibbs. "Tell me again."

Joseph sputtered out the words. "Birch convinced Forbes he'd join with British forces to take Washington down, so he's on his way to meet Forbes and some other men who say they'll do the same. They will take the British loyalty oath, but the authorities know of the place and time and are on their way there now. People will be arrested, and Birch's name is on the list!"

"Who turned him in? Was it Tom Hickey?"

"I don't know. Nobody's seen Tom for a couple of days, but we can't let Birch be caught up. We have to get to him first."

"We have to hurry. Washington demands absolute secrecy, so if Birch gets taken into custody, we can't reveal his mission or even offer clemency. He'll suffer the consequences just like all the others, and they could be severe. Follow me!"

An hour later, a muscular man with curly brown hair and a scar on his forehead pounded his fist on the door of the boarding house. When no one answered instantly, he pushed his shoulder hard against the door, and it swung open. He brandished a large kitchen knife at the eight men standing in the small front room and shouted, "Where is he?"

Forbes bolted from his chair and grabbed Joseph's shirt pulling him forward while two other men took him by the arms.

"Who the hell are you?" asked Forbes in a scratchy voice. "What do you want?"

Joseph spotted the tall, blond Birch Johansen leaning against the mantle by the fireplace, and shouted, "You! You! You rotten Swede! You won't mess with my woman again! I'll cut you into little pieces! Your doodle first!" Five men standing near Birch protectively grabbed their crotches.

Joseph, with two quick outward thrusts of his strong arms, shoved the men holding them to the floor, and after another quick move to Forbes, Joseph was free and forcing his way through the shocked men toward Birch. He pointed at him again, still screaming, "I'll cut you good!"

Birch backed away from the fireplace, his eyes widening with alarm. "Now listen," he said, holding his hands out and moving behind the other men.

"He wants you," one of them said, "not me." He pushed Birch toward Joseph.

"Listen, she came to me. It was her idea, not

mine." He dragged a cushioned chair in front of him, and as Joseph got closer, he shoved it over in Joseph's direction. "Stay away from me!"

Joseph easily pushed the chair out of the way and continued to move ever closer to his quarry. He grabbed the fire poker and shook it in the air. "You can't run far enough to get away from me! The streets of New York will never hide you!" The other men quickly got out of the way, moving to the corners of the room.

Birch leaped over a stool and made a dash for the door, but Joseph stayed right behind him, still swinging the poker in one hand and the knife in the other and shouting about Birch's doodle.

Both Birch and Joseph bolted to the street. Birch darted to the left while Joseph hesitated on the small stoop. "Right, you blackguard! I'm right behind you! Right!" he shouted.

Birch, finally realizing what Joseph was trying to tell him, changed directions, and ran down the street to his right as Joseph jumped off the stoop and darted after him, still menacing the poker and his knife and shouting vile things. At the end of the block, Birch dashed around the corner of the building but skidded to a stop just before he ran into a horse hitched to a delivery wagon. Caleb Gibbs sat high on the seat. "Get in the back. Pull the cover over you. Hurry!" said the captain.

Joseph caught up to Birch and pushed him toward the back of the wagon where the two of them slid under the canvas covering the wagon-bed. Birch barely had time to pull in his long legs before Gibbs slapped the reins and the horse started forward, turning in the opposite direction from the boarding house and moving at a fast trot down the street.

The men from the boarding house chasing after Birch and Joseph turned the corner, only to find the street empty. They ran all the way to the next block before realizing that the men they were following were nowhere in sight.

Gilbert Forbes, lagging behind, huffing and puffing, leaned against the wall of the building. He gasped out to the men. "They're gone. We've better things to do." All headed back to the boarding house to complete the oath taking and decide their next plan of action.

Minutes later, the men in the boarding house were surrounded by Continental soldiers, arrested, and dragged away in chains.

After hearing William Leary's testimony before the committee, Tom Hickey was arrested with counterfeit money in his pocket, and along with twenty other suspected conspirators, imprisoned in Bridewell Prison. Issac Ketchum, the man who failed to get the counterfeit paper for Issac and Israel Young, now turned jail house snitch, shared a cell with Hickey.

"What they'd catch ye doing?" asked Hickey of the man sitting on a bench in the middle of the crowded cell.

"They think I was buying paper to print fake money, but I wasn't. I swear I wasn't."

"Lots of falsely accused men in here. But they got no idea what I know about things, bigger things than fake money."

Ketchum turned his back to Hickey. *The fastest way to get a man to talk is for him to think you don't care.*

He didn't have to wait long before Hickey tapped

Ketchum on the shoulder. "Want to hear about something really important?"

"What could you know that's important?"

Hickey scooted closer to Ketchum, and speaking in a low voice, said, "I know that Washington isn't long for this world, and once he's gone, the so-called revolution dies with him."

"You know something I don't? Something nobody knows?"

"I know plenty, and they'll call me a hero when the old man breathes his last. We'll get paid in British gold that's worth something."

Ketchum leaned close and grinned. "Tell me how I can get in on this."

"Ye can't. Ye ain't a member of the old man's personal guard. We're the ones who know him best, the ones he trusts."

"You know these men? You know their names?"

Hickey stood and walked away before turning back to say, "If I get what I want in return, I know all their names, every last one of them, even his favorite." He moved to the wall and leaned against it.

When the guards brought in the porridge that would serve as supper, Ketchum whispered into one man's ear. An hour later, Ketchum was led out of the cell to the office of the prison official who at once took him higher up the chain of command to report what he had heard.

Chapter Nineteen

Joseph lifted the flap on the corner of the tarp, finally letting fresh air into the stuffy wagon. "We're out of the city," he said. "But stay where you are. We can't take any chances that someone might see us."

"What was going on in the city?" asked Birch. "Why did you take me out? I was so close to getting all the information and names we needed."

"That's the problem. You were too close. Arrests are being made, and everyone is spilling their guts, and we couldn't risk your name coming up. Uncovering this scandal could threaten confidence in the revolution, and if you're arrested, we can't help you."

Birch smiled, and in a playful scolding tone, said, "I should say thanks, but you threatened my doodle!"

"Exactly what I wanted to do." Joseph gave his friend a playful punch. "I got right to the heart of the matter, so to speak, and it convinced all the others. Did you see their faces?"

"No, I was too busy running away from the man with the knife! So where are we headed?"

"We're going to the church a few miles away where Sophic is inoculating some new recruits against smallpox, and the patients are quarantined. It will be safe until things die down and you can rejoin the guard."

A wistful look came over Birch's face. "Sophie."

****

The wagon carrying the fugitive and his rescuers arrived at the church hoping to find a quiet, isolated place, but instead found it bustling with activity. Men stood on ladders painting the wooden exterior and gutters a bright white while women hung freshly washed sheets and blankets to dry on ropes strung between trees. Dirty water slopped out of the washtubs dragged through the church backyard by pairs of women and then dumped out, creating a small pond of soapy water at the edge of the woods.

As Birch and Joseph crawled out from under the canvas and stretched their legs, they wondered if they were in the right place. This temporary smallpox hospital was supposed to be undisclosed to the general public, but here it was overrun with locals.

Birch approached a woman tugging a dry sheet off the line. "Excuse me, but what's going on here?"

"We're getting the church all spruced up, inside and out, a sort of spring cleaning. Thanks for coming to help. You can work with the men doing the painting." She draped the sheet over her arm after folding it and dropped it into a basket. "Well, hop to it," she said. "We have a lot to do before nightfall."

"Yes, ma'am."

Bewildered, Birch and Joseph walked up the steps to the front door, now freshly painted black, opened it with the brass handles, and went inside, nearly tripping over a mop sweeping across the floor. Even more people worked inside. Women wiped down the benches with rags while men polished the railings and baseboards.

"Here to help?" asked the man with the mop.

"No, we're looking for someone, the doctor," said Birch.

"You're too late."

A sick feeling dropped into his gut. "What do you mean, too late?"

"She's leaving for Philadelphia tomorrow. She's got some sort of work to do there. Pastor said she was here to do something for the war effort. Don't know what, and don't care if it will get the Brits out of the country. You know what I mean."

Birch nodded.

The man put his hand up beside his mouth to hide his words. "I found a couple of men's shirts and a pair of breeches under a bench, makes me wonder what was going on, but Pastor Jones said it was God's work, so I just burned the clothes before anyone else saw them. Are you sure you're not here to help? We could use it."

Joseph interrupted. "We're also looking for her assistant, Justine. Where is she?"

"Lydia," the man shouted, "have you seen the doctor and her helper?"

"Out back."

Rushing through the chapel and out the side door into the yard, they were suddenly stopped by a sea of white linens flapping in the wind. Birch brushed aside as many sheets as he could until one smacked him right in the face, nearly knocking him down. He tugged it off his head.

"Hey!" came a familiar voice. "Quit pulling on it. If it falls on the ground, you'll wash it again yourself!"

Birch peeked his head around the edge of the sheet. "No problem. I've washed sheets before."

"Birch!" cried Sophie. "You came!" She jumped

into his arms and smothered him with kisses. "I'm leaving for Philadelphia tomorrow, and I thought I wouldn't see you!" Before he could answer, she covered his mouth with hers again.

The women helping with the sheets and blankets ducked their heads, embarrassed by this display of affection. "Close your eyes," said one woman to a young girl.

"But what if they're married?" the girl answered.

"Still close your eyes. Their private business should be done in private." The girl put her hand over her eyes but snuck a quick look through open fingers.

"Where's Justine?" asked Joseph, but before Sophie could answer, he spotted his wife running toward him from the soapy pond.

She ducked under a row of sheets and nearly crashed into him. "Joseph! My love!" He lifted her and spun her around.

"Is the war over?" asked Sophie, her arms still around her husband's neck. "Are you back to stay?"

Birch shook his head. "No, the war will go on for a while if the Brits have anything to do with it, but I'll be staying here with you."

"Wait," said Joseph. "We need to talk somewhere more private."

The four of them headed around the church to the side where no one was working.

"They said you're going to Philadelphia, and I'll be going with you," Birch said. "It'll be safer for me there."

"Safer?" said Sophie with her hands on her hips. "What's going on? Are you in danger? Tell me now."

"I can't tell you everything, but I've been working

on something for the general. Let's just say a plot's been uncovered, a dangerous plot, and I could have been arrested."

"Arrested?" She put her hand to her chest to calm her racing heart.

"Rest easy, Sophie," said Joseph. "Birch was undercover, but we got him away in time. No one knows we're here, and as soon as Birch is in Philadelphia with you, he'll be out of reach. All will be well."

Justine held her husband at arm's length. "What about you? Anybody want to arrest you?"

"No, my love. I used a false name, but Birch could only get in good with the traitors by being himself. They had to think he was one of the Life Guards, and that he could be recruited to join them."

In unison, Sophie and Justine cried, "No!"

Both men tugged their women close. "No worries. The plot's been broken up and everyone responsible is in custody," said Joseph. "But we couldn't risk Birch being arrested."

"Joseph got me out in time," said Birch, "and now we're headed for Philadelphia, so no need to worry. All is well, especially now that I have you in my arms." He kissed the top of her head.

"What about us?" asked Justine. She grinned. "Are we going to Philadelphia, too? I've never been to a big city."

"Sorry, my love, but we're heading back to camp. I investigated counterfeiting of Continental money, and I might be called to testify against the counterfeiters."

Justine gasped. "Could you go to jail?"

"No, my love. No one knows who I really am, so

I'm safe." He paused. "Want to go for a walk? Maybe into the woods over there?"

Justine winked. "A walk? You just want to stroll through the fresh air?"

"No, ma'am," said Joseph with a wink of his own, and they were off, hand in hand.

Sophie raised her eyebrows. "If you help me get these sheets down and folded, we can go on our own stroll."

"All right. Let's hurry!"

Two hours later the chapel and churchyard were empty. The dried sheets, brooms, and rags, along with the empty paint buckets were gone, and all that remained was a peaceful church waiting for the next Sunday gathering. The three remaining smallpox soldiers had been taken to private homes in the area to finish up their recovery, while Sergeant Murphy marched the rest of the men back to camp to get started with their regular training. Joseph, Justine, and Caleb Gibbs took the wagon and caught up with the soldiers, leaving Birch and Sophie alone, safe in the church.

Sophie and Birch walked hand in hand across the yard. Blooming flowers filled the air with sweet smells while the sun warmed everything its rays touched. A gently flowing stream rippled at the back of the yard that divided the church property from farms in the distance.

A wooden bridge, well-used by parishioners coming to services, crossed the stream, and the couple stopped to sit on the edge with their feet dangling just above the clear water. Having walked in comfortable silence, he now turned his eyes to her, saying, "Every time I'm away from you, I realize how I wasn't certain of what I wanted or where I was going, but then you make it all so clear." He added, "Without saying a word."

"How do I do that?" She locked both of her hands over his as if he might disappear if she didn't hold on tight.

"The same way you do everything. By being you. By the way you see the world, you bring color to it, and now I feel things I never imagined I would."

She tenderly cupped his face, her eyes shimmering. "Birch, you mean everything to me. I worried every day it would end in disaster, that I'd never see you again, never see the sparkle in your blue eyes or feel the warmth of your hand around mine."

He gripped her hand tighter and leaned in, their foreheads touching. For Sophie and Birch, the world faded, leaving them alone with each other. "We'll face whatever comes together, always."

They sat in contented silence until Birch leaned back on his hands. "Joseph rescued me. You should have seen his performance as an angry husband swinging a poker and threatening to cut off my doodle!"

Her cheeks rounded into a smile. "I wish I had been there to see that." Then she pushed out a strong breath. "No, I'm glad I wasn't. I've seen a lot of danger, a lot of blood and injury, and I hate it, but I've always endured it, but just thinking it might happen to you shatters my spirit. Promise me, you won't put yourself in harm's way again."

"I wish I could promise that, but I'm a soldier until the war is over. There'll be danger."

She nestled against him. "I know, but just promise

me, you'll be all right."

"I promise."

As the sun slowly slipped behind the trees, and stars began to twinkle, they sat close in each other's arms and spoke wistful promises that, despite the unknowns of war, they would share countless tomorrows.

"Let's go inside," said Sophie. "I've missed you so. I want to feel you again."

In silence, they walked hand in hand across the yard and through the back door of the church that led to Pastor Jones' quarters. His furnishings consisted only of a bed, a desk, and a wood stove. Stacked on four open shelves were two sets of dishes and glasses and eight books, three of them Bibles. All he needed, and tonight it was all the two of them would need.

"Looks perfect," said Birch as he slipped her apron off over her head and slid her shift off her shoulders and down to the floor. He leaned in to kiss her neck. His mouth slid down her bare shoulders to her firm breasts and then to her stomach. As he went farther down her body, she ran her fingers through his hair and released soft sighs of pleasure.

"Some nights I think I might forget how you feel or how you taste."

"Then I'll be there to remind you."

After finishing his exploration of every part of the woman he loved, he lifted her to the bed and took off his own clothes. Now they lay beside each other with nothing to keep them apart.

The next morning, when the sun peeked through the freshly cleaned window, they knew their time together was ending. He caressed her until she tugged him deep inside her, and they didn't leave each other's embrace until they were both fully satisfied.

Once dressed, they ate slices of apple and leftover porridge and packed up what remained of Sophie's smallpox inoculation supplies. After carrying everything outside, packing the carriage, and hitching the horse, they left for the safety of Philadelphia.

Then the world fell apart.

****

On their third day on the road to Philadelphia, suddenly six Continental soldiers on horseback surrounded Birch and Sophie. The soldiers crowded around the carriage, forcing them off to the side of the road.

"Are you Birch Johansen?" asked one of them in a commanding voice.

"Yes, sir, I am. How may I help you?"

"Step out of the carriage, please. Ma'am, you may stay seated where you are."

"What's going on?"

"Step out of the carriage, or we will drag you out."

Sophie put her hand on Birch's arm and held him back. "You can't do this," she said to the soldier. "You're making a mistake. This man is my husband and has permission to travel with me to Philadelphia."

"Yes, ma'am. My name is Captain Nichols, and we have the authority to arrest him, ma'am. We've been sent to do just that. Step out now."

"It'll be all right, Sophie. I'll find out what's going on." Birch pulled out of Sophie's grip and climbed out onto the road. To Captain Nichols, he said, "I am a lieutenant in General Washington's Guard."

"We know," said Nichols as two others took Birch

by the arms. He fought to keep the third from locking manacles around his wrists. "Hey, stop!" hollered Birch as he flailed his arms until the three overpowered him and the chains clicked in place.

"No!" cried Sophie, jumping out of the carriage, fury in her voice and on her face.

The captain spoke firmly. "Birch Johansen, you are expelled from all rank and authority and are being charged with treason and sedition. We are taking you back to Bridewell prison for trial."

"You've made a mistake!" said Sophie. "He's been with me for the last three days."

"We know, ma'am. The pastor at the church reluctantly said you were headed to Philadelphia, and we followed you. We have testimony that Johansen kept company with one Gilbert Forbes, along with William Green and Thomas Hickey who, including several others, have also been arrested. All have testified freely that the lieutenant is a co-conspirator of a treasonous act."

"And what were they offered for testifying so freely?" asked Sophie sarcastically.

None of the men answered until Captain Nichols said, "Get back in the carriage, ma'am, and Sergeant Rhodes will ride with you to Philadelphia."

"Do what he says, please, Sophie," said Birch over his shoulder as two soldiers dragged him to a horse, hefted him into the saddle, and linked his manacles on the saddle horn. "Captain Gibbs will sort it all out. It'll be all right. This is a mistake."

Sophie gave Nichols a withering glare. "I'm not going to Philadelphia," she said with that familiar look of determination Birch knew so well. "I'm going with you." She climbed back into the carriage and picked up the reins.

"Sergeant Rhodes will still ride with you."

"Only if he sits there quietly because I'm going with my husband."

The sergeant gawked in disbelief that a woman would speak to his captain like that. "Are you certain, ma'am?"

"Never surer of anything."

Nichols sighed and said, "Do as she says."

"Yes, sir," the sergeant said. He took a seat next to Sophie, but when he tried to take the reins from her, she slapped his hands, saying, "I'll drive!"

****

The trip back to the army camp was an ordeal. The captain kept a fast-moving pace, saying to one of the others, "If I move fast enough, that woman won't be able to keep up, and I can leave her behind. I've had enough of her interference."

She proved him wrong despite the ache in her arms and the hunger in her belly.

Birch tried to slow the pace by asking, "Can we stop for a bit? Our horses are tired."

"No," answered Nichols. "They can go another five miles before we stop, and everyone can stretch their legs and relieve themselves."

"Sophie," Birch called over his shoulder. "Are you all right?"

"Don't worry about me, Birch. But Sergeant Rhodes keeps falling asleep. I think he's exhausted."

"I didn't fall asleep!" protested Rhodes. "I swear, Captain, I didn't fall asleep!" He leaned over toward Sophie and whispered, "Are you trying to get me in trouble?"

She smirked. "As often as I can."

They ate hardtack and biscuits from the soldiers' packs while they traveled, and Captain Nichols refused to stop to sleep until it was too dark to see the road, and then only when there was someplace to lock up Birch.

The first night Captain Nichols shoved Birch into a small closet in a seedy tavern and posted a guard outside the door. He said to Sophie, "You can sleep in a bed if you can pay for it, or you can sleep on the floor."

"I'm not leaving my husband alone with the likes of you." She curled up on the floor. The soldier on guard gave her his jacket that she gratefully rolled up for a pillow.

The second night Birch and Sophie found themselves locked in a cold, damp, empty icehouse. "They left us blankets," said Birch as he unfolded one of them and laid it on a bale of hay meant to hold ice cut from the river in the winter. "We can snuggle in close." He flipped open the second blanket.

"At least they took the manacles off your wrists. I wish they hadn't kept them on your ankles. I'll try to pad your ankles inside your boots so they don't chafe so much. Bring that bucket of water over here, please."

Captain Nichols had rummaged through her doctor's kit before handing it to her, having removed anything sharp along with some things that weren't. After soaking the hem of her dress in the water, she gently washed over the raw skin on his wrists. Tearing strips off her underskirt, she wrapped his wrists and then his ankles as best she could.

"Hopefully this will help," she said. "I wish they'd let me bring in my full medical bag. Then I might have been able to put some ointment on." She looked up at his face. "I feel helpless, and I don't like it. I'm not used to it."

He pulled her into his arms. "This is all a mistake, and as soon as we get into the city, Captain Gibbs will straighten it out. We should be there tomorrow, and then this will all be over. I promise you."

But in the back of his mind, he knew no one would stand up for him or expose his role as a Continental spy. General Washington couldn't take the chance since acknowledging any threat to his life would make him appear weak. Birch was on his own, and unfortunately, so was Sophie.

They clung to each other on top of the bales of hay, staying as far off the wet floor as they could. They spoke only a little but absorbed each other's warmth as each sent up silent prayers.

Neither of them slept very much.

Chapter Twenty

The following afternoon, they arrived in New York City, where Birch demanded to be brought before Captain Gibbs. His request was ignored. Instead, the soldiers dragged him through the streets in chains, past a hostile crowd of men and soldiers he had once considered friends and comrades. They jeered and shouted while the officers made only feeble efforts to hold the mob at bay.

Men reached out and tore at Birch's clothes. "Traitor!" His sleeve ripped off in their grip.

Men stepped out to spit on him. "Turncoat! How could you betray the cause?"

"Take this!" shouted a soldier as he threw a rock at Birch. It caught him on the cheek, and blood dripped down his face to his neck.

"How do you like this?" bellowed another man. The stone landed square in his chest. Birch grunted and doubled over, only to be forced up by the guards and dragged forward.

Birch glimpsed Joseph, Justine, and Sophie standing at the edge of the crowd near the wall. Sophie reached out for him and called his name, but before he could answer, he was yanked inside the prison walls.

The heavy iron gate slammed shut.

"He didn't do it!" cried Sophie. "He didn't do it!" No one could hear her over the crowd noise except

Joseph who answered, "I know," before wrapping her in his arms.

****

As he was led through the courtyard of Bridewell prison, Birch gagged on the overpowering smell of unwashed men, rotting flesh, disease, and filth that permeated every part of it.

"Get used to it, traitor," said one of the guards who used his key to unlock the first of many gates and doors. "There'll be no fine living with Washington's special guard here. You'll wear what you have on until the day they drag you out. If you thought you were above the rest, you ain't now."

"A cat-in-the-pan is what you are," said another in a gravelly voice, "a man flipping from one side to the other. The lowest of all the scum we've got in here." He gave Birch a smack on the back of the head. Birch stumbled and bit his lip but didn't fall.

Standing outside a crowded cell, the guard unlocked the door while another one removed his wrist and ankle chains and shoved him inside. He called out to those already there, "Here's more company for you! Play nice, lads."

Birch looked around at the other prisoners' faces. Clearly, they had no intention of playing nice, no intention of playing at all. "Fresh meat," murmured one.

Two prisoners advanced toward him. As soon as they were within arm's reach, Birch hit each one in the face, one after the other with two quick punches. They both staggered back with bloody noses while Birch swept a defiant stare over the faces of the other prisoners. "If you want a piece of me, it'll cost you."

Any other men who might have had thoughts of besting the new prisoner fell against the wall and sat down. Here was someone who would fight back, and they didn't want to bother with him if he weren't easy prey. Birch continued to scan the cell until his gaze landed on a dark-haired man squatting in the corner, chained to the wall. One Thomas Hickey. Tom still had an obvious bruised eye and a scabbed-over cut lip from their last meeting.

"Good work, Lieutenant," said Tom, dragging out the word "lieutenant." "Ye show 'em who's boss."

"I had older brothers who taught me how to handle a bully before a bully handled me." Birch ground out the words. "Why was I arrested? What have you done to me?"

Tom sneered. "Ye put me in this hellhole."

Birch's eyes narrowed as he gave Tom a vicious look. "What are you talking about?"

Tom smiled wickedly. "Don't play like ye don't have all yer buttons. It was ye who turned me in, told 'em about the sham money."

"It could've been one of your gambling pals."

"Nah, their necks are on the line, too. What I need is a way out of here. I needed a bigger bargaining chip. None of these bums could help me, but you could. Nobody'd believe any of the scum in here could turn me over, so I had to pick a ripping-good fellow, a bang-up soldier, an out and out fine gentleman. Someone who just might stand in my stead at the trial." He grinned. "And guess who came to mind?"

Birch glowered at him.

Tom stood as best he could with the manacles gripping his ankles chained to the wall. "See that grimy piece of dirt over there?" He pointed to a dirty bearded prisoner across the cell. "Issac Ketchum, a rat if I ever saw one. He asked why I was in here the night I came, so I said I'd been slumming bad money, and maybe I let it slip where the fake money came from, and maybe I'd let him in on the deal, and maybe I knew something more, something that would change the war."

"He believed you?"

"About the money and everything else. I said I was a real patriot, just playing at being loyal to the crown, and I knew stuff that might bring Washington down, stuff that might end the general once and for all. I told him I knew about a plot to kidnap and murder the old man. All I had to do was mention a few names, well, really only mention one name. And if the right people knew, we'd be heroes, entitled to a good reward, so like any good telltale, Ketchum told the guards who took him to the officers. That's why I'm chained to the wall, but you'll be my ticket out of here." He tapped his chin as if in deep thought before saying, "At our trial, I think I'll even bring up a tear, right here." He ran his finger down his dirty cheek. "About how I got suckered into the scheme to be a turncoat by someone wiser and smarter who called me his friend, and about how when I wanted to pull out, he beat me." He pointed to his battered face.

Birch cried out, "You bastard." He grabbed Tom by the shirt. "Now we're both in the stew. Who did you claim was trying to kill Washington?"

Hickey's eyes opened wide, full of mock innocence. "Ye, of course. Ye're the one who told me about it and asked me to come in on the plot, but I tried to refuse."

"You liar! Your lies will get us both hanged!"

Tom pushed Birch's arms away. "Not me. I'm a low man in the scheme of things. Some of the twenty lads taken with me will testify to that. I just passed fake money, but other, more important fellows, planned to end this war by getting rid of our beloved general. And only the 'perfect soldier' could plan something that big, someone like...ye."

Birch put his hands on Tom's chest and slammed him back into the corner. "They'll never believe you."

"They already have. How do you think ye got here?" He laughed. "What will Sophie think of ye now?"

Birch reared back; his fist clenched. "This is still about Sophie?" he snarled. "You attack my wife, and then you get me into this?" Just before he landed his punch, the cell door clanked open, and four armed guards walked in. One of them announced, "Front and center! Thomas Hickey, Birch Johansen, Matthew Lynch, William Green. You're being transported to a military prison for trial."

Loud protests went up among the prisoners, but the guards quickly forced their way through the cell and dragged out the men they wanted. Once outside, the four prisoners were led away to places unknown.

Chapter Twenty-One

June 1776

The morning air was oppressive in the courtroom of the military court-martial of Thomas Hickey and Birch Johansen. On orders, the windows stayed closed, and the soldiers and guards sweltered in their full uniforms with obvious sweat stains on their underarms and collars. The tribunal of twelve officers serving as judges used their handkerchiefs to wipe off the drops of sweat on their arms and necks, but it gave them little relief.

All this was in a vain effort to keep the trial confidential, but the crowd still heard all the details from eavesdroppers at the courtroom door who took turns running outside to spread the word.

The military officers serving as judges sat in high back chairs behind a table across the back of the courtroom with the witness box to the left in front of them. The accused were at tables behind spindled half walls while the Judge Advocate stood at a podium with papers, ink, and quill to take down the proceedings.

Colonel Samuel H. Parsons, heading up the tribunal, pounded his gavel until all were quiet. He read the charges from the official documents in his hand. "Thomas Hickey and Birch Johansen are hereby accused of treason and mutiny, as well as secretly communicating with the enemy for the most vile purposes—specifically, plotting the assassination of General George Washington."

When word of this reached the crowd outside, their protests, jeers, and even some cheers were silenced by threats of arrests by armed guards.

"How can they do this?" said Sophie from near the steps of the courthouse. "How can the charges go from counterfeiting to treason? On what evidence?"

Joseph moved in close to Sophie and Justine. "The truth will come out. Birch will be set free. Don't worry."

Inside the courtroom, the officers serving on the court all nodded to Colonel Parsons that they were ready to begin testimony.

The Judge Advocate, William Tudor, spoke. "Thomas Hickey, you have been arraigned on charges of treason and mutiny. How do you plead?"

"Not guilty," answered Tom.

"Birch Johansen, you have been arraigned on charges of treason and mutiny. How do you plead?"

In a steady voice, Birch said, "I request a defense attorney."

"None is necessary. How do you plead?"

"Not guilty!"

"We are ready to hear witnesses," announced Colonel Parsons.

Tudor called out, "William Green, come forward and take the stand."

The small man walked on shaky legs to the witness box and stood behind the short wall.

"How are you involved in this case?" asked the colonel.

"I just wanted to fool the Tories. I didn't really

want to turn traitor."

"Just tell the court what happened."

"I, uh, met with Mr. Gilbert Forbes at the Corbes tavern, and we talked politics. After a time, Mr. Forbes asked me to enlist with the British and I would be paid. I didn't want to do it. I just said I did so I could cheat the Tories and find out who was behind this plan. I told Tom Hickey, and he agreed to go along with it, so I gave him two shillings to seal the deal."

"What did Mr. Hickey do then?"

"Well, Mr. Forbes told him about a plot to kill the general, and Hickey said he'd see about finding more men to join. He found ten men."

"Do you know their names?"

"No, sir. Hickey wrote their names on a piece of paper, and I gave it to Mr. Forbes. That's all I know. I swear, that's all I know."

"Did Gilbert Forbes mention the names of any of these men?"

"No, sir, but I did meet both prisoners once, and we talked about men who fought for the colonies but were really loyal to the British, and Johansen gave me a dollar."

Birch jumped to his feet. "Liar! I never gave you anything, ever!"

"Take that man in hand," said the colonel to the guards who put their hands on Birch's shoulders and forced him back into his chair. "There will be no further outbursts. Private Green, you may step down but keep this man in custody."

William Tudor announced, "We call Gilbert Forbes to the stand."

As William Green walked past the prisoners, Tom

hissed under his breath, "Ye'll pay for this." Green's eyes widened, and he ran out the door of the courtroom with the guards close behind him.

Gilbert Forbes did not wear his usual white jacket as he approached the witness stand. Instead, he wore a ditto suit made of a light brown linen with matching shirt, breeches, and a short jacket, and he'd buffed his shoes to a bright shine.

Birch leaned over to whisper to Tom, "Who let him out of his cell to get cleaned up?"

Tom grunted and shrugged.

Forbes did not look at either defendant as he faced the courtroom.

"What do you know of these proceedings?"

"I did speak with William Green on several occasions, and we drank to the good health of His Majesty, but it was Green who hounded me to join in the traitorous plot. After a time, I gave in."

"What about the note with the names of other men on it?"

"Yes, Green did give me a paper with five names on it, Tom Hickey's and Birch Johansen's included. Then I gave Hickey one dollar, but Johansen wouldn't accept any money. He said he would do it because it was the right and just thing to do."

Birch started to stand again, but the soldiers on either side of him forcibly shoved him back down. The chair legs scraped on the floor.

"Mr. Forbes, why did you pay Hickey for those names?"

"Not for the names. I only wanted to assure him he would be safe. I paid with the money I had gotten from Mayor Mathews. He assured me that British ships would be prepared to accept these men who had signed on. I also want to say that Johansen delivered a letter to Governor Tryon as proof of his loyalty and willingness to cooperate."

"Do you know what this letter contained?"

"No, sir, only that it could not fall into George Washington's hands."

"Did Johansen take the letter himself and give it to the British?"

Forbes nodded. "Yes, sir."

"How much money did Mayor Mathews give you?"

Sweat dripped from Forbes' forehead into his eyes. He wiped it off with his sleeve. "He paid me one hundred pounds."

It was now close to the noon hour, but there'd be no break. The heat in the room was beyond stifling.

The next witness was Issac Ketchum. He spoke loudly and clearly as if he'd already been rehearsed. "In the jail, Thomas Hickey spoke to me about how he and some others, including Johansen, were going to turn themselves in to the British as soon as British ships landed on shore. An official group had been formed with officers appointed, and Johansen was one of the leaders."

This time Birch fought off the guards and stood, spitting out the words, "Liar! No one ever appointed me an officer of anything like that, and I never accepted any such position! How dare you say that?"

"Sit that man down!" shouted the colonel. "Another outburst from you and you'll be taken from the courtroom in chains. Do we understand each other?"

Birch slowly sat down and pounded his fists on the table. He didn't answer.

"Mr. Ketchum, do you have anything else to add?"

"Only that Mr. Hickey told me there were eight members of George Washington's special guard involved in the plot."

"Thank you for your service in helping to bring these men to justice. You are dismissed." As Ketchem walked out, Colonel Parsons looked across the room to the defendants' table. "Thomas Hickey, do you have anything to say in your defense?"

Tom's face turned dark and vicious. "I only agreed to what Forbes said so I could cheat the Tories and get some money. I never wanted to change coats. Never."

"You may be seated. Birch Johansen, do you have anything to say in your defense?"

"Yes, sir. I deny all the charges brought against me, deny all the inuendo, and all the accusations. Everything said against me in this court is completely false. If you will allow me to testify, I will tell you what I know, which will prove my innocence."

The colonel paused before saying, "Is that all, Mr. Johansen?"

"Yes, sir. I'm asking for a chance to testify to the truth."

"Do either of you have any factual evidence to support your claims or factual evidence that the testimony here was false?"

"No, sir."

"No, sir, only my word."

"Then the court will be dismissed so we can render our decision. Take all the prisoners back to their cells. I will notify you when we reconvene. In the meantime, air out this room. Open the windows, light candles to help with the odor, and use paper fans to move the stale air. Court dismissed." He banged his gavel twice. All the judges stood and left for the large hall behind the courtroom to deliberate.

Two hours later the court reconvened. When all were ready, Colonel Parsons asked the defendants to stand. "You may announce our verdict," he said to the Judge Advocate who stated in a clear, steady voice, "The prisoners are found guilty of a breach of the fifth and thirtieth rules of the Articles of Rules and Regulations for the government of the Continental Forces."

Tom held his face and shoulders in a defiant stance while Birch dropped his head and leaned his arms against the table.

"Both prisoners will suffer death for their crimes by being hanged by the neck until dead."

****

A wail left Sophie's throat when soldiers announced the verdict to the crowd outside of the courthouse minutes later.

"Quiet," said Joseph. "We can't draw attention to ourselves. We might be arrested as accomplices. Quiet, let me think."

Justine gathered Sophie close to her and led her away.

"We must find a way! I cannot watch him hang! I cannot," sobbed Sophie as her tears fell on Justine's shoulder.

****

June 26, 1776
The official proclamation nailed to the courthouse

pillar read in bold print: To be hanged by the neck until dead!

"What are we going to do?"

Sophie sat on the cot inside Captain Caleb Gibbs' tent. Her hands shook. "This isn't right! It's not justice! I'm begging you! We have to stop it!"

"I apologize again, doctor," said Caleb, his face pale from the full realization of the consequences of Birch's conviction. "I didn't anticipate he'd be arrested or that he'd be sentenced to hang. I am so sorry. I let him down."

Sophie stood with her fists clenched. "You gave him this assignment. You knew he'd take it and give it everything he had just like he always does. And now you're getting him hanged."

"I take responsibility," said Caleb in a solemn voice. "I thought he might be arrested as a conspirator, but never did I imagine he'd be accused of being a ringleader. How the charges grew into a hangable offence, I don't understand. But, please believe me, there's nothing I can do."

"Just go tell them he's innocent! I'll go tell them he's innocent! He was on a mission sanctioned by you and General Washington. They'll have to let him go!"

"Please, understand. I'm sorry, but it won't work that way."

"What about my Joseph?" interrupted Justine. Her deep brown eyes widened. "He was on the same mission, to catch the counterfeiters and traitors. What if he's arrested?"

Joseph put his hand on her shoulder. "You don't have to worry about that. I won't be charged with treason because counterfeit money is pretty much common knowledge, but the men Birch worked with had a plot to kill Washington, something very different."

"If that plot ever became public knowledge, His Excellency will look like he couldn't protect himself," said Captain Gibbs, "and it would seriously damage support for him. The trial shows other conspirators that the general will fight back with severe consequences."

Sophie pounded on the captain's chest with her fists. "If we win the war but lose Birch...I'll...curse you until the day I die!" Caleb tugged down Sophie's arms and held them at her side, but she continued her tirade. "You must stop the hanging! Do you hear me? You have to. You need to! Say the word and stop it!"

Caleb gulped down the guilt lodged in his throat. "I wish I could just say the word, but I can't. I'm sorry."

Sophie shook off his grip and fled back to Justine's arms, sobbing.

"I've never seen her like this. She's usually so strong and practical," said Justine as she patted Sophie's hair. "We have to think of something. Joseph, think of something."

Suddenly Sophie straightened up and wiped her eyes with her sleeves. "Don't talk about me as if I'm not here." She gave a loud sniff and rubbed her nose with her other sleeve, saying, "When I was a child, and I cried when we lost a patient, my father used to take me into his office and stand me in front of him. He'd say, 'You can never know how strong you are until being strong is all you have left.' Strong is all we have left now, and we will be strong for Birch. Who's got a plan?"

Chapter Twenty-Two

June 28, 1776

The scene in the field near the Bowery in New York City was like no other.

Over twenty thousand people made their way to watch the hanging of the traitors, Thomas Hickey and Birch Johansen, but the mood of the crowd was more like a family picnic than a somber reminder that death comes in many ways during a war. Old friends and relatives greeted each other with smiles, hugs, and claps on the back. Children chased each other around the spectators to the adults' annoyance.

The multitudes of strangers in the park consisted of men, women, and children from every social level. Although the wealthy grumbled about having to stand so close to the riffraff, the poorer classes simply enjoyed the spectacle as the first fun they'd had in a while.

Soldiers stood on all sides of the quickly built gallows with their muskets slung across their backs. Some wore grim expressions while others tried to hide their troubled consciences. They knew the men about to be hanged for treason, and that betrayal cut deep.

Braver children ran under the gallows to taunt the soldiers, but they soon discovered the men quickly put a stop to it by lowering their weapons directly at the mischief-makers who ran away screaming.

Washington had ordered every soldier not on duty to attend the hanging, wanting it to serve as a cautionary tale for any others with thoughts of wavering loyalty. These soldiers were scattered throughout the crowd, some on the edges, others within the spectators, all on the lookout for anything that might disrupt the proceedings. They'd been warned to be on the lookout for malcontents who would rather see a fight than a hanging, as well as loyalists wanting to disrupt any proceeding led by patriots, and even the few who might protest having a hanging at all. A riot could easily break out with so many people with so many differing opinions so close together.

****

Sophie pushed back the dangling straws from her hat, trying to keep the ends from poking into her eyes, while hoping they would still cover at least part of her face. She pushed a cart in front of her, one that held hot coals under a tray of small meat pies with folded-over baked crusts. The heated handle had already left red burn marks on her palms, but she ignored them and kept moving through the crowd, shouting, "Hot meat pies! Get 'em while they're hot! You can't watch a proper hanging without one!"

People stopped Sophie and paid the penny she charged for each pie, often asking, "How do I know these are fresh?" She always answered, "Eat it and if you get sick, I'll pay for your funeral."

"Where will I find you for payment?"

Ignoring the question, she gave the cart a shove, pushing the buyer aside, and continued through the spectators, chuckling to herself. "You'll be dead, so you won't need to find me." She shouted, "Hot pies!"

Sophie, who stayed close to the front of the scaffold, spotted Justine at the back of the throng beside a small fire with a grill laid over the logs, shouting, "Ale! Mulled cider for the ladies and the children! Get it hot!" She dipped her metal pitchers into the barrels of ale and cider, set them on the grill to heat up, and poured drinks out of two more pitchers into the leather mugs most people dangled from their belts for an event like this one. "Fresh off the fire! Warm your hearts and your stomachs!" Every few minutes she paused and searched the crowd until she found Sophie in her straw hat with a big red feather on it blowing in the wind.

Dozens of people surrounded Justine's table, holding out their mugs, urging her to fill their mug first. The odor of so many excited and unwashed bodies closing in around her nearly choked her, but she held her breath as often as she could and gave them what they wanted. Drinkers dropped their pennies into a tin on the table, which she emptied into her apron pocket every time she turned her back to refill her pitchers.

Just as she was about to fill up one of her pitchers again, a grimy man with dirty nails, missing teeth, and a particularly powerful odor waved a knife under her chin. "Give me your money, you hay bag!" he demanded. Then he spit at her, and the glob landed on her cheek. She promptly threw a full pitcher of hot cider into his face. He dropped the knife and ran away screaming, "You hay bag!" while the remaining customers cheered. They didn't want anything to interfere with getting a good drink, and many men and women were already quite drunk with still an hour to go before the anticipated event.

Exactly what she counted on.

Standing close to the steps on the left side of the scaffold were two men, both dressed all in black with black hoods over their heads and only their eyes peeking out of two round holes. Most thought they'd been recruited from out of the city to protect their identities from retaliation by friends or relatives of the condemned. However, two women, one in a straw hat and another standing by a small fire, knew the name of one of the hangmen, Joseph Gallagher.

Justine kept an eye on her man beside the gallows between customers while he stood quietly waiting to do what everyone thought was his duty. If he were discovered, or if the real hangman was found tied up in a field across the river, he'd most likely hang, too, but he'd risk it to save his truest friend.

Joseph took a deep calming breath and sent up a silent prayer that he'd be able to do his job exactly as they had planned it, to do it at exactly the right time, and that he could escape in the chaos before the soldiers realized what had happened. If he were late by even three seconds, the entire plan would go awry. He could not fail!

Two other men sat atop the seat on each of the coffin wagons situated directly under the trap door below each noose. One was the local undertaker. The other was a captain in the Continental Army. Only one would be paid a standard fee to take care of the body. The other gladly risked his own life to save a man he had knowingly put in danger.

Caleb Gibbs straightened his back on the seat of the coffin wagon under the left-hand trap door. His black hat, black suit, and heavy black scarf were too big for him, but by tugging the hat down and lifting the scarf over his chin, they disguised him well. He sweated under the wool garments in the June heat, but that mattered little, a small price to pay for what he had done.

As was typical at military hangings, as soon as each prisoner was declared dead, the rope on the noose would be cut and the body would drop directly into the undertaker's wagon. The driver, after slamming the lid to the coffin shut, would leave the area at once to take the body to a pauper's cemetery, escorted out of the park by ten soldiers walking beside the wagon. There would be no tolling of the church bells for the prisoners, and they would be buried in unmarked graves in different cemeteries, so no one would ever know where to find their bodies or know their names. A final insult for their crimes.

Four soldiers stood around each wagon, waiting to be part of the escort when the body was carried out. The other required six would step away from their post around the gallows and follow each coffin wagon. For the wagon on the left, once free of the crowds and onlookers, and the soldiers had returned to their camp, Caleb would drive to a designated cemetery off the New York islands. There, under the cover of darkness, he'd open the plain wooden casket, send "the body" on his way, and bury the empty box.

Caleb's eyes followed Sophie's red feather through the crowd as well as the sunlight flashing off Justine's pitchers. He didn't dare look toward the two hangmen.

At exactly eleven a.m., four drummers entered the field playing a solemn cadence as the two prisoners, closely surrounded by armed soldiers, trudged to the foot of the gallows steps. Jeers and cheers went up, nearly drowning out the drum cadence.

Blood drained from Sophie's face when she saw him. Her heart raced, and her stomach clenched, but she knew what she had to do. She took a deep breath and shouted at the top of her lungs, "Hot meat pies! Fresh buttered scones! Get 'em right here!" Some people turned and reached for a pie while others tried to block her way so they could get a look at the condemned men. She pushed all of them aside with her cart, knocking a few down who protested loudly, but she kept moving and never took her eyes off the man of her heart.

She had to get into the right position if she was ever going to see him alive again.

****

Birch, the buttons and stripes torn from his uniform, shuddered at his first sight of the gallows with its two thick rope nooses swinging in spine-chilling rhythm with the wind. The sun cast an eerie shadow over the preacher and the army witnesses standing behind the ropes waiting for the condemned prisoners.

Birch sucked in his breath. Not that he feared death. He'd been preparing himself for that all night, but it choked him that he'd never see Sophie again, never hold her hand or kiss her lips. For the day after the verdict was laid down, he'd heard her calling his name from the outer area of the jail, but the guards wouldn't let her in to see him, no matter how much she begged. Her tears couldn't persuade them, but Birch felt each one hit his soul like a hammer. Despite the injustice of everything he faced, knowing the love of his life was in pain was more than he could bear. His silent tears were not for himself, but for her.

He thought he heard her voice above the crowd. He scanned the crush for whoever had shouted, "Meat pies," but he couldn't find the sound again above the deafening crowd noise. A guard beside the steps said, "Hear that, traitor? They can hardly wait to see you dangle!" The man laughed. "Colonel says he figured over twenty thousand people, city dwellers and soldiers, came to see the end of you."

Birch didn't respond to the man's remarks or even turn his head. He didn't care about any of the watchers except one, and he frantically searched for her. He had to have one last glimpse of the woman who inspired him to be the best version of himself, the woman who had saved him from an ordinary life.

Thomas Hickey, also stripped of his buttons and stripes, shook his shoulders against the arms that held him. He answered every remark with a pitch of his body against his jailors' grip, but they held him tight. He stomped his feet and growled with every step toward the gallows. Turning his head back toward Birch, he spit out, "See you in hell!" followed by a wicked laugh. His foot hit the first step of the scaffold, and the crowd went silent.

Soldiers led Tom up the stairs and across the scaffold to the noose on the right with the first hangman walking directly behind him. A few of the men watching cheered but were silenced by the ones who came to see a hanging and didn't want anything to disturb the anticipated moment of death.

"Do you have any last words?" asked the preacher standing nearby.

Hickey's eyes seemed to fill briefly with tears, but he wiped them off with the flat of his hand, and his eyes darkened as he shouted, "General Green, listen and be careful or ye will join me here!"

"Who's General Green?" asked one of the guards behind Hickey.

The second one shrugged. "Who knows?"

With that, the hangman slipped the noose over Tom's head and tightened it around his neck. "May God be with you." He stepped to the side and without hesitation pulled back the lever releasing the trap door. The door gave a loud thud as it opened. As Tom's feet and legs fell through the hole, the crowd cheered. A handful of women may have shed tears, but most of the people watching felt exhilaration at the death of a traitor.

Tom's neck broke at once, and he died, but the hangman left his body dangling until nearly ten minutes later when he verified the prisoner's death. As soon as he shouted, "He lives no more!" the man cut the rope, and Tom's body dropped to the undertaker's wagon below. The body landed with a dull thud followed by the sharp crack of the coffin lid being forcibly closed. Ten soldiers marched beside the wagon as it moved slowly out of the park. The crowd grew silent again until the wagon was out of sight, but soon the witnesses grew restless, and the commotion started up as they waited for the second execution.

Sophie sucked in her breath and held it as Birch was escorted up the steps on the scaffold. He stopped under the remaining noose on the left and stood straight and tall, his eyes still searching for Sophie.

"Move! Out of my way!" she shouted. "Get out of my way!" as she rammed her cart into people who refused to listen to her. Everything had to happen at just the right time and in just the right order. She had to get in position before it was too late.

Birch's eyes again searched the mass of onlookers. "Where is she? One last look," he pleaded. "One last look!" He gave up, regretting that her last memory of him would be with a rope around his neck and dropped his head before raising it again and standing straight with his shoulders back. Even though this hanging was a travesty, he had pledged to risk his life for the cause of freedom, and he would proudly be the sacrifice George Washington needed. He hoped Sophie would eventually feel the same way despite her grief in the years to come.

He faced forward and prepared himself for what was to happen when the second hangman walked right up to him, put his hand on his shoulder, and spoke quietly into his ear.

Birch's eyes opened wide.

The hangman stepped back, and again the priest asked if the condemned man had any last words. Birch turned his head briefly to give another glance at the hangman before saying loudly, "You may not remember me, but never forget that the fight for freedom is worth it." He took another slow breath. "I'm ready."

The hangman reached up and draped the noose around Birch's neck, moving the knot to the back and ever so quickly leaving an unnoticed small gap between the rope and his neck. The hangman whispered, "Be ready." Stepping back to the edge of the platform, he put his hand on the lever of the trap door in the floor.

That was the signal!

Joseph counted to five in his head, keeping his

timing perfect, exactly as they had practiced the night before. Justine also counted to five in the same perfect timing. Then she tossed a small metal tin used to hold kitchen supplies into her fire. The gunpowder inside exploded with an ear-shattering bang, creating a mass of black smoke. People nearby panicked, running in every direction, anything to get away, dragging with them other spectators who didn't know what was going on. Soldiers ran toward the sound and the smoke, but the multitude pushed them back in their own rush to escape. Pandemonium reigned.

Justine threw another canister into the fire. More noise and more smoke.

At the same time, Sophie, now standing directly in front of the scaffold, lit the short fuses on her covered tins filled with gunpowder and baking soda with the red-hot coals in her cart. Like Justine's canisters, they were designed to make enormous clouds of thick smoke. She tossed them, one after the other, six in all, along the front of the gallows. Within seconds the gallows were hidden behind the smoke. She tossed three more, obliterating the platform completely. People standing in the front panicked, covering their faces with their hands and hats against the choking smoke. They ran, dragging their children by their arms, and again the soldiers could do nothing to stop them.

Gibbs pulled his scarf up to cover his mouth and nose as the pungent smoke billowed in front of him in hideous thick clouds. He coughed and wiped his watering eyes as he struggled to keep the frightened horse and his wagon in place while he waited for the thud of Birch falling into the coffin.

By now the smoke from Sophie's canisters had

billowed up, and Joseph could no longer see the crowd. And the crowd could no longer see him. He counted to five again at the same even pace. On the count of five, Joseph pulled the lever back, but, with a cracking sound, it caught on an uneven cut in the opening and stuck. Joseph hurriedly pushed it forward and tried again. This time he put all his strength into it and wrenched the stick back. The lever released, and the trap door opened.

Knowing he had only seconds to act, he pulled his short sword out from under his shirt and, with a quick strong swing of his arm, sliced the now taut rope just above Birch's head. The prisoner fell through the hole in the floor and collapsed into the open coffin below. Gibbs said in a hoarse voice, "Get down and stay down!" before he quickly slammed the coffin lid shut. Slapping the reins, he urged his panicking horse through the crowd and out of the field into the fresh air. Half of the coffin escorts were overcome by the smoke and could not follow the wagon. The rest had left their posts to help calm the panicking people.

Caleb kept his horse moving through the masses until he was out in the open. Once beyond the park, Caleb traveled as fast as he could, staying close to the river until he was out of sight.

In the chaos, Sophie and Justine left their fire and cart behind and got lost in the masses of people pushing out and away.

Joseph pulled a scarf over his nose and mouth and crouched down, watching his women through the drifting smoke until they were off the grounds before he dropped through the open hole in the floor. As soon as his feet hit the ground, he took off running toward the back of the scaffold. No soldier was there to stop him, so he had a clear path into the Bowery part of the city where he hid himself until the next morning when everyone was to meet at a designated area near Washington's New York headquarters on Richmond Hill estates.

****

Hidden in the woods, and ready for the escapees, were two wagons loaded with supplies enough to last for several weeks, along with maps marked with safe houses and out-of-the-way areas where they could find shelter. Caleb Gibbs was the only one who knew the wagons had been packed on General Washington's orders. Even though Tom Hickey's lies had been exposed, the upmost secrecy was still imperative for both the general and the escapees. The future support for the war depended on it.

That night the women crawled under the piles of provisions to sleep until their men caught up with them the next morning, but the joyful reunions were short-lived. They had to be on their way to safety, and it would be months before they saw each other again.

Captain Caleb Gibbs claimed sickness until he rejoined his regiment with no one the wiser. Joseph and Justine headed north while Sophie and Birch turned west. On the run now, they would stay in isolated places until the uproar and the questions about the smoky end to the hanging at the park subsided. No one knew how long that would take.

****

Three hours after the hangings, in the field still smoky but empty, soldiers were charged with taking down the scaffold and cleaning up the area as best they could. A soldier picked up a straw hat with a large red feather on it from the ground, which surprisingly hadn't been trampled too badly. "Won't my Hilda like this?" he said, holding it up for the other men to see.

Another scrounger filled his mug with Justine's leftover mulled cider and drank it down in one long gulp. With his foot, he stirred the remains of her fire until only ashy coals were left. He then picked up the grill, now cool enough to handle, and carried home his prize.

The next day General George Washington issued a statement about his formerly trusted soldier. *"The tragic fate of Thomas Hickey, executed today for mutiny, treason, and treachery, should serve as a warning to every soldier in the army. The General urges all soldiers to steer clear of such disgraceful crimes, which tarnish a soldier's honor and harm the country they are sworn to serve, whose pay they earn and nourishment they receive. To avoid such offenses, the best approach is to stay away from situations that may tempt you, especially the company of immoral women. According to Hickey's own dying confession, it was such associations that led him down a path of wrongdoing, ultimately resulting in his untimely and shameful death."*

Chapter Twenty-Three

April 1777, after ten months in hiding
A wagon filled with everything needed to set up a new household, driven by Jasper Mountney and his wife, Annabelle, stopped at an empty two-story brick building on a lonely road about three miles outside of Williamsburg, Virginia. No one used this road very much since a newer, wider road existed a mile to the north and made for much easier traveling. But a busy road was not what the Mountneys wanted. This one would suit them just fine.

"We're here, So…S…Annie," said the man. "I have to get used to that new name."

The man had his long yellow hair tied back in a queue to keep it out of his blue eyes. He brushed back the runaway strands. "I'm sure glad to get rid of that wig I had to wear. Feels good to have the wind in my hair."

Annie reached over and untied the ribbon around his queue. "Let all of it loose now." He grinned as he turned his head, so the wind could blow it away from his face. His neck carried a red scrape around it, and although slowly fading, it would never go away completely, just like the memory of what caused it.

His wife tucked her long auburn hair tightly into her ruffled linen cap. For months, she had pulled the cap down to her eyebrows to hide any stray locks, but today she pushed it back and felt the sun on her face.

Both smiled. "At last," she said. "I don't think I could have taken much more of living in tents and broken-down sheds to avoid being recognized. We owe such gratitude to General Washington, and especially to Captain Gibbs for setting this place up for us so we could stay in hiding and still be of use in the war effort."

"Caleb took quite a risk in speaking to Washington on our behalf a couple of hours before the hanging. He could have been court martialed, maybe even executed. Good thing he convinced the general I was innocent, and of what we were up to that morning, and we couldn't have survived these past months without his influence, however secret it had to be."

"Someday we'll repay Caleb with more than just words. But for now, we'll be glad for a house with a real roof to keep out the rain! This place looks sturdy enough."

She walked back and forth surveying the brick two-story house that they'd been told had been empty for about three years. "I see just a couple of places that need patching, and the roof seems to be in pretty good shape. We won't know for sure until the first heavy storm. This just might be a workable tavern after we get it cleaned up."

Jasper took down a heavy trunk from the back of the wagon. "I'm betting some critters have already found a nice home in it."

She walked up the steps, pushed open the door, and peered in. "Lots of space…and dust and more than a few spider webs. I don't see any critter holes or larger nests…yet." Pointing inside, she said, "We can put the bar here and put tables over there, maybe four or five. Come look."

She stepped on the first two boards of the flooring by the door and heard a loud creak. Startled, she jerked her foot off and tried it again. The same loud creak. "At least we'll know if anyone comes in," she called over her shoulder.

Jasper wiped dirt off one of the panes of the front window and peered in. "This will do quite well for us. Far enough out of town so folks won't be checking up on us, and close enough for soldiers to drop by for ale and a quiet place to talk. A fine place for us to hear what's going on with the troops that pass through."

"Yes, Jasper, it's a proven fact that ale loosens all tongues. I want to see the kitchen."

She walked to the back of the tavern and pushed open the top half of a Dutch door leading to the kitchen and leaned over it, looking around. "Quite nice. Needs to be cleaned up but will do just fine. Let's see what's upstairs."

Jasper carried the trunk inside and set it in the middle of the room. "We'll be comfortable here, and we can be useful...and safe, especially me, Jasper, the walking dead man."

"And, Annabelle, his living wife." She laughed. "Now let's get unpacked and open for business."

The next sunny day, Annabelle and Jasper walked into Williamsburg and talked to a few of the store owners, explaining they were opening a roadhouse and inn on the road outside of town, and they hoped to get their support.

"Our inn will be for travelers who aren't going on the main road and shouldn't take any business away from you here in town. To anyone who stops with us on their way to Williamsburg or other points north and south, we will gladly mention your establishment." Most of the shopkeepers were agreeable and weren't concerned about losing business to the Stag Horn Tavern. Others just shrugged, too busy with their own shops to respond or care.

One owner said, "Other businesses have tried to start up on that road, but all failed because it's in a lonely, out-of-the way spot. We'll be glad to have you come work for us if you don't make a go of it."

Those were the words Jasper had been waiting to hear. They were code to let him know that this shop owner was a patriot, and his shop was a safe place if trouble came up. For the last ten months, a courier from General Washington had carried messages about similar safe places near wherever they were. Although they hadn't had to use them, the two escapees were grateful that one was nearby now.

Jasper's reply to confirm acceptance was, "We're confident in the future, and we thank you very much for your support."

The shop owner nodded.

Two weeks later the Stag Horn Tavern opened for customers.

Two nights after that, Annabelle dished up six dinners of mutton meat pies, pea soup, and biscuits to a family planning to start up a farm a mile or so away. Two British soldiers walking on their way from Williamsburg to their latest camp also stopped in for mugs of ale, which a friendly Jasper served up from behind the bar.

To the family at the tables, Annabelle said, "I

promise I'll have something sweet the next time you come in. We just found a supplier of foodstuffs we can count on, and he's promised apples, red and green. How does pie sound?"

The family nodded between bites of hot food. "We don't know if we'll be able to come here again, might be too busy getting our crop planted, but we will certainly tell others."

"So how about if I bring you a pie as a housewarming gift when I get them made?" The two children nodded their heads up and down vigorously until the mother agreed.

But business from the locals was not what brought Annabelle and Jasper here. It was the war.

Jasper set mugs of ale in front of the two British soldiers standing at the bar. A boney private took a long drink. His red coat hung sloppily from his shoulders. "We stopped on the chance you would serve us," said the young man with a thick English accent. "Do you have many loyalists around here?"

"At least one," said Jasper with a wink. "But I don't advertise that. Too many so-called patriots pass by here, but you're safe with me for now. I'll warn you if trouble comes in. How's the war treating you?"

The soldiers drank down their brew and ordered another, which Jasper quickly set in front of them. Ale and loose tongues made a fine combination for picking up confidential information.

"The campaigns in New York were brutal, and now we are travelling around from battle to battle. The two of us are taking a short break tonight before we move on."

The corporal standing next to the private scratched

under the edge of a bandage on his hand. "The land in this part of the country had to have been created in hell. Thick forests and so many hills to climb, not like the English countryside at all. General Burgoyne has a notion to cut off New England from the rest of the colonies, but we can't afford to lose any more men just to satisfy his wild ideas."

The first soldier picked up his mug and moved to a chair beside the fireplace. "Fightin' these backwoodsmen is like fightin' a ghost. First, ya see 'em, then ya don't."

"Watch your language, private. You don't want to start talking like they do, swallowing the ends of words, and picking up that colonial drawl. Proper English, please."

"Want something to eat?" asked Jasper. "Annabelle can bring you something from the kitchen."

"That would be fine," said the corporal. "Supplies are running low, and hard tack doesn't fill your stomach."

Jasper poked his head into the kitchen. "Got any stew left for two hungry soldiers?"

"Be right out. Just have to heat it up," answered Annabelle.

"Any Frenchies been in here?" asked the private. "We hear George Washington's got help from the French now."

"I haven't seen any Frenchies here, but what kind of help?" asked Jasper. "We don't get much news."

"Somehow Washington convinced the French king that he just might win this war, so the French are giving out supplies, weapons, and even sending officers to help with battle plans. Just what we need, more of

England's enemies over here."

Annabelle set bowls of steaming hot stew, with more vegetables than meat, on the table in front of each man.

"This smells delicious, ma'am," he said as he picked up his spoon and scooped up a mouthful.

"Eat up. Don't let me interrupt. You men keep talking." On her way back to the kitchen, she winked at Jasper.

"Another mug, sir," said the private.

"It'll all be on the house," said Jasper as he poured two more mugs. "Can't let you Brits go thirsty. Where are you headed next?"

"North."

"We have Fort Ticonderoga back again, so now it's on to the Hudson River valley. The fighting will be rough. We took back New York City, but now we're spread too thin over too wide an area, and Philadelphia is proving a hard fight. You'll pray for victory for us, won't you?"

"You can count on it," said Jasper firmly. "Do you want a room for the night? We got two upstairs."

"No, but thank you, sir," said the corporal. "We can't stay long. We're supposed to be scouting out the area, and we're expected to meet up with our troops about five miles north of here."

"A couple of regiments, I'd guess," said Jasper.

"A couple, and then some. Come on, lad, drink the last of the ale you'll have in a while. Thank you for your hospitality."

Jasper escorted the soldiers to the door and waved as they walked away. He called after them, "Fight for King and country!"

After they were out of sight, he said under his breath, "Thanks for the information."

****

Another week later a teenage boy drove his horses up to the front of the Stag Horn Tavern in a wagon loaded with goods slated for delivery.

Jasper stepped into the doorway as soon as he heard the rattle of the wheels coming down the rough road. "Hello there, Abraham! Good to see you. Any trouble heading here from Philadelphia way?"

"Nah, I take the back roads the Brits don't know about." The well-muscled dark-haired boy jumped off the wagon seat. He landed awkwardly on his left club foot but righted himself quickly as he said, "I brought you all kinds of good stuff, sir, vegetables, a barrel of flour, and a bucket of cream, but it might be butter already with these rough roads!" He had an infectious laugh, and Jasper couldn't help but laugh with him.

"I even got a couple of chickens and wire to build a coop. Won't have beef again for a while, confiscated by soldiers passing through, and I've got another book. Mr. Shepherd wants to trade with you again."

"Good, because I have a book for him."

Annabelle greeted Abraham with a tight hug. "So good to see you. After we get everything unloaded, you must tell me all about the storekeepers, Moses and Edith, and I can rewrap your foot while we talk. Is the store going well?"

The boy grinned. He had two missing teeth on the left side of his mouth, but few people noticed because he was so enthusiastic when he spoke. Abraham loved life, and his limp didn't hold him back from enjoying every moment.

"They lost supplies when the lobsterbacks nearly cleared out the mercantile, stole everything is what they did, but after the army moved north, he's back in business. General Washington sent some of his soldiers home to get their farmland ready to plant, and they'll share what they grow with the army and with Mr. Shepherd at the store. Mistress Shepherd said next time they might bring the barrels of ale themselves so they could visit you." His chest puffed up. "They'd leave me in charge of the store!"

Annabelle put her hand on his shoulder and sighed. "Wouldn't it be fine to see them again, and fine that you'd be running the store? Has Edith said anything about being with child?"

Abraham blushed and shrugged. "Not as I can tell, but she's like a mother hen to all the kids who come in the store for penny candy every day. I don't know how she gets any work done with all of them underfoot. I try to shoo them out, but the lady herds them back inside like she can't get enough of their grubby faces."

"Edith's always been like that, taking care of everybody." Fond memories flooded her mind. How she wished she could see Justine and Joseph again, but she knew she had to remember and use the names Moses and Edith for the boy's sake.

Abraham and Jasper unloaded the wagon, and Annabelle stored everything in the kitchen and cold cellar. They rested over leftover cold meat and cheese on bread.

Jasper handed a slim book to Abraham. "Now make certain Moses gets this, and where is the book he's got for me?"

"You two sure do a lot of reading. Seems I'm

bringing books every time I come." Taking a volume from inside his jacket, he said, "Here's the book."

"You can't leave without something to eat on the way. I've got leftover stew to take with you in a crock." She lifted his hand. "And I'll see what I can do for that scrape on your palm. How'd you get it?"

"A barrel slid off the delivery wagon, and I tried to stop it." He dropped his eyes to stare at his crippled foot. "But I couldn't get my balance. The molasses still spilled in the mud. I thought he'd take the cost out of my pay, but he didn't. I had to clean it up, but the street will be sticky for a long time."

As Annabelle cleaned his hand and rewrapped his foot to give it more stability, two more British soldiers rode up to the tavern, leaving their horses at the water trough out front. "Got anything to eat?" asked one. "We can pay in British coin, take it or leave it."

"Of course, I'll take it, welcome," said Jasper. "Sit right down. I'll bring you some ale while you wait. On the house for those men in red. Annabelle, got any more meat left over?"

"I'll get it."

"We're in a hurry," said the soldier. "Need to meet up with our regiment."

"No problem." Jasper set the mugs on the table. "So how is the war treating you?"

The redcoats eagerly shared what they knew, especially after downing their third mug.

Abraham watched the soldiers silently. Seeing redcoats here, and at the store, was not unusual for him, and he knew better than to ask questions.

****

That night, with the curtains drawn in their upstairs

bedroom, Birch pulled the candle close as he leaned over his desk to decode the message Joseph left in his book, using letters marked with small dots on the pages. Birch would then rearrange them in the right order, using a unique pattern Joseph sent every time they exchanged books.

Birch had orders to supply Joseph, living in a small town near Philadelphia, with any information about British troop movements in his area, and Joseph sent Birch news of what might be coming his way.

"I've got a lot to send to Joseph this time. We've had soldiers from both sides stop by the tavern, and do they love to talk." He scribbled a couple more dots on the page. "I keep the ale flowing for this very reason, to loosen tongues, most of which should stay shut."

He had learned the numbers and movement of troops, how supplies were holding out, and much more. He also included in his code how the Brits were becoming discouraged and that a major victory by the Americans could break their spirits.

This time Joseph's translation, among other things, read, "Captain Gibbs stopped at the store. He wanted to come see you but thought it would be too dangerous. Washington has used what we sent him."

Later that night while lying next to each other in bed, Sophie whispered, "This place could be home for us, like the store is for Joseph and Justine. I would like that."

Birch stared at the ceiling. "Don't get your heart set on it. This is the fifth place Washington has sent us in the past couple of months, and it may not be the last. We're doing valuable work for the war effort, and don't forget I'm supposed to be dead. If anyone finds out the general knew I escaped, he'd lose all respect and maybe the war."

"But we haven't seen Justine or Joseph since the hanging, and I so miss them."

"I know. Let me make it up to you." He rolled over on top of her. His lips met hers as his hands tugged her nightdress up above her waist. Suddenly they forgot all notions of war, codes, and secrets. They had each other and that was all that mattered.

****

"I am interested in renting a room," said the man.

Sophie studied his face. He was probably in his forties and carried himself in a very self-assured manner. He was handsome with wavy buckskin-colored hair, a well-trimmed dark mustache that curled on his cheeks, and a dark mole just below his right eye. He wore a green jacket with a yellow silk scarf tucked into his collar. He looked very sophisticated, too sophisticated for this part of the country.

"Have we met before?" she asked.

"I'm sure not. My name is Hiram Beckett, and I am interested in renting one of your rooms."

"Of course, will this be for tonight?"

"No, it will be in three days. I will not be spending the night, instead I'll be using the room for a meeting with a few of my acquaintances. We will need the room for several hours starting at sundown. I would also like a table and six chairs instead of a bed if that is possible."

"It's a bit unusual, but it is possible."

"I'll pay in advance and include a bonus for the unusual requirements."

"Thank you. I'll have the room ready Thursday

evening."

Hiram tipped his cap. "If we find the quarters acceptable, we may be returning on a regular basis. Thank you, madam."

After supper, Sophie told Birch about the odd request of a guest. Imitating his quality accent, she lifted her nose and said, "If he finds our establishment acceptable, he will honor us with his company in the future."

Birch gave her a questioning look. "What did this man look like?"

"Not as tall as you with sandy brown hair, a fancy mustache, a dark green jacket…"

Birch interrupted her. "A yellow neck scarf and a mole under his eye?"

"Yes, do you know him?"

Birch paced in front of the bar, gliding his hand along the edge. "I think I might. Did he tell you his name?"

"Hiram Becker or Beckett, something like that."

He pinched his lips inward before he spoke. "I met him at the tavern with Gilbert Forbes. They were standing in the shadows, but I saw him pay Forbes in gold coin and heard him congratulate Forbes on bringing the right men to him. I even heard him say 'Governor Tryon thanks you.' Later, Forbes introduced him to all the men at the table, including me."

"Would he recognize you?"

"Maybe he wouldn't remember, but we can't take the chance."

"What do you suppose they're meeting about?"

"I don't know, but I'd sure like to find out."

"Why do you suppose they came way out here?"

"We're out of the way, away from the prying eyes in town, and I bet Gibbs and Washington would be very interested to know anything these men have to say."

****

Three nights later, Sophie greeted Hiram Beckett and five other men as they entered the Stag Horn Tavern. "May I offer you gentlemen a drink of ale or sliced chicken made just today?"

"You may send up the chicken at eight o'clock," said Hiram, "but until then we require complete privacy. Please direct us to the room."

The six men followed Sophie upstairs to the largest of the rooms on that floor. Five of the men took their seats in the chairs while Hiram pulled the curtains tightly shut at the two windows. "Madam, you are excused," he said abruptly.

Just before she closed the door behind her, one of the men asked, "Where is your husband?"

A chill ran down Sophie's spine. "He's out back cutting some firewood."

"I don't hear any chopping."

"He's back deep in the woods. Would you like me to get him?"

"That won't be necessary. You are excused," said Hiram.

Sophie went downstairs to the kitchen to finish preparing the chicken slices, all the while trying to calm her racing heart. She knew exactly where Birch was, and it wasn't deep in the woods.

Her husband crouched inside a large wardrobe left by the earlier owner in the corner of the room where the strangers met. He'd cut a hole in the top so he could get air, but it was still stuffy and uncomfortable inside. The wood smelled musty, and several splinters jabbed his backside. His long legs were already cramping from folding them up inside the narrow space. Sweat dripped down his neck, but he barely had room to lift his arm to wipe it off.

He wiped his hands on his breeches, knowing he could not get the pages of the notebook he held wet. With the charcoal writing stick in his hand, he sat poised to write down what he heard. Sophie had notched the pages in the notebook so in the dark he could feel where the next line should be. It wasn't a perfect system, but they'd have better luck deciphering what he'd written if the words didn't run into each other too much.

Birch listened and learned.

"We all know why we are here," said a deep voice. "Captains Smalley and Winston, along with Lieutenant Carter are looking for our assistance."

Another voice with a British accent said, "We want to thank you men for offering your support and knowledge about this area. As we increase our presence here and parts north, information about the land, the availability of decent roads, and names of loyalist supporters will be increasingly helpful to our troops."

Birch wrote down what he could until he heard a chair scrape against the floor.

The man with a deep voice said, "I need to stretch my legs a bit." He must have walked over to the window as another voice said, "Don't open the curtains. The light from the lanterns will shine for miles."

The first man then walked over to the wardrobe and knocked on it. He slapped the front and both sides, jarring Birch each time. "This is certainly a fine example of craftsmanship. Seems out of place in this backwoods country. Wonder what they keep in here." He put his hand on one of the knobs on the door and jiggled it. "This is silver," he said. "Carved and very fancy. Any silversmith would be proud of the workmanship." He jiggled it again. The door opened a crack.

A sliver of light pierced the darkness inside. Birch held his breath.

Just then a knock at the door to the room startled everyone, including the man curious about the wardrobe. "Oh, the food is here," he said. "Set it on the table." He pushed the wardrobe door closed.

Birch breathed a quiet sigh of relief. Next time he'd tie the handles closed with a string on the inside.

He heard Sophie set the plate with the slices of chicken and cut up apples down in the center of the table. "I have a pitcher of water in the hall along with six mugs. I'll bring them in."

Birch heard the tray with the pitcher and the mugs slide across the table. "Enjoy, gentlemen," said Sophie. "Let me know if you need anything else. I'll be right downstairs."

The meeting in the upstairs bedroom of the Stag Horn ended at exactly nine o'clock. Outside, the men lit small lanterns they'd brought with them. Three men rode away on horses while the other three crowded into a carriage. "We will return to the same accommodations next week," said Hiram. "Have everything ready in exactly seven days."

"I will, sir," answered Sophie, who quickly ran upstairs to let Birch out of the wardrobe.

He unfolded his stiff legs with a groan and leaning

on Sophie made his way to the writing desk in his bedroom and sat down. "I must get this into code as soon as possible before I forget, so I can send it to Joseph so he can get it to the general."

"What did you hear?"

"British troops are on the move, but they're very low on supplies and morale. That's why some non-military men were here, to see if they could help. They mentioned a couple of loyalist supporters in town who might come to future meetings. The military men also named a couple of possible battle sites, and if Washington knows where they are, he can get there first and be ready."

"How are we going to send it? Abraham's not due here for another week. Can we wait that long?"

Birch laid down his quill and took her hand. Staring at nothing at all, he said, "I don't think we can. We might have to use mail delivery from the post office in the Williamsburg general store, but letters are frequently opened, and snooping eyes might read it. If that's the case, sending a message in code would make someone suspicious, and if we don't use code, then any words about the military, like war or soldiers, certainly would."

Sophie put her arms around Birch's neck and leaned her head against his. All at once she stood up straight. "I have an idea! How about I write to Justine, a newsy, how-are-you-friend letter while you bury the code inside it? You know, make it look like I can't spell or put the dots over the words like ink splotches or some sort of decoration."

Birch grinned. "You, my dearest wife, are a first-class spy. Let's get started."

Five days later, a chatty letter from Annabelle Mountney written to Edith Shepherd arrived at the Shepherd Mercantile in the small town just south of Philadelphia. Edith was overjoyed to hear from her dear friend, and Moses Shepherd was equally as excited to hear the news from Jasper. He quickly sent that "news" on to the nearby Continental camp.

A month later, Abraham delivered supplies to the tavern, and he returned to the store carrying a dark blue knitted shawl with a note attached saying, "Pay careful attention to how I covered the buttons to match." Edith removed the buttons sewn down one side of the shawl and discovered tiny strips of paper laid under the yarn covering. Again, Moses was eager to decode the strips into a message he sent to General Washington.

The next month Captain Caleb Gibbs received a book from an unknown sender. The note tucked inside the first page read, "Enjoy this account of woe and sacrifice to come." Confused at first, he quickly recognized the patterns of dots and splotches over or beside the words on each page. "I taught them well," he said to himself before relaying the British troop movements to the general.

After six months of weekly meetings, Hiram Beckett paid Sophie for the use of the room, saying, "This is the last time we will meet at your establishment." And she never saw him or any of the other men again.

Chapter Twenty-Four

August 1781, the war continues
Justine jumped down from the wagon and ran into the Stag Horn Tavern, shouting, "Where are you? Sophie, where are you?"

Sophie came out of the kitchen drying her hands on a towel, which she dropped on the floor as she ran into her dear friend's arms. "You came! You're here!" They hugged and danced around holding each other's hands.

Sophie held out Justine's arms to get a better look at her. "You look wonderful!"

"So do you," said Justine. "When's the baby coming?"

Sophie patted her bulging belly. "I'm hoping by the end of summer or early September. Can you stay that long? Please say you can stay that long."

"I wouldn't miss it! Where are the other two? Abigail and Agnes?" Two sandy-haired girls came through the front door dragging the hands of their father, Birch, and Joseph. "Come in, Mama wants to see you!" shouted three-year-old Abigail with two-year-old Agnes right behind. "Look who's here! They're the ones you always talk about! Our godparents!"

Hugs, kisses, and smiles all around.

After supper, the grownups sat around the fireplace while the girls fell asleep on blankets on the floor. Both girls refused to leave their already much-loved Justine and Joseph to go upstairs to their beds. "Just this once," said Sophie.

"Tell us the news," said Birch.

Joseph paused. "I wish this could be a totally social visit."

"We wanted to spend as much time together as we could before…" said Justine.

"Before what?" asked Sophie. "Before the baby's born?"

"Unfortunately, no," said Joseph. He cleared his throat and shifted in his chair, but didn't speak.

"What is it?" said Sophie.

"We got here as fast as we could after we got the message. I brought Justine to stay with Sophie. Birch, we have to leave tomorrow morning."

Birch stood; his face grim. "You better tell me why. I won't leave Sophie, not with the baby on the way, without knowing more, a lot more."

Joseph dropped his head and spoke softly. "For the past four years, Justine and I have gotten comfortable with life at the store, and you've done the same here at the tavern. We both did our jobs and passed along vital information to General Washington, but now he needs us to do something more."

"You're not going back to the fighting, are you?" asked Sophie with a quiver in her voice. She took Birch's hand. "We've done our part for Washington. He can't mean to send you back."

"No, he doesn't mean to send us back. He means to send us forward."

By daybreak Birch and Joseph were gone.

"Where's Papa?' asked Abigail the next morning. "And Uncle Joseph?"

Justine picked up both little girls, Agnes and Abigail, and set them on her lap. "Girls, listen carefully to me. For a while it is only going to be us ladies, you, me, and your mother. We need to all pitch in to help, no complaining, only helping. We can do this. Right?"

"Right," said Agnes determinedly.

Abigail hesitated. "When will Papa and Joseph be home?"

"We don't know," said Justine. "George Washington asked them to help him win the war."

"Papa told us what he did in the war, and how he met Mama in the war. Did you know Mama is a doctor?"

"I did, and we don't have to be afraid. We're strong women with strong minds. We know what to do and how to do it, whatever it is."

Both girls nodded. "Can we go help Mama put the clothes on the line?"

Justine set the girls on the floor. "Good idea. I'll be there in a minute."

The Johansen girls ran out to the backyard while Justine stared out the front window, whispering, "Come home, please. I need you Joseph, and Sophie needs Birch. Come home to us and make the world right again." She wiped a tear from her eye. She mustn't let the girls see her cry.

****

Joseph explained the details of their mission to Birch as soon as they got on the road at sunrise. "The general has convinced Cornwallis he is fortifying his troops to defend New York City, but instead he's coming here to Yorktown to force a British surrender. The tavern is only a little over an hour's ride away, but

257

Washington is on a three-hundred-mile march, at least four more days to get here, but since we were so close, he sent us to give him details about what he's walking into."

Birch and Joseph stopped two miles out of town, left their horses hidden in a stand of trees, and walked the rest of the way until they heard the noises coming from the British camp just below Yorktown on the York River along the Atlantic coast.

"You do realize that since we're not in uniform, we could be hanged as spies," whispered Joseph.

"Wouldn't be the first time."

Birch put the spyglass to his eye. He could see hundreds of redcoats sweating and straining to dig, move, and pack dirt into high mounds below the city. "Clever," he said. "If they build enough of these redoubts, they'll be protected, and it'll keep anyone from getting close enough to attack. Since they believe Washington is still in New York City, it looks like they're using the time to prepare for any future raids. They're in a perfect position to still get supplies from the ships at sea, but no one can get close to them. Look for yourself."

Joseph looked through the glass. "With them on the higher ground with these redoubts, we could be slaughtered in a frontal assault."

"I'm moving up to get a better look," said Birch. "You keep filling in that drawing of the Brit fortifications, and I'll let you know if there's anything else we need to add. Then you can take it to Washington's forward soldiers."

Leaving Joseph, Birch crept close to the camp until he crouched down, hidden behind a cluster of trees and bushes. He counted the number and memorized the locations of the redoubts below the city.

Then he heard a branch snap and heavy breathing.

He froze. His eyes flickered. Very slowly he turned his head to see what was behind him. He hoped it was an animal and not a redcoat.

It wasn't a redcoat.

It was a German Hessian soldier, a mercenary fighting with the British, identified by his blue uniform and tall, peaked hat on his head. He pointed his musket directly at Birch. The Hessians were notoriously brutal, so Birch stood and turned around with his hands in the air.

"Hello," he said.

The man grunted and said, "*Halt, kein reden.*" Birch didn't understand the words, but the soldier waved his musket, indicating that Birch should move toward the British camp. Turning his back to his captor, he started forward with his hands still in the air.

This is bad. If I'm not shot here in the woods, I'll be a prisoner, and it wouldn't take long for them to figure out what I'm doing here and why.

"*Schneller bewegen!*" shouted the soldier.

Again, not knowing what it meant, Birch kept his same deliberate pace. A few more yards and they'd be out of a sloping gully and within sight of the British lookouts.

The Hessian said, "*Nicht schießen,*" but it didn't sound like an order. It was more like a plea.

Birch kept walking until he heard a familiar voice say in a whisper, "Get back here, Birch. It's me."

Birch turned to see Joseph with his musket pressed against the Hessian's back, and the Hessian motionless.

Birch quickly grabbed the weapons from the Hessian, his musket as well as his sword and pistol. "How'd you know where I was?"

"Wearing moccasins, we don't leave much footprint, but you break off branches every once in a while," said Joseph. "What should we do with him?"

"Tie him to a tree and gag him while we get out of here."

"He'll talk if they find him, and they'll know we were here."

"If we shoot him, they'll hear the shot."

"Not much choice. Tying him up will give us more time," said Joseph as he nudged their prisoner over to a tree and motioned for him to sit down.

Birch laid the German's musket and pistol on the ground. He took Joseph's rope and started to wrap it around their prisoner.

The enemy soldier suddenly lurched forward, grabbed his own pistol off the ground, and fired.

The ball shot upwards, hitting Birch in the back of his shoulder, tearing the muscle and leaving a jagged hole. It then moved up and out the top of his shoulder, grazed his collarbone, and barely missed his cheek. Birch fell to his knees.

Immediately, Joseph turned his musket on the Hessian and fired. The man fell dead.

"Birch! Birch!" He lifted Birch to his feet.

Birch stifled a moan.

"We have to move fast. Can you walk?"

"I'll have to."

Birch leaned heavily on Joseph, who now also carried three muskets over his back and three pistols tethered to his belt.

"Leave me," said Birch, breathing hard. "It's more important to get the report to the general."

"We do it together or not at all. Tie your jacket over your shoulder. It should slow the bleeding at least a little."

They only stopped moving twice to tie the jacket tighter and to let Birch rest for a minute.

"Am I leaving a blood trail?"

"No, your jacket's soaking it up."

Back at their camp, Birch collapsed on the blanket draped over his saddle. Blood seeped down his shirt and his pants while the edges of the jacket were soaked with it. "I can't make it any farther," he said quietly. "Go get Sophie." He closed his eyes and leaned back against the saddle.

Joseph readied his horse. "I'm leaving two loaded muskets and two pistols with you. I'll be back as soon as I can. Don't die on me until then."

"I'll try…my…best."

Joseph rode the fifteen miles to the tavern as fast as the horse's endurance allowed. He returned with Sophie and a wagon, fearing Birch wouldn't survive the nearly four hours it took to get back to him.

"He's still here!" he shouted to Sophie as she caught up. Kneeling beside his friend, he said, "He's still alive!"

He ran back to help Sophie down from the wagon. Then he took a bucket of water from the back to rub down the exhausted horses. "Are we in time?"

"Toss me my bag."

Her first words to her husband were "I thought I told you not to get hurt. When will you listen to me?" She scowled but then kissed him firmly on the mouth.

Birch smiled and groaned. "Are you really a lady doctor?"

"You better hope so!" Sophie leaned in, her pregnant belly pressing against him.

The blood flow from his shoulder had lessened, but it started up again as she cleaned out the entry and exit holes. She debrided what she could and, using thick pads of cotton cloth, tightly wrapped the arm and shoulder. "We have to get him back to the Stag Horn so I can clean this out thoroughly. Help me get him into the wagon."

Birch leaned heavily on both of them as they slowly made their way to the wagon. Once Birch was lying on the quilts and bedding gathered there, Joseph quickly tossed in Birch's saddle and tied his horse to the back.

"Can you find the way by yourself?" Joseph asked Sophie. "I have to deliver the information about the British fortifications to the advance soldiers for Washington."

"I can manage just fine. You go save the war."

****

General Washington, grateful for Joseph's information, now planned his strategy for the fight at Yorktown. At night, his troops built their own redoubts in complete silence, moving closer and closer to the British fortifications each night, and Cornwallis never suspected a thing until it was too late.

On October 17, 1781, a lone British drummer boy beat "parley" on his drum, followed by a British officer waving a white flag. Two days later the British and Hessian troops marched with their heads down through the American and French troops in surrender.

Justine changed and dressed Birch's shoulder every day under Sophie's watchful eye as Sophie cared for her newborn son.

After the signing and ratification of the peace treaty between the American colonies and Great Britain in Paris on January 14, 1784, Birch, Sophie, and their children packed up and left for home in Cambridge, Massachusetts. Dr. Samuel Dougal greeted them with open arms.

The only thing Birch and Sophie left behind in Virginia was a hand-carved stone over a small grave at the edge of the woods. It read: *George Washington Johansen, age 20 months. Born September 15, 1781—Left this earth June 10, 1783—Loved for eternity.*

Chapter Twenty-Five

Thirty years after the end of the Revolutionary War—1813

The little house where Birch had met Sophie and her father now stood between two larger brick buildings, both family-owned residences, on a street lined with similar houses. A small wooden sign nailed over the door read "Dr. Sophie Johansen."

Birch tapped his cane on the step leading to the front door. His rheumatism pained him on rainy days like today, and he needed extra support for his leg, but he still couldn't make himself take the last step into the house, not yet. How was he going to tell her he'd resigned from the Massachusetts legislature after being a state senator for nearly twenty-five years?

She'd been begging him to retire for the last five years, saying, "We need time for each other with nothing, and no one, making demands on us. We've done our duty for this country. Now it's time for us." But he hadn't been ready. He wasn't sure what made him decide to retire now. He just knew it was time.

Stepping up onto the small porch and sighing deeply, he put his hand on the doorknob. From inside, he heard the laughter of the youngest of his eight grandchildren, twins, Lily and Rose. His news could wait until he'd had his fill of hugs and kisses.

"Poppie," shouted Lily. A tow-headed six-year-old

jumped into his arms, quickly followed by auburn-haired Rose latching onto his leg. These twins were as different as night and day in their looks and personalities, with the only thing they had in common being bright blue eyes. He so adored them, and they adored him. They visited often, but it was never enough for Birch.

"Now let me sit down," he said as he hooked his cane over the back of the chair. "Then I can hold you both."

Between snuggles and kisses, he glanced up at the doorway leading to the kitchen and saw the most beautiful woman he ever knew leaning against the door frame. Her rich auburn hair was now streaked with white, but the wrinkles around her eyes didn't diminish their vibrant green color. With her thumb, she twirled the silver wedding ring with the blue stones around her third finger, a habit of hers for all the years she'd worn it.

"You're home early today," she said. "No laws to pass for the good of the state?"

"Just home early to spend time with you and these little imps."

The girls giggled and leaped down from the chair. "We're helping Gram with supper," said Lily. "She let me peel the carrots."

Sophie nodded with a wink.

"And I peeled the potatoes," said Rose.

Again, Sophie winked. "The pieces may not all be the same size, but they'll taste just as good, won't they, girls? Maybe better. Why don't you two get out the bowls and spoons for the stew and set the table? We will need eight tonight."

The girls ran into the kitchen as Birch asked, "Who's coming for dinner?"

"Our girl, Agnes, brought the grandgirls over today, so she and John could finish painting their parlor. They should be here any time. Justine and Joseph are coming, too. She's still recovering from her lung infection, so I invited them. Their two boys are in the city for the next two weeks to finish getting the store ready since Joseph retired.

"But it was an even more exciting day because I got two letters from our other two children. One from Abigail and, if you can believe it, one from Young Joe, written in his own hand no less. It's been so long since we've heard from him that I wasn't sure our wayward youngest son remembered where we lived or if he could even write!" She handed him two letters. The envelopes were open, and the letters peeked out of both.

A loud crash of pottery hitting the floor and shattering came from the kitchen.

"You better see to that," said Birch, "while I read these." He started with Abigail's, a beautiful woman who looked just like her mother. Her passion, however, was not for medicine, but for teaching, and she often taught at the University of Pennsylvania. It'd been a struggle to get admitted, but like her mother, she never gave up.

Dearest Papa and Mama,

Marcus and the children are doing fine. Marcus has been busy building two houses just outside Philadelphia. The city keeps expanding, and so does the need for competent builders. Lydia chose a honey cake for her eighth birthday. Callum pretended he didn't care about her cake because he'll be thirteen in three months and is too big for such things, but I caught him sneaking a lick with his finger. We'll be home for Christmas, and we'll be bringing a surprise, one more grandchild for your collection. I think he or she will come in October. If it's a boy, we want to name him George after the child who died when you and Mama were in Virginia. If it's a girl, we'll call her Georgia. Is that all right with you? We miss you and love you!

Enclosed is a picture Lydia drew of you and Mama. Good likeness, I think!

Love, Abby

"Of course, it's all right to name him George. We'd be honored," he said to himself. "Both the baby and the general would be proud." Then he unfolded the drawing. It showed him riding on a horse, or at least he thought it was a horse. It could have been a camel. His likeness had bright yellow hair standing up on end. "I guess my stark white hair now wouldn't show up!" The drawing also showed Sophie holding up some sort of stick, most likely her scalpel. Sophie's hair in the drawing was as red as the stripes on the flag while both had five fingers on one hand and six on the other. "Yes, a good likeness!"

He then opened the letter from Joe, their youngest, named after their dearest friend, Joseph Gallagher. Joe was a career soldier, and so far, he'd remained relatively unscathed despite the fighting last year to claim territory in southern Canada. Recently he'd been deployed to defend the expanding western edge of the United States of America.

Dear Pa and Ma,

Sorry it's been so long since I've written, the fighting over expanding our borders continues, and it keeps a soldier busy. Sarah and the children remain in Ohio, and I get home when I can. Our four little ones are fine, although they aren't so little anymore. I don't understand it, but somehow, they keep growing while I'm away! They're all doing very well in school. Lucas is only seven, but he wants to go to university to be a doctor! Where he got that idea, Ma, I don't know!

I'm thinking about retiring from the army and probably will do it next fall. Sarah wants me home and everyone wants me away from any fighting. If it works out, we want to move back to Cambridge. (I can see the smile on your face already!)

Give all our love to everyone!

Young Joseph

Sophie came in from the kitchen. "Did you read the part about Young Joseph retiring? It gives you something to think about, doesn't it, if your son retires before you do?"

"I'm glad you brought that up."

"Really? You usually complain that I'm harassing you."

"No need for that anymore. Today was my last day in the Massachusetts legislature."

Sophie gasped. "Really?"

"I finally announced it, and a new senator will be appointed to replace me until the election in the fall. They gave me a certificate and everything. Want to see it?" He handed her a decorated piece of finely printed linen paper with his name in bold letters at the top.

As she read it, she said, "Why didn't you tell me? I would have come."

"I wanted to surprise you, and it wasn't much of a celebration, anyway. They sat down and passed a vote on a bill before I was even out of the building. But it doesn't matter because spending time with my beautiful wife has been on my mind for a while now. In fact, it's been on my mind since the day we got married."

"We'll celebrate tonight. I think I can whip up a carrot tea cake. The girls can help me get it ready, and it can bake while we eat."

"My favorite. My only job now will be to bother you as often as possible. After a while, you'll be sending me back to work."

She laughed. "Never."

She fell into his lap and kissed his face all over, his cheeks, his neck, even his nose, until Lily and Rose came in the room and, putting their hands on their hips, said almost in unison, "Kissing again? Aren't you and Gram too old for that?"

"Never!"

HISTORICAL INFORMATION

Patriot's Blade is a novel of historical fiction. While the central events of the book are true, my characters and their activities within those events are fictionalized. In some cases, I have altered dates and certain quoted remarks to suit my character's timeline or view of that event. I do my best to respect the overall historical accuracy of the time period within the storytelling process.

The early engagement of the Revolutionary War was misnamed. Two hills sat one right after the other, with the higher called Bunker Hill and the lower called Breed's Hill. The soldiers chose the lower of the two hills (Breed's) to begin the fight, but the name Bunker Hill endured.

The British were confident it would be an easy task to defeat these untrained backwoods men and then sail home to England as the victors. The British fought as they always had, in formation, but the colonist farmers and woodsmen fought independently and slaughtered the British in the first two assaults. By the time the British generals changed their tactics for a third offensive, the colonists were almost out of ammunition. During the hand-to-hand combat, the colonists defended themselves with their hunting knives but were at a distinct disadvantage with the British having the longer reach of their muskets and attached bayonets. It was brutal, and while the British claimed the victory, their casualties were three times those of the colonists.

The British also had not expected how the landscape in the Americas differed from that of England. The colonial roads were rugged, the land heavily forested, and the weather humid. The British were not prepared.

Complicating the colonial side, George Washington knew there was more to this war for freedom than winning or losing isolated battles. He had to engage the support of all thirteen colonies, but as General of the Army, he inherited a militia consisting of a ragtag bunch of untrained men, most of them soldiering for the first time. After the battle of Bunker Hill, the British retreated to the city of Boston, which Washington put under siege, and he wisely used the waiting time to train and equip his men. But to turn them into a consistent and united fighting unit would take much longer.

The siege of Boston went into months with no movement on either side until Henry Knox suggested that the general secure the cannons from the abandoned Fort Ticonderoga in upstate New York to use against the city. Washington agreed, so in the dead of winter, men, sleds, and horses retrieved fifty-nine cannons on an expedition known as the Noble Train of Artillery. It is noted that most drawings of the trip show oxen pulling the sleds, but Knox could not come to an agreement on price, so in reality he had to use horses.

The cannons arrived at Dorchester Heights above the city of Boston on January 25, 1776. Then it took nearly two months for the powder for the cannons to arrive, and when it did, the Americans began firing on Boston on March 2. The British awoke to find themselves in the direct line of fire. They retreated to Nova Scotia, Canada, on March 17, giving Washington his first significant victory. Washington's army then marched to New York City where he correctly surmised the British would attack next.

During this time, conspiracies abounded, many of them instigated by the British-appointed New York Governor William Tryon. These included the printing of counterfeit money intended to bankrupt the new colonial government along with plans to get rid of Washington permanently by whatever means possible. Washington first discovered the treachery when he intercepted a coded letter written by Benjamin Church, who had been writing to the British enemy for months with details of the Continental progress. The events referred to in this book of how the letter came into Washington's hands are true. I, however, used Sophie and Willow to convey the letter to Washington when it was really Church's mistress who did so.

The incident where Birch delivers a confidential letter to General Washington was based on the true story of Elias Nexson who, when told to give the letter to Governor Tryon, made certain General Washington got to read it first, and so the colonists were ready for the eventual invasion.

Washington's trunks containing the papers, money, and battle plans, were transported under the supervision of Captain Gibbs and guarded by His Excellency's Guard—the Life Guards. After the war, Gibbs packed one of the trunks with historic papers and carried it home for safekeeping. However, a fire destroyed the trunk thirty-one years later, and nothing remains of these papers.

My characters Birch, Sophie, Joseph, and Justine are fictional, but their activities in combating the spread of smallpox—a curse Washington was convinced could kill more men than musket balls—were real. However,

Washington did not order inoculations until 1777, but I moved the date earlier to get Sophie involved sooner.

The trial of Thomas Hickey was adapted from the actual court account, but I included Birch Johansen's name and actions for the sake of the storyline. At that trial, David Mathews, the appointed mayor of New York City, was accused of carrying money from Governor Tryon to Gilbert Forbes to pay for rifles, muskets, and men willing to betray their country. He admitted to taking money, but he claimed he warned Forbes of the danger he was in and forbade him to come to his office. Mathews' explanations were not enough for his release, and he spent two more months in jail before being sent to Connecticut for supposed safekeeping. Mathews escaped and returned to the now British-occupied New York City where he resumed his duties as mayor. The other men who testified received only mild consequences such as bare minimum prison sentences, and only Hickey received the ultimate judgement.

The traitorous threats to the new country and its leader were real, but my characters' roles in unraveling these plots are fictional. The names and activities of the counterfeiters—Ketchum, Young, and Dawson—are true along with the activities of Governor Tryon, Mayor Mathews, and Gilbert Forbes.

While all these conspirators deserve condemnation, David Mathews has his disgrace written on a plaque in a public playground located in the Bronx. Part of the inscription reads: "The British-born Mathews was installed as the Loyalist mayor. Mathews was known as a thief, an embezzler, and a spendthrift."

One reason for the eventual colonial victory was

that Washington himself was a genuine spymaster. He ordered the creation of a secret code called the Culper Code, along with an underground message delivery system, which brought him invaluable information on British movements and schemes. Read my book, *Desperate Hope*, for a fictional account of Birch's sisters, Daisy and Tansy, and their involvement in this elaborate spy system that stayed secret until the early twentieth century. A fascinating true history of the spy ring can be found in a book entitled *George Washington's Secret Six* by Brian Kilmeade and Don Yaeger.

The story of Birch hiding in the wardrobe to overhear British Loyalists plots and plans is based on the true story of Lydia Darragh who hid in a closet and took notes when military officers met in her upstairs rooms. Later her husband wrote the notes into code and layered them into the buttons of their son who visited his uncle, Lt. Charles Darragh, of the Continental Army who then passed the information on to his superiors.

Dr. Samuel's phrase "You never know how strong you are until strong is all you have left" is a paraphrase of something Bob Marley said many years later. When I first read it while doing my research, I thought it had to be a generation-old saying, so I labeled it as such.

Thomas Hickey was indeed hanged in front of 20,000 witnesses, the largest number of spectators for a hanging ever, but all the other conspirators were eventually freed.

I created the plan Sophie, Justine, and Joseph carried out to rescue Birch, and I had fun working out the timing and researching how someone could survive a hanging. The truth is that, in reality, no one could escape death unless the rope broke or had been cut, so I had Joseph do the deed. Hickey was the only one to suffer the ultimate penalty that day.

The day after the hanging, British warships entered the harbor, and the battle for New York City began shortly thereafter.

The strategy of General Washington at the battle of Yorktown was to build redoubts beyond those of the British and do it in complete silence. Now hidden by their own redoubts, they came close to the British fortifications before the redcoats discovered them. They attacked at night and were upon the British before they knew what had happened. The battle of Yorktown essentially ended the war.

I hope you enjoyed this storyline inspired by the true history of our country. You can contact me at my website www.SusanLFurlong.com with comments and see my other historical fiction books. Research fascinates me, and you can't make this stuff up!

All my books are available on my website, on Amazon, and on most other online sellers in both paperback and e-book.

A word about the author...

Susan's love for history fuels her resilience against the sneezes and coughs that old books give her as she delves into research for unique historical events to inspire her historical fiction romance novels. Susan captures her readers' imagination with a highly enthralling style, chronological events, and smoothly flowing narratives that keep one's eyes glued on her novels from the first page to the last.

She has written two non-fiction books and four novels set in historical Scotland. A recent release, *Desperate Hope*, is the first in a series, Whispers in the Shadows, set during the American Revolution. *Patriot's Blade* is the second. When Susan is not combing through history piecing together plots and characters for her next novel, she writes, directs, and performs with a music and drama group.

For more information about Susan's books, visit her website at www.SusanLFurlong.com .

Thank you for purchasing
this publication of The Wild Rose Press, Inc.

For questions or more information
contact us at
info@thewildrosepress.com.

The Wild Rose Press, Inc.
www.thewildrosepress.com